It was time fo...
that would fina...
question: W...

The silence in the room was taut with suspense as Judge Brown slid a letter opener under the envelope flap. Her agonizingly slow rip of the paper had the same effect on the room's occupants as running a fingernail down a blackboard.

All drew in deep breaths when the judge extracted two sheets of paper. "For the benefit of the record," the judge stated, "let it show that I've removed individual reports on blood drawn on September fourth by a hematologist at Good Shepherd Hospital laboratory. One report is for Kipp J. Fielding III, the other for Michael L. Cameron, M.D."

Faith had her fingers crossed that Michael's name would be inside that envelope—that DNA testing would prove Michael was the babies' father.

Judge Brown perused first one sheet, then the other. "My stars!" she burst out. Both papers slipped from her fingers and fluttered to the floor. The judge's eyes, indeed her whole face, reflected her shock. Composing herself with an effort, she bent and retrieved the pages.

"In my twenty years of serving in various capacities with Family Court," she said, "I've never run across anything like this...."

Dear Reader,

Two separate and quite diverse incidents served as catalysts for this story. First, my daughter had twins, the only multiple birth in our family, as far as we know. Helping out after the birth of the babies, I found that twins are far more than twice the work of having a single child. Two babies had four adults working twenty-four hours a day...to the point of being comedic. Or it would have seemed funny had we not been so blasted tired. Several years ago I'd written a story that included twins (*Trouble at Lone Spur*), but I knew I wanted to do another one. Infants this time. A story dedicated to all the hardworking parents of multiples.

Sometime after I'd returned home, and recovered from the hectic pace of my visit, the second kernel for this story germinated. I read a two-inch article in a local newspaper about a precedent-setting custody case involving twins. Voilà! A storyteller's delight—a twisted plot device if I ever saw one. My story has virtually nothing in common with the actual case. That's the real fun of writing. The story becomes uniquely a writer's own. I hope you enjoy learning how twins Nicholas and Abigail end up with the loving parents they deserve.

Roz Denny Fox

P.S. I love hearing from my readers. Write me at P.O. Box 17480-101 Tucson, Arizona 85731.

BABY, BABY
Roz Denny Fox

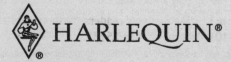

TORONTO • NEW YORK • LONDON
AMSTERDAM • PARIS • SYDNEY • HAMBURG
STOCKHOLM • ATHENS • TOKYO • MILAN • MADRID
PRAGUE • WARSAW • BUDAPEST • AUCKLAND

If you purchased this book without a cover you should be aware
that this book is stolen property. It was reported as "unsold and
destroyed" to the publisher, and neither the author nor the
publisher has received any payment for this "stripped book."

ISBN 0-373-70902-1

BABY, BABY

Copyright © 2000 by Rosaline Fox.

All rights reserved. Except for use in any review, the reproduction or
utilization of this work in whole or in part in any form by any electronic,
mechanical or other means, now known or hereafter invented, including
xerography, photocopying and recording, or in any information storage
or retrieval system, is forbidden without the written permission of the
publisher, Harlequin Enterprises Limited, 225 Duncan Mill Road,
Don Mills, Ontario, Canada M3B 3K9.

All characters in this book have no existence outside the imagination of
the author and have no relation whatsoever to anyone bearing the same
name or names. They are not even distantly inspired by any individual
known or unknown to the author, and all incidents are pure invention.

This edition published by arrangement with Harlequin Books S.A.

® and TM are trademarks of the publisher. Trademarks indicated with
® are registered in the United States Patent and Trademark Office, the
Canadian Trade Marks Office and in other countries.

Visit us at www.romance.net

Printed in U.S.A.

BABY, BABY

PROLOGUE

January 4

MICHAEL CAMERON TURNED UP his coat collar before he stepped out of the cab. He took care to shield his medical bag from the cold, relentless rain blowing into New York City. "Keep the change," he told the cabby, thrusting a folded bill through a slit in the window. Hunched into his topcoat, Michael stared up at the window of his luxury midtown Manhattan penthouse. Now he wished he hadn't asked his secretary to phone Lacy and forewarn her of his arrival. She would be furious at his leaving her in the lurch again. "As if I have a choice," he muttered, taking the front steps two at a time.

Bettis, the attendant on duty, opened the building's main door. He extended Michael a large umbrella. "Nasty weather, eh, Doc?"

"Thanks." Michael shook wet hair out of his eyes as he ducked under the canvas. "Nasty all right, but at least it hasn't turned to sleet." He lingered, making small talk. The longer he avoided the scene that surely awaited him upstairs, the better.

"Home early today, huh?" Bettis closed the umbrella and reached around Michael to press the button summoning the private elevator. "Big evening, I guess." The older man winked. "Saks delivered Mrs. Cameron's new dress. Oops. Don't tell her I spilled the beans. I think she planned to surprise you.''

Michael frowned as he entered the elevator. ''Lacy bought a new dress for tonight? Damn,'' he muttered. Keeping the door ajar with his bag, he pushed back one cuff to check a flat gold watch. ''I need a cab out front by two, Bettis. I'm scheduled on a five-twenty international flight. In this weather, traffic to JFK will be hell.''

The doorman nodded briskly, but his eyes were sympathetic as Michael let the door close. Michael hoped he hadn't revealed his own unsettled feelings. It galled him to think the staff had probably discussed his rocky marriage—although it shouldn't surprise him that Bettis was aware of his and Lacy's problems. After all, the doorman occasionally dated the Camerons' housekeeper.

Michael dug for his door key as the elevator glided to a stop outside his apartment. Could he really blame staff for talking when the situation between him and Lacy had gone from bad to worse over the past ten months? That was why he'd arranged a night out, hoping to mend their latest rift. An unexpected trip was the last thing he needed. But there was no other option. Throwing back his shoulders, Michael braced for battle as he moved to insert his key in the lock.

Surprisingly, the door swung inward. Caught off balance, Michael pitched forward, hands flailing, as Lacy flung herself at his chest. The key flew in one direction and his bag in the other, and Michael's arms circled his wife's too thin frame. His shocked sputter ended with a mouthful of Lacy's fine blond hair. She paid no attention to his incoherent gurgle, only fused her mouth with his as she stripped him of his coat, jacket and tie.

"Mmm, Michael," she whispered seductively. "When Maxine phoned to say you were leaving the clinic early, I sent Mrs. Parker to a movie." Lacy's momentum propelled Michael into the bedroom where they both toppled onto a king-size bed.

"Lacy, what the...?" He'd barely lifted himself onto his elbows when she unfastened her peachy satin robe to expose naked skin. Pressing her lips against his, she wound around him again. The kiss smothered his second attempt to speak. With sure fingers, she unbuckled his belt and released the zipper of his slacks

"I see you're ready, too," she cooed, leaving his mouth long enough to run a wet tongue from his navel to the bulge of white cotton springing from the open zipper.

Michael exhaled swiftly. "La...c...y." Her name was a groan ripped from his tortured lungs as she quickly slid over his erection with grasping hands and initiated a frenzied ride.

Release came for Michael before he caught his breath. The speed embarrassed him, yet he was more concerned about their rough coupling. It'd been weeks since they'd said two civil words to each other, let alone had sex. "God, Lacy, are you all right?" he gasped, raising his torso enough to ease her aside.

She pouted as she slid to the edge of the bed. Tossing her shoulder-length hair, she matter-of-factly retied her robe. "I thought this would be an incentive for you to come home early more often, Michael. Heaven knows your technique needs practice."

He winced, as much at her underlying rebuke as the bright lamp she'd snapped on. "Lacy, what exactly did Maxie Lucas say when she phoned?"

"That you asked her to let me know you were on

your way home. Why?'' Her blue eyes narrowed in sudden suspicion.

Michael rolled off the bed and raked an unsteady hand through tousled brown hair. ''Maxie was to warn you that I was on my way home to pack. The fourteen-year-old Norwegian girl I told you about has moved to the head of our transplant list. I got a call an hour ago. We have a match. I'm flying out tonight.''

A crash followed by breaking glass brought his head spinning around. Lacy, her pretty face contorted by anger, had cleared the nightstand with a sweep of her hand. Pill bottles lay strewn amid jagged pieces of glass from their smashed wedding photo.

''Dammit! I didn't set out to disappoint you, Lacy. But I *am* the chief surgeon on the international heart-lung transplant team. I'd expect you, of all people, not to begrudge a child her chance.''

''I don't need a doctor now, Michael. I need a husband.''

One of his eyebrows shot up to meet a rain-wet lock of hair.

''I hate that superior attitude you get, Michael. Almost as much as I hate that the first question out of your mouth after we made love was, 'Are you all right, Lacy?' ''

''Not this argument again,'' he growled. ''Getting over-tired, flu, colds—anything causing undue stress can still put your transplanted organs in jeopardy. Dammit, I don't like arguing, Lacy. If it wasn't such awful weather in Norway, I'd take you with me.''

''Wouldn't that be fun?'' she drawled sarcastically. ''I could sit around a hotel while you spend twenty-four hours a day at the hospital. No, thank you, Michael.''

''Then call Faith. She didn't have any time off at

Christmas to visit, but maybe she'd like a break from Boston now. You two can take in some shows. I don't think she's seen the apartment since you redecorated this last time.''

"That's because my sister spends as many hours at *her* hospital as you do at yours. I'll go to the beach house—again. The sailing crowd doesn't treat me like an invalid." Her last words were muffled as she pulled a suitcase from the closet and flopped it open on the bed. With an aggrieved air, she folded a new silk dress that hung on the closet door.

"I refuse to be made to feel guilty about this, Lacy. I was a surgeon when you married me, and I'm a surgeon still. Name one thing you've ever wanted that I haven't given you."

"Your time, Michael."

He gestured helplessly, then turned away to shed his remaining clothes. He strode into the bathroom and wrenched on the shower, returning to the bedroom just long enough to yank a black flight bag from the closet. "I took an oath to heal, Lacy. It's what I do."

"Amen. Not a day goes by that you don't ask if I've taken my pills. If I'm doing my breathing treatments. If I'm warm enough. Et cetera, et cetera."

"A few precautions seem a small price to pay for enjoying a normal life."

"Normal?" Lacy paused in the act of pulling on a pair of slacks. "Normal women's lives don't revolve around endless checkups and buckets of pills, Michael. The don'ts in my life outweigh the dos. Don't walk in the rain, Lacy. Don't play in the snow. Don't climb mountains. Don...don't have children."

Michael's jaw tightened. "Your anti-rejection drugs

place you at risk. Add to that the normal stress of carrying a child—but you know all this, Lacy.''

''Yes, Dr. God. Tell me again how normal I am.'' With jerky movements, Lacy tucked in her blouse and began flinging clothing into the suitcase.

''There's adoption,'' Michael ventured after a pause. ''But we'd need to solve our differences first.''

Stone-faced, Lacy continued to fill the case as if he hadn't said a word.

Doubling a fist, Michael smacked the door casing on his way into the shower. When Lacy wore that closed expression, there was no discussing anything with her. Meanwhile, it was getting late. A kid in Norway counted on him. Lacy had been given a second chance. Why in hell couldn't she appreciate the fact?

By the time Michael dried off and dressed to travel, Lacy had packed the third in a trio of matched luggage. Michael folded two suits and several shirts into his bag. ''How long are you planning to stay at the beach?'' he asked, eyeing her growing pile of luggage. Not waiting for her answer, he took his shaving kit into the bathroom to fill.

''Why would you care?'' She elbowed past him and scooped an array of cosmetics into an overnight case.

''You're my wife. Why wouldn't I care?'' His bafflement increased when she slammed the lid, tossed the small case with the others, then went to pick up the phone.

After punching in a series of numbers, she spoke into the receiver. ''Bettis, this is Mrs. Cameron. Call the garage and have them send the Mercedes around. Then please come to the suite and collect my bags.''

''It's pouring rain,'' Michael said quietly. ''If you must go today, call the car service to take you. I'll arrange a few days off when I get back from Norway. We'll drive back to New York together.''

"Go to hell," she said in a voice that dripped honey.

"Lacy, dammit!" He faced her across the bed. "Why do you always have to pick a fight before I go on a trip?"

"And you're forever off on one, aren't you? For all we're together, I may as well be single. I...I've made up my mind, Michael. I'm filing for divorce."

"*Divorce*," he said in a strangled voice. "God, Lacy." His knees buckled and he dropped heavily to the bed just as a sharp rap sounded at the front door. Michael couldn't force words past the lump in his throat. He knew things hadn't been good, but—

Lacy left the bedroom. Moments later she led Bettis in to get her bags. The doorman eyed the broken glass. He made no comment, only gathered the cases as Lacy directed.

Michael caught her wrist or she would have gone without saying goodbye. "Don't do anything rash until I get back," he begged in a low voice. "Give me a chance to put things right. I'll take a few weeks off. We'll go to the Bahamas or something."

She jerked from his hold. "It's over, Michael. I've never been anything more to you than your first transplant."

"That's not true."

"Yes. Find another star patient. I want a man who sees me as a woman."

Stunned, Michael watched her walk away. It was some time before he stood and resumed filling his shaving kit. He studied the hands reaching for his razor. A surgeon's hands. His skill had brought them together. Well, technically, Lacy's sister, Faith, had brought them together. She was a nurse at the Boston hospital where Michael had done his residency. Lacy was the one who'd demanded he set up practice in New York.

How had they gone from building a future together to...contemplating divorce? With hands not quite steady, Michael knocked a packet of pills from a shelf in the medicine cabinet. Absently he retrieved it. Lacy's birth control pills. In her haste she must have forgotten them.

Michael dashed out of the apartment to catch her. Halfway to the elevator, he stopped. This was a full dispenser. Probably an extra that Lacy's gynecologist had given her in case they had to travel on short notice.

A shiver coursed through Michael's body as he recalled what had happened earlier. Replaying the scene in his mind, he felt his blood begin to flow again. Granted, Lacy could be impulsive, but she wasn't foolhardy. Those were just angry words she'd thrown out, hoping to make him stay home. Her threats had become habit—a way to manipulate him. And he'd refused to bend. They were both at fault.

Sighing, he retraced his steps. He'd phone her the minute he reached his hotel in Trondheim. Once he turned the patient over to her own team for follow-up care, he'd talk to his partner about taking time off. Dominic would understand.

Michael finished packing and wrote a note to the housekeeper, letting her know that he and Lacy would be away for a week or so. He felt better for having a solid plan in place. Shifting his bags, he locked the door and went down to meet his cab.

CHAPTER ONE

August

A PERSISTENT RINGING dragged Faith Hyatt from a deep sleep. As one hand fanned the air above her nightstand in an effort to silence the sound, her sleepy brain insisted the call had to be a wrong number. She'd just come off two weeks of back-to-back shifts at the Boston hospital where she worked. Half the staff was laid low by flu. Maria Phelps, who scheduled shifts, had promised Faith four uninterrupted days off.

"'Lo," she said in a raspy voice, burying the receiver in the pillow under her ear. Faith covered a yawn and tried to focus on the voice at the other end of the line.

In spite of exhaustion, she shot upright. Her head and heart began to pound, and the receiver slipped from her shaking fingers. Scrambling to find it in the dark, she brought it to her dry lips again and croaked, "Gwen, you're positive the woman admitted through E.R. is my sister? Lacy Cameron?"

Long used to being ejected from bed in the middle of the night, Faith turned on a light and found clean clothes as the caller relayed details. "Yes," Faith said, bending to tie her sneakers, "It's possible she'd revert to Hyatt now that she's divorced. I'll be there in ten minutes, Gwen." Smack! The receiver hit the cradle. Faith's mind continued on fast-forward as she splashed cold water on her face, brushed her teeth and ran a comb through her short brown hair.

Her last contact with either Cameron had been in June. It was now the end of August. Lacy's husband, Michael Cameron, had thrown Faith for a loop when he'd phoned late one night in early June to inform her that he and Lacy had divorced. At the time Faith had been crushed to think her sister hadn't confided in her. But family ties had never meant to Lacy what they did to Faith. In fact, it was pretty typical of Lacy to arrive here in the middle of the night after months of silence, expecting her big sister to haul herself out of bed and put in an appearance at a moment's notice. Lacy had always thought the world revolved around her needs. And when hadn't Faith turned herself inside out for family? Sighing, she strapped on her nurse's watch and rushed from the building. Lopsided though the relationship was, she and Lacy were bound together by blood.

Faith set out to jog the four night-shadowed blocks that separated her apartment building from the hospital. Passing the corner deli, she realized she hadn't asked Gwen what was wrong with Lacy. No one detested being sick more than Lacy did. As her worry increased, Faith broke into a run.

At last, lights spilled onto the street at the corner where Good Shepherd had stood for over fifty years. Breaking her stride only long enough to press the button that operated the front doors, Faith rushed into E.R.

"Hi, Cicely." Breathing hard from her sprint, Faith latched on to the plump arm of a passing nurse, another friend. "Gwen phoned. About my sister," she managed after the next deep breath. "Do you know where she is, or which doctor admitted her?"

"Finegold. He sent her up to Three East. Said he'd

do a complete workup after he finishes the emergency surgery that brought him in tonight. Your sister just dropped in, said she hadn't seen a doctor. Finegold ordered tests, which Lacy refused until after you see her." The nurse rolled her eyes. "The great Finegold doesn't take kindly to anyone vetoing his edicts. I don't envy you having to unruffle his feathers."

Faith gave a puzzled frown. Finegold was senior staff gynecologist. "Uh...Cice, did Lacy say why she happened to be in Boston at this hour? She lives in New York City." Faith frowned again. "Or she did. Perhaps Newport, Rhode Island, now. Her husband, er, ex, said she'd received their beach house in the divorce settlement."

"I thought her chart listed a Boston address, but maybe not. Uh-oh. Hear those sirens? Headed our way. You'd better get out of here, girl, while the gettin's good."

"You don't have to tell me twice." Faith ran and boarded the elevator as two ambulances screeched to a halt under the portico. Loudspeakers began to drone the names of staff who were needed in E.R. Doors opened and nurses spilled out.

By comparison to the E.R. chaos, the third-floor ward was silent. Faith stopped at the nursing station and spoke to a nurse she knew. "You admitted my sister, Lacy Camer...er, Hyatt." Shedding her coat, Faith tossed it over a rack. "May I see her?"

Two nurses at the desk appeared to be relieved. "In 312," one of them said. "We hooked her up to oxygen, Faith. It was all she'd allow."

"Lacy hates hospitals." *Especially this one.* First, their mother had been chronically ill. She was in and out of Good Shepherd for years. Then, in college, Lacy

had developed degenerative cardiopulmonary disease.
Faith stared into space as memories of those unsettled
years crowded in. Her sister had been terrified of their
mom's cystic fibrosis. On their mother's bad days—and
there were many—care of the household fell to Faith.
She was just seven when she first assumed responsibility for her baby sister, since their dad could only afford
part-time help. About the time Lacy hit her teens, life
became doubly traumatic for Faith, who by then attended nursing school at night. Her sister rebelled and
refused to help take care of their mom. In spite of everything, the family had endured—until worse tragedy
struck.

Mrs. Hyatt died and shortly after that, Lacy fell ill.
Their dad folded inside himself. Only good thing hap-
pened that year—Faith met Dr. Michael Cameron, Good
Shepherd's rising star of heart-lung transplant surgery.

As she turned away from the nursing desk and approached her sister's room, Faith guiltily recalled the
secret crush she'd once harbored for the handsome, bril-
liant surgeon. The man who'd ultimately married her
sister. How fortunate that Michael had never had any
inkling of how she felt. Before she'd begged him to
take Lacy's case, Faith had rarely drummed up enough
courage to even smile at the man. He'd left her tongue-
tied and feeling giddy. Nurses didn't feel giddy. It
wasn't allowed.

Hearing that Dr. Cameron had fallen in love with her
more attractive, more outgoing sister really hadn't come
as any big surprise to Faith. The *real* shocker came
when Michael telephoned to say he and Lacy had split
up.

Now Faith wished her shyness hadn't kept her from
asking pertinent details. Michael had volunteered noth-

ing—merely mentioned he'd been out of the country
and he didn't know about the birthday gift Faith had
sent Lacy until a full month after her twenty-seventh
birthday. Michael promised to forward her package to
the beach house, which he said Lacy had received in
the divorce settlement. He'd signed off, leaving no
opening for questions of a more personal nature.

Faith, who'd observed numerous doctors' infidelities,
took for granted that Michael had ended the marriage.
She knew from experience that all sorts of attractive
women stood ready to trap doctors who were as successful and handsome as her former brother-in-law. Few
men had the integrity to walk away from such easy bait.
Michael had fallen off the pedestal she'd placed him
on, and that disappointed Faith. She wondered if her
reaction was a result of being more mother than sister
to Lacy; after all, mothers resented people who hurt
their kids. Lacy had probably been humiliated by Michael's defection. That was, Faith had decided, the reason her sister had slunk off in private to lick her
wounds. The reason Lacy had never returned any of her
calls.

Refusing to dwell on those unhappy circumstances,
Faith cracked open the door to Lacy's room. Her legs
refused to step over the threshold. Was that motionless
body in the bed her once-vibrant sister? Perhaps this
wasn't Lacy's room.

Letting go of the door, Faith tiptoed to the bed for a
closer look. She gasped as her eyes lit on the patient's
swollen belly. She stumbled backward a step, not wanting to startle a stranger.

But…no. The hair, the features, were Lacy's. *Her
sister was pregnant.* Faith muffled an involuntary cry
as the room spun wildly. It was impossible to stop sta-

tistics from running through her head. How many heart-lung transplant patients had successfully delivered babies? She battled the hysteria clogging her throat. Because of Lacy's condition, Faith regularly sought out articles concerning organ transplants. She remembered reading in a discarded medical journal about one young woman's successful delivery. *One*. And that woman's journey hadn't been easy.

In spite of her reluctance to disturb Lacy, Faith must have made a noise. The dark lashes that brushed her sister's pale cheeks lifted slowly, revealing unfocused blue eyes. "Faith?" Lacy's voice was thin, breathless. Even with a steady infusion of oxygen, it was obviously a struggle to talk and breathe simultaneously.

"Lacy, honey." Faith dragged a chair to the bed and sat, grasping the cold fingers. She rubbed gently, trying to share her warmth. "Michael told me you were living at the beach, Lace. I tried calling—left quite a few messages—but you were never at home. Or were you too sick to return my calls?"

Pulling free, Lacy groped in a bedside cabinet. "We, ah, haven't got much time. In my purse…papers for you to sign." There was no question that she considered her request urgent.

"Hush. Save your strength. Admission forms can wait." Faith recaptured her sister's hand. "I understand Dr. Finegold ordered some tests. If you'd prefer, I'll notify your own obstetrician and the two doctors can consult first."

"I haven't seen an obstetrician since I moved to Boston. That was…three months ago. The papers…are from my attorney. Sign them, Faith. K-keep a copy and mail the other. Envelope is attached. I'm giving you full custody of m-my baby, in case…'' The icy fingers tightened on Faith's hand.

"Custody? Oh, hon, I know you feel rotten. It's tough enough going through pregnancy alone, to say nothing of getting sick.'' Tears squeezed from Faith's eyes. "Why didn't you tell me you were pregnant? Did you think I wouldn't help? I'll be the best aunt ever. And you'll be a wonderful mom.''

Lacy again tried to reach the cabinet. "Sign… papers,'' she panted.

Faith knew it could spell disaster to upset a patient in Lacy's condition. "Okay, if you'll lie still, I'll sign the blasted forms.'' She hurriedly found Lacy's purse and retrieved the documents. Without reading a word, Faith dug out a pen and wrote her name beside every X. "There,'' she exclaimed, tucking one copy into the pocket of her uniform and the other into a stamped envelope. "All done. Now will you please relax?''

Lacy tossed her head from side to side. "After it's mailed.''

Faith heaved a sigh. "You always were stubborn. There's a postal box right outside the entrance. I'll post this after the doctor examines you.'' Faith was no stranger to bartering with Lacy. Once it had been a game with them, everything from coaxing her younger sister into eating oatmeal to doing her homework.

"Now.'' Lacy's demand was punctuated by a siege of choking that turned her lips blue.

"Hey, hey. Breathe slow and easy. See, I'm on my way to the mailbox. I'll just have the duty nurse page Dr. Finegold. Oh, and Lacy, Finegold may act gruff, but he's the best OB-GYN in Boston.''

Once Lacy's choking eased, Faith scurried out. After stopping at the nursing station to ask them to hunt up

Dr. Finegold, she completed her mission as fast as humanly possible. Lacy's condition frightened Faith more than she wanted to admit. She was afraid her sister needed more than an OB-GYN. She needed a pulmonary cardiologist.

Passing a pay phone in the hall, Faith was tempted to call Michael. He, more than any heart-lung specialist, had the expertise to help Lacy. But she dared not contact him, not without Lacy's consent. Maybe now that those all-important papers were dispatched, her sister could be persuaded to listen to reason.

Inside the room again, Faith met Lacy's anxious eyes with a smile. "Mail gets picked up from that box at six in the morning. Now let's discuss you. I think we should call Michael. Whatever happened between you two, Lacy, he's one of the world's leading transplant authorities. Plus," she said around a quick gulp of air, "he's your baby's father."

"No. Well, probably not." Lacy's voice rose and fell convulsively. "Sit. Listen."

Faith found that her legs wouldn't hold her. She thought she was beyond shock. Obviously not. Recovering marginally, she sank into the chair, gathered Lacy's clammy fingers and kissed the white knuckles. "I'm here for you no matter what, Lace. I won't call Michael. But don't ask me not to hate him for booting you out."

"Michael, ah, didn't boot me out." Lacy's fingers fluttered. "He...we—he was so rarely home. He loved his work. M-more than he loved me."

"That's doctors, Lacy. Surgeons, especially. I thought Michael was different. The times I visited you, he seemed so devoted. I thought you had everything, honey."

"Isolation. Drawers full of pills. Endless poking and prodding by my follow-up team." Lacy ran a restless hand over her swollen stomach. "I quit taking everything when I found out I was pregnant."

"Oh, Lace! You shouldn't have stopped the anti-rejection pills. Your body needs them to function properly."

"Yes, but I..." After struggling to catch a breath, Lacy whispered, "I...want her to be perfect. N...or...mal."

"You know it's a girl?"

Lacy shook her head and cradled her abdomen again. "No. I haven't consulted a doctor. I just call my baby Abby. You remember my best friend in high school? Abi...gail?"

Faith's flicker of a smile was soon replaced by a frown. "So, if you're not having Michael's baby—then whose?" She bit her lip and glanced away. "I'm sorry to be nosy. But it occurred to me that if you cared for a man enough to make love with him, he ought to be here seeing you through this."

Lacy grew fretful again. "I...I—K-Kipp's on the U.S. sailing team. We, ah, met the day I left Michael. After I fi-filed for divorce, I...I stopped at the club. Kipp...well," she explained haltingly, "he was lonely, too. The next day he took me sailing and we, ah, made love on the boat. In the weeks after, we danced, sailed, combed the beach. He brought me flowers. Kipp never treated me like a...a...an invalid." Lacy took a long time to finish her sentence.

"Sounds...wonderful." Faith didn't want to hear more, and Lacy should rest and save her strength. "Dr. Finegold ought to be out of surgery by now. I'll go see what's keeping him." She rose and started away.

Lacy plucked at Faith's arm. "Let me fin…ish. Kipp's team went to Florida for a race. H-he phoned every day." A weak smile lifted her blue-tinted lips. "I expected him to visit when the team returned. He didn't. A few days before he was due back, I got sick. Flu, I thought. I went to the clinic for antibiotics." She labored to catch her breath. "And…learned I was pregnant."

Again the room fell silent except for the muted puff of oxygen combined with Lacy's raspy breath.

"Shh. We can talk after you've recovered." Lacy's breathing had changed. Her respiration had become so shallow and erratic it frightened Faith. "It's obvious the guy didn't stick around. But don't you worry. I make enough to hire a nanny to help with the baby. Lie quiet now, please," Faith begged.

Lacy wouldn't be denied. "I'd never been to Kipp's house. He always came to mine." Color splashed her ashen cheeks. "I…found his address and dr…ove there." Tears flowed from the corners of her eyes.

Wanting to save her sister pain, Faith wiped the tears away with her thumbs. "Please don't do this, Lacy. Some men are just jerks. Forget him."

"I…I…parked and was admiring his house. His…his wife came out to…see if I was lost. I didn't know he was m-m-married." Tears rolled over Faith's thumbs and onto Lacy's pillow.

"The bastard!" Faith couldn't help herself. She wished she could have five minutes alone with the man responsible for causing her sister this agony.

"The…irony, Faith. Kipp and his wife separated because she couldn't conceive. They ar…gued over adopting. His dad, a bigwig on Wall Street, wants a grandson to carry on the family name. Kipp…dropped by later.

To apologize. Seems his wife heard of a new fertility treatment. He felt obligated to l-let her try it.'' Lacy's thin body was racked with sobs. "I...he...doesn't know about the baby. I don't want him to.''

Straightening, Faith adjusted the oxygen hoses. "Oh, sweetie, don't do this to yourself. You're getting all worked up and it's sapping what little capacity you have to breathe. I'm going to get a doctor.'' Increasingly worried because Lacy's skin felt clammy and her face now had a waxy cast, Faith sprang up and hurried across the room.

She yanked open the door and bumped into someone coming in. "Dr. Finegold!'' she said, tugging him inside. "Faith Hyatt, sir. I've assisted you on post-op rounds. This is my sister.'' Letting go of his sleeve, Faith waved toward the bed. "Lacy is a post heart-lung transplant patient,'' Faith whispered. "At the onset of pregnancy, she quit taking her anti-rejection meds. Please, she needs help.''

The doctor walked to the bedside and swiftly began an exam. Each time he paused to write in the chart, his scowl deepened. "Who did her transplant?''

"Dr. Cameron. Michael Cameron,'' Faith added, darting a guilty glance at Lacy.

"I only know him by reputation. Get him on the phone. Stat! Meanwhile, see if our staff cardiologist has ever assisted with a post-transplant delivery. And while you're at the desk, Hyatt, order a sonogram.''

At each barked order, Faith nodded. Everyone on staff knew Finegold expected blind obedience. Still she dragged him aside. "You wouldn't know, but Lacy is Dr. Cameron's ex-wife,'' she murmured. "She won't authorize calling him.''

"She's been assigned to my care, Nurse. I'm making the decisions."

"Yes, sir." As Faith turned and grasped the door handle, Finegold swore ripely. She felt the flap of his lab coat as he hurtled past her and bellowed into the hall. "Code blue. Get me a crash cart, on the double." Racing back to the bed, he tore away blankets, sheets and the flimsy oxygen lines and started CPR.

Faith's senses shut down totally until a cart slammed through the door accompanied by a trained team whose purpose it was to restore a patient's vital signs. For the first time since she'd become a nurse, Faith didn't see a patient lying there. She saw her baby sister. Pictures swam behind her eyes. Lacy as a newborn. Taking her first steps. Starting school. Going on her first date. A hospital-room wedding that had somehow led to this debacle. If Michael Cameron had been more of a husband, Lacy would be well and happy and living in New York. Lacy might not blame him, but Faith did. He'd promised to care for her sister in sickness and in health—until death parted them. Panic filled her as Finegold ordered the paddles applied to Lacy's thin chest.

Lacy's body jumped and so did Faith's. She didn't breathe again until a technician gave a thumbs-up sign, meaning Lacy's heartbeat had resumed.

"Dammit, dammit, dammit," Finegold cursed, yanking the stethoscope out of his ears to let it flop around his neck. "We have a pulse but it's thready. Clear me for an O.R. This woman doesn't have a snowball's chance in the tropics if we don't take the baby. How the hell far along is she? What kind of prenatal care has she had? Get Epstein, Carlson and Wainwright to scrub.

Round up an anesthesiologist.'' Finegold all but foamed at the mouth.

As he barked orders, Faith grabbed his arm. ''My sister hasn't had any prenatal care, but I'm familiar with her heart problems. Let me scrub with you.''

The doctor shook her off, never slowing his steps toward the door. ''I know you're qualified to assist, Hyatt, but you aren't in any shape. Take a seat in the OB waiting room. I'll find you when I'm finished.''

''But I *want* to help!''

''Pray,'' he said, spinning on a heel. With that, he flew down the hall.

The hardest thing Faith had ever done, outside of burying her mother or maybe waiting anxiously through Lacy's long and tedious heart-lung transplant, was to step aside while they wheeled her out of the room. Even though Faith heartily disliked clingy relatives who impeded the progress of staff readying a patient for surgery, she doggedly kept pace with the squeaky cart. At the elevator, she elbowed aside a technician and kissed Lacy's cheek.

Weighted eyelids slowly opened. Oxygen tubes from a portable tank pinched Lacy's nose. IVs ran in both arms. ''Take c-care of my b-baby. L…li-like you did me.'' The dark pupils of her eyes swallowed all but a narrow ring of blue. It took every ounce of her energy to breathe. Still, she reached feebly for Faith's hand.

Faith closed the icy fingers between her palms. ''We'll take care of your baby together.'' Hardly aware that the elevator door had slid open and someone on the team had roughly disengaged their hands, Faith's wavering promise bounced off a rapidly closing door. ''You fight, Lacy. Hang in there,'' she cried in a fractured voice.

THE WAIT SEEMED INTERMINABLE. At about five in the morning, Faith walked to the phone to call her father, just to hear his voice. He and she were all that was left of Lacy's family. But Dwight Hyatt had escaped into a dreamworld when his beloved wife died. Though only fifty-six, he resided in an assisted-living facility. He played checkers with other residents, watched TV and occasionally went on supervised outings. He recognized Faith at her weekly visits, but he rarely asked about Lacy unless prompted. More times than not, he didn't know Faith when she telephoned.

Fighting a sense of disorientation, Faith did as Dr. Finegold ordered. She prayed—until she ran out of words and tears. Three hours had passed when she wandered over to the waiting room coffeepot and poured a third cup of sludge. Through the window, she noticed that pale golden threads had begun to erase a solemn gray dawn. The promise of a sunny day lifted Faith's spirits and gave her hope, the first she'd had throughout her long, lonely vigil.

Muffled footsteps intruded on her optimistic moment. Glancing up, she experienced another rush of relief at seeing Dr. Finegold striding toward her. He untied his mask and dropped it wearily as he drew closer, still wearing full blue scrubs. The cup of muddy coffee slipped from Faith's fingers and splashed across her feet.

Even at a distance, she recognized the look on Finegold's face. ''No, no, no!'' The scalding coffee seeped through her socks, but Faith felt nothing until a crushing pain descended and great, gulping sobs racked her body. She stumbled and fell heavily into the nearest chair. She wasn't aware that tears obscured her view of the approaching man or that they dripped off her cheeks when she stared mutely up at him.

"I'm sorry," he said brokenly. "We did everything we could. Her heart and lungs had been overtaxed for too long. Without anti-rejection drugs..." The doctor shut his eyes and massaged the closed lids. "God, I'm sorry," he repeated, as he continued to loom over Faith's shuddering frame. "This part never gets easier," he said quietly, shifting from one foot to the other.

"And the baby?" she finally asked in a wooden voice.

"Babies," he corrected, pulling out an adjacent chair and sinking into it. "A boy and a girl. Both underweight, but scrappy as hell. My best guess is that your sister was seven to eight months along. The male baby weighed in at four-two. The female, an even four. I put in a call to Hal Sampson. If you want a different pediatrician, I'll cancel him."

"Two?" Hysteria tinged Faith's tearful voice. "Twins?"

"Yeah. None of us were prepared. With no history, we were flying by the seat of our pants." Leaning forward, the doctor clasped his hands between his knees. "You've got a lot to deal with. I suggest visiting your niece and nephew before you tackle the unpleasant chores that face you. I think they'll give you the will to do what needs to be done." He stood then, and gripped her shoulder briefly. "Well, I have to go complete the paperwork."

"I, uh, thanks for all you did." Dazed, Faith rose. Automatically blotting her eyes, she stood and held on to a chair back. Order and organization had always been her greatest strengths. Dependability ran a close second. In an isolated portion of her brain, Faith knew she could get through this ordeal by focusing on one task at a time.

Task one: Mop up the coffee she'd spilled.

Task two: Welcome Lacy's babies into this harsh, cruel world.

Task three: See her sister properly laid to rest.

Only after she'd done those things would Faith allow herself to think about the future. Struggling with a fresh surge of tears, she groped in her pockets for a tissue to wipe up the coffee. In doing so, she encountered her copy of the custody agreement. In sad hindsight, Lacy's urgency became all too clear. Lacy must have sensed how badly off she was if she'd had custody papers prepared. Oh, why couldn't she have had the care to preserve her own health?

She hadn't. And Faith had promised to be the babies' guardian. She would do a good job of it, even if right now her loss seemed too great to bear.

Once she'd mopped up the spill—but before she notified the mortuary who'd handled her mother's funeral—Faith took Dr. Fincgold's suggestion. She made her way to the nursery. With her first glance into the isolettes, she lost her heart to these two tiny scraps of humanity. The baby swaddled in blue screwed up his red face and bellowed, letting the world know he was a force to be reckoned with. His sister pursed a rosebud mouth and slept on, the barest hint of a sigh raising her chest.

A pediatric nurse placed a bolstering hand on Faith's shoulder. "I'll get you a mask, gown and gloves if you'd like to hold them."

"May I?" Faith's heart fluttered with both joy and sorrow. Joy for herself. Sorrow for the sister who'd never comfort these little ones with her touch.

She made an effort to curb her sadness and concentrated on counting the babies' fingers and toes. "Oh, aren't you sweethearts? It takes both of you together to weigh what your mama did at birth." Lacy had been a solid eight pounds. Faith rocked them and talked on in a low murmur, determined that they should start life hearing about the good, fun-loving side of their mother. "Your mama loved you," she whispered. "She gave up her own life for you. I'm going to make sure I bring you up the way she would have wanted...."

Soon after, Faith fed both babies with special tubes the nurses prepared, tubes designed to teach the babies to suck properly.

By staying, rocking the dear little bodies and holding them close, Faith was able to delay dealing with her loss. Dr. Finegold was right, she decided, staring at the babies who were now curled up, sleeping peacefully.

Lacy's twins gave her the strength to go on. To take the next step, complete the next task.

CHAPTER TWO

THE TELEPHONE WAS RINGING when Faith walked into her apartment the next afternoon. She'd spent most of the morning attending to the numerous details associated with Lacy's funeral. The cloying scent of funeral-home flowers remained in her nostrils. Although she'd walked home in the late-summer sunshine, she still couldn't warm up.

Physically and mentally drained, Faith considered letting her machine take a message. The red light already blinked, so there were others. News traveled fast in a hospital. It was probably someone from the staff wanting to express condolences. But what if it was the funeral home? The director had said he'd be in touch if any problem arose. Maybe she'd neglected something important.

She snatched up the receiver on the fifth ring. After an initial exchange of hellos, it was a minute or two before Faith realized the caller was the hospital's chief administrator.

At first all she heard was his mention of the twins, and she panicked. Her heart flew over high hurdles, while her ears recoiled in fear. She could only think that something had happened to Lacy's babies, even though they'd been fine when she stopped by at ten. The nurses had assured her the babies were healthy, small as they were.

Little by little, Faith's training kicked in, and she relaxed enough to make sense of what Dr. Peterson was saying.

"I don't understand," she ventured shakily when she thought she finally had his message straight. "Two men are at the nursery asking to see the twins? Both claim to be the father? Who are they? How do they…" Her voice trailed off, but before Dr. Peterson could say another word, Faith drowned him out. "It doesn't matter. Allow no one near Lacy's babies. No one but me. I'll be there in five minutes. Tell the nursery staff to have the men wait in the room at the end of the hall."

The taste of fear grew stronger after she dropped the receiver and bolted for the door. The *how,* the *why,* the *who* all whirled in a muddle through Faith's sleep-deprived brain. She'd hardly closed her eyes since Lacy had reappeared so abruptly in her life…and then vanished for good. Had it really only been last night?

The *how* fell into place before Faith reached the sidewalk. Local newspapers had built a headline story out of the death of Michael Cameron's first multiple-organ transplant patient. Faith had briefly glimpsed today's front page. At the time, she'd only registered pain—to think Lacy wasn't to be allowed dignity in death. Her sister had despised the condition she thought had stolen her independence. Lacy had been terrified of becoming a burden to others. She would have hated having her weaknesses exposed to the world.

As she hailed a cab, it struck Faith that the *who*—the two men making demands at the hospital—wasn't really any great mystery. One of them would be the great Dr. Cameron himself. The other, probably the married playboy. Kipp, the sailor with no last name.

It wouldn't be long before Faith ferreted out the *why,*

she thought grimly as she paid the driver, and quickly entered the hospital by a side door. Not that anything either man had to say would change the facts. Lacy's last request had been for Faith to keep her baby safe from the likes of those two. She had papers saying so.

For good measure, Faith stopped by the admitting office and ran off two copies of the custody document. If, by the time she reached the nursery, she still felt as hostile toward the men as she did now, she'd rub their noses in the truth. Neither one of them had loved Lacy enough to stick by her during her pregnancy. As far as Faith was concerned, the jerks didn't deserve to set eyes on the twins—and that went for the actual birth father, as well as Michael, who must suffer delusions of being the dad. Why else would Dr. Cameron be here throwing his weight around?

Staff members glanced at Faith curiously as she hurried along the corridor and took the back stairs two at a time. Obviously the grapevine had spread the word. An interested crowd would be lurking behind the potted plants in the expectant fathers' waiting room.

Thanks to one of the larger rubber plants, Faith was afforded a good view inside the room before anyone noted her approach. Her breath did a half hitch that she couldn't control. Michael Cameron stood near the window. His brown hair, still dark and thick, was mussed as if he'd run a hand through it several times. The inscrutable Dr. Cameron, who rarely, if ever, had a hair out of place.

No matter how hard Faith tried to control her feelings, her heart always did a slow somersault when she came across Michael unexpectedly. It irritated her that she never seemed to have that reaction to other men— eligible men.

Today Faith commanded her heart to be still. She wanted to study these two analytically—the men who'd been her sister's lovers. Cameron's summer khaki suit looked new. He wore a pale cream shirt and a tie that matched the gold flecks in his hazel eyes. He appeared more gaunt than when she'd last seen him more than a year ago, the previous May, at Lacy's twenty-sixth birthday.

Good. Faith hoped his new leanness had something to do with the breakup of his marriage and wasn't because he'd joined a fancy health club. She couldn't tell if he was suffering. His smoldering regard centered on the room's other occupant. But the man at whom Michael glared appeared oblivious of the daggers coming his way.

Sun-bleached hair fell in a perfect cut above the second man's well-tanned brow. An expensive navy blazer hung loose over pristine white pants. Faith couldn't determine the color of the stranger's eyes. They were trained on a magazine with a sailboat on the cover.

Both men exuded an air of comfortable wealth. Faith could only hope their behavior would be as civilized as their appearance. Taking one last deep breath, she moved around the plant and into the room.

Michael was the first to notice her. He uncrossed his arms and straightened away from the window, feeling a jolt of recognition. Faith Hyatt had always been so different from Lacy. He doubted he was alone in finding it hard to believe they were sisters. Tall, blond Lacy had had an athletic build—or rather she had before she'd decided it was chic to be model-thin. She wore makeup with flair and was always experimenting with hairstyles. His ex-wife had been happiest when surrounded by people. Faith, however, was small-boned and quiet to the point of being difficult to talk to. She seemed content to spend hours on her own, yet she had a rare ability to calm the sick with a touch. If she wore any lipstick at all today, she'd chewed it off. Her fresh-scrubbed look made her seem much younger than her thirty-four years. Something about this woman had always fascinated him.

Michael had first met Faith the year before he'd completed his residency. Even then, she'd worn her walnut-brown curls in a pixie cut that emphasized her huge dark eyes. Serious eyes that studied him now as if he were an unwanted specimen under her microscope. Not surprising. She'd played mother bear too long. Lacy had been her cub. Naturally she'd transfer those nurturing habits to Lacy's babies. *His* babies.

From the minute Michael had seen the article in the *New York Times,* describing Lacy's pregnancy and her reputed refusal to take her anti-rejection meds, many things that hadn't made sense to him before the divorce fell into place. For instance, Lacy's little speech about normal women her age having kids. Her odd behavior that day. The unused packet of birth control pills he'd found after she'd virtually attacked him at the door, frantically initiating sex. A lot added up now—now that it was too late to help her. But it wasn't too late to help their babies. The infants were said to be about four weeks premature, and that made them his. Period. Nothing left to discuss. He scowled in the other man's direction.

Because Faith's steps slowed as she entered the room and her uneasy brown eyes seemed to be searching for an escape route, Michael took pity on her and softened his harsh expression. Crossing the room in long strides, he reached for her trembling hand. "I'm sorry Peterson disturbed you, Faith," he murmured. "You must have a million more important things to do today than rush down here. I can't tell you how shocked I was to read about Lacy's death in the *Times*. The report indicated she'd stopped her anti-rejection meds. I wish you'd called me when her pregnancy became obvious, Faith. Whether or not Lacy was mad at me, someone on her transplant follow-up team should have followed her prenatal care."

Faith swallowed. "Lacy never contacted me. She never returned any of my calls The first I knew she was pregnant was when they admitted her to the hospital. She'd had no prenatal care, Michael."

The other man in the waiting room rose and glanced at the couple engaged in conversation. Closing his magazine, he walked to the center of the room. "You're Faith, Lacy's sister? I'm Kipp Fielding III. The news story I read in our paper said you'd spent time with Lacy before she, uh, went into surgery. She and I were...ah...quite close in January and February. Did she by chance mention me?"

Faith's head snapped up. She tugged her hand from Michael's fingers. "As a matter of fact, Mr. Fielding, she did have a few things to say about you. Except that she never revealed your last name—so you *could* have remained anonymous." A rustle near the room's entrance forced their heads around. Two nurses stood in the hall, chatting with a technician who was rearranging items on a lab cart. Faith knew at once that all ears were tuned to what was being said inside. Gossip lightened the tedious work at the hospital, provided a distraction from pain and death. In the past, Faith had been as big a participant as the next person. However, now that it involved someone she loved, she had second thoughts about the passing of possibly harmful rumors.

"Gentlemen, let me call Dr. Peterson and see if there's a conference room available where we can talk with more privacy."

Kipp buried his hands in his pockets. "I don't see what there is to talk about. That baby boy is my son. He's a Fielding. I intend to take steps to insure his birthright."

"Now wait a damn minute." Michael wrapped long fingers around Kipp's jauntily striped tie. "Maybe you can't add, Fielding, but I can. Lacy and I were still married in January. Those are my children she carried."

A shrill whistle split the air. Both men swiveled toward the source. They gaped at Faith, who calmly removed two fingers from unsmiling lips. "Maybe you two don't mind airing your dirty laundry in public. It so happens it's my recently deceased sister you're maligning. Have you no decency?"

Michael dropped his hand. "You're absolutely right, Faith." He cast a scowl at the eavesdroppers. "I agree we need a private place where we can settle this issue."

Confident that she'd soon set both men straight, Faith went to the house phone and punched the hospital administrator's number. "Dr. Peterson, please. This is Nurse Faith Hyatt. He phoned me at home earlier. I'm here in the hospital now." She tapped her toe while she waited for him to come on the line. When she'd explained the problem, he told her the conference rooms were all in use but offered the use of his office. "Thank you," Faith said. "We'll be right down."

Peterson brushed her effusive thanks aside. "It's an honor to have Mike Cameron here. I'm on my way to the cafeteria. I'll have them send over a tray of coffee.

Oh, Nurse, when your business winds down, perhaps
Dr. Cameron might take a moment to tour our new heart
wing. His stamp of approval would be a boon to Good
Shepherd.''

Faith sighed. "I'll tell him." She had no doubt he'd
prefer a tour of the heart wing over a trip to the funeral
home. Of course, she was probably foolish to even think
Michael might ask to pay his last respects to his former
wife. Hadn't Lacy said Michael loved his work more
than he loved her? If that was how things stood between
them when they were married, why would he alter his
attitudes after their divorce?

"Does Peterson have a room or not?" Michael spoke
near her ear, making Faith jump.

"Um, yes. His office. He also said he hoped you had
time to tour our new heart facility when we've completed our business.''

"Not today. Maybe later in the week. I'll catch him
and explain. Once we iron out this mess, I plan to spend
an hour or so with my babies. And after that..." He
swallowed. "Uh...if you have no objection, Faith, I'd
like to see Lacy.''

His chin dropped to his chest and his eyelids closed,
and she realized she'd misjudged him.

"Of c-course,'' she stammered. Seeing Michael so
emotional triggered her own bleak feelings again. "The
service is tomorrow. It's very small." She named the
funeral home. "Lacy didn't have many friends left in
Boston. Although...I'm not sure of that.'' Suddenly
flustered, Faith clasped her hands and frowned at her
fingers. "Perhaps I should have an official funeral notice placed in the afternoon paper." Peering up at Michael through her eyelashes, she asked him, "Were you
aware Lacy had moved back to Boston?'' Unexpectedly

her eyes filled. She had to blink hard to contain the tears. "That's another thing I don't have any explanation for—why she didn't let me know. It might have made a difference if she had." A tear did creep out and slip down her cheek.

Michael gently clasped her upper arms. "Don't beat yourself up, Faith. It's taken me some time since she asked for the divorce to realize that Lacy always did what Lacy wanted, and to hell with how it affected others. I believe she planned this pregnancy from the get-go. It wasn't accidental."

Kipp broke into the conversation. "Look, I need to catch the three-o'clock shuttle back to New York. Do you suppose you two could take care of family business after we settle my parental rights?"

Faith felt like hitting his supercilious jaw. "I imagine your wife is expecting you home at the usual time. Does she have any idea where you are and what you're doing, Mr. Fielding?"

"Wife?" Michael repeated, bristling.

The well-placed barb brought a wave of crimson to Kipp's tanned cheeks. "Shelby doesn't know yet, Ms. Hyatt. I assure you she'll welcome the boy into our home once the details here are finalized and I have a chance to tell her. Shelby has wanted to adopt a child for some time." Lowering his voice, he said hesitantly, "My father hasn't favored adoption. He's pressed for a blood grandson. And now he has one."

Faith cocked her head to one side. "Lacy had twins, Mr. Fielding. A boy *and* a girl. You've only mentioned her son. But then girls can't carry on the family name, can they?" she said coolly. In an even colder tone, she added, "Lacy's son will never be Kipp Fielding IV if I have any say in the matter. And I have a lot of say."

Michael stepped between the two combatants before Kipp could rebut. "Shouldn't we go to Dr. Peterson's office before we shed blood on this shiny tile?"

Faith clammed up immediately. She hadn't intended to lose her temper. And she'd forgotten their audience. Aiming pointed glances at the bystanders still lurking in the hall, she squared her shoulders and marched past them. Michael and Kipp fell in behind her. Michael, though, paused at the nursery window and leaned his forehead against the glass. He cupped both hands around his eyes in order to see better.

"Lacy's babies are in the premie unit," Faith informed him stiffly.

Backing away from the window, Michael joined her. "The paper said they were approximately four weeks early. Are they well, Faith?"

Kipp halted midstride. "They are, aren't they?" he demanded. "The article I read said the boy was under weight." He stuffed his hands into his pants pockets. "Lacy never told me she'd had organ transplants. Is there a possibility her son will inherit her medical problems?" he asked, sounding both worried and unsure.

Michael shot him an incredulous stare. "I'm a good surgeon, Fielding, but no one is that perfect at cracking open a chest. If you and Lacy got down to bare skin, fella, it'd be hard to miss her scar."

A flush streaked up Kipp's throat. He fingered his tie.

"Stop it, you two." Faith pasted a smile on her face for the gray-haired woman seated behind a desk outside Dr. Peterson's office. "The world doesn't need to know all the sordid details of Lacy's history. Both babies are in good health. Hal Sampson examined them. Michael, you remember him—he was pediatric chief when you were here."

"Yes, I remember. Sampson's top-notch."

The men dropped back and let Faith address Peterson's secretary. "Mrs. Lansing, I phoned Dr. Peterson a few minutes ago. I'm Faith Hyatt."

Nodding, the woman rose and led the trio into an oak-paneled room. She pointed out a tray with a coffee carafe and cups that sat on a low table. While she withdrew, but before she closed the door, Michael poured Faith a cup of coffee, and then one for himself. "Still take cream in yours?" he asked, passing the carafe to Fielding so he could pour his own.

"Yes," she said, surprised he'd recall such a mundane thing. "Too much straight caffeine gives me jitters. Today, especially, I've got enough acid running in my stomach to charge a battery."

Michael gazed at her over the rim of his cup. "I'm sorry so much has fallen on your shoulders, Faith. How is Dwight handling Lacy's death? Has he been any help, or are you having problems there, too?"

She perched on the edge of one of the three chairs someone had arranged in a triangle around the coffee table, and clutched the hot cup to warm her suddenly cold fingers. "I tried telling Dad we'd lost Lacy. He got it all mixed up in his mind and thought I was talking about Mother. The doctor had to sedate him. I decided there wasn't any sense in putting him through the grief of attending her service."

"What about your aunt Lorraine?"

"Still on the mission field in Tanzania. When things calm down, I'll write her a letter. Or perhaps I should try calling her via the field office. But maybe it's pointless to worry her when she can't come." She broke off abruptly. "Why this pretended concern, Michael? Your obligations to the Hyatt family ended when the divorce was final. By the way, exactly when was that?''

"July." Michael shifted his gaze to Klpp Fielding. "The divoroc wasn't my idea. Lacy filed in January while I was on a medical mission to Norway. I phoned her at the beach house to ask her to reconsider. She refused to talk, and said she had company. It was too late, anyway—she'd already filed the papers. That was January fifth. Two days later, divorce papers arrived by courier at my hotel." He massaged the back of his neck. "I might have convinced her to drop the request if I'd been able to make it home the next week as I'd originally planned. But we ran into complications with the transplant and I couldn't leave Norway until much later. By then, her lawyer and mine had pretty much settled the particulars. Mine said I shouldn't contest. He said she was seeing someone else."

"That would be you," Faith said testily, her soft brown gaze hardening as she pinned it on Kipp.

"Yes, it would," he returned without a hint of shame.

Faith's gaze never wavered. "I guess you forgot you had a wife."

"Shelby and I separated before Thanksgiving. I assumed she intended to get a divorce—not that it's your business. Having spent the holidays alone, I felt at loose ends. Lacy was lonely, too." His lip curled slightly. "She said she was on her own a lot. Her husband devoted his life to his career." Meeting Michael's angry glare, Kipp continued speaking to Faith. "Lacy hadn't been out with her husband in months. She'd never been sailing. Had never dug for clams. You'd have thought I'd given her diamonds when I bought her flowers. If ever a woman had been neglected, it was Lacy Cameron."

Michael clenched a hand in the front of Kipp's shirt. "Damn you, Fielding! I didn't neglect my wife."

"That's enough." Faith pulled a tissue from her handbag and mopped up the coffee Michael had spilled when he vaulted from his chair. Their macho posturing irritated her so much she forgot to be shy. "Lacy did feel you were obsessed with work, Michael. But Kipp, although you treated her like a queen for a few weeks, that hardly makes up for concealing the fact that you were married."

The men gaped at Faith's furious scrubbing. They both frowned, and Michael recognized the anger in her movements as she wielded the tissue. The table was more than polished to a shine when she finished.

Michael broke the silence first. "Lacy had all of my heart and as much of my time as I was able to give." If he sounded hurt, he thought dully, it was because he still had his moments. "I took an oath to heal." He thought Faith should understand that, even if Lacy had somehow forgotten.

Getting to her feet, Faith tossed the sodden tissue into the trash. While she was up, she dug in her purse again and removed the copies she'd made of the custody agreement. She shoved one into each man's hand. "What drove either of you to do what you did doesn't make any difference to Lacy now. In seeking love, my sister obviously made some bad choices. Maybe even selfish ones. But in the end, her decisions weren't selfish. No matter how difficult it was for her to breathe when she was admitted, her focus was on the life that had been created within her."

"Custody papers?" Kipp skimmed through the stapled packet. "She can't do this. Her babies have a father." The man scowled openly at Faith. "You just admitted that Lacy was in distress during her last hours. Any attorney worth his salt will prove you coerced her into signing these. Not only that, who witnessed your signatures?''

''I didn't instigate this agreement. Lacy brought it with her, Mr. Fielding. If there was duress involved in the signing, it was directed toward me. Lacy refused all treatment except oxygen until I not only signed the forms but mailed them to her lawyer. If you'll check closely, on page three she acknowledges my signature, And someone notarized each line Lacy endorsed.''

Faith wasn't about to tell them Lacy's witness signature had already been in place when she herself signed the document. That didn't change the facts. Lacy had watched her sign. Most importantly, the agreement represented her wishes.

A range of emotions flitted across Michael Cameron's face as he read the document from start to finish. Sadness. Longing. Grief. But Faith didn't see anything like resignation as he folded the papers and tucked them into the inside pocket of his suit jacket. While his eyes darkened sympathetically, his jaw remained tensed, his posture determined—as though they'd entered a fight ring and the bell had rung.

Fielding drained his cup and thumped it back onto the tray. Wadding a paper napkin, he threw it into a nearby wastebasket. ''Lacy told me a little about her childhood. I recall she said her mom was an invalid. And that you sacrificed your youth to run the household, Ms. Hyatt.''

''I was the oldest child. If Lacy had been born first, it would have been the other way around,'' Faith stated flatly.

Michael moved forward. ''If you have a point, Fielding, I'd like to hear it. But don't try to say Lacy slandered Faith. I know she admired her sister.''

Faith gave him a surprised glance. She and Lacy had grown closer after Lacy's marriage—and before her divorce. Faith was pretty sure familial love had existed. But admiration? Her heart swelled at the thought. During all those troubled years, she would have settled for a simple hug from her sister. Faith roused as Kipp spoke again.

''My point is that Faith missed the things kids do for fun. Lacy said Faith never participated in school activities. No dances. No sports. No guys. A while ago, you two talked about her ailing father. If she assumes care of two infants on top of that, I think she's kissing any chance for a normal life goodbye. This is when she should concentrate on meeting someone and getting married.''

A startled gasp escaped Faith's lips. But she was too embarrassed by Kipp's rundown of her life to make any comment. More like her *lack* of a life. He'd managed to make her sound pretty pathetic. Oh, she'd dreamed of falling in love, she'd even had a brief affair with a hospital accountant. He'd ended the relationship, eventually marrying another nurse and moving to another state. Faith continued to hope for marriage and a family someday. But she never felt as if she needed a husband to be complete. Her life hadn't been all that bad.

Michael, too, seemed astonished by Kipp's blunt statement. Since no one interrupted, Kipp hammered his point home. ''I'm offering you an out here, Faith. Shelby and I have a six-bedroom home. It sits on three acres. She's able to devote all her time to motherhood. I made some inquiries this morning. I know how much you earn. And I know you work some oddball shifts. I sincerely doubt anyone would think you derelict of duty if you signed Lacy's babies over to their natural father."

"You're claiming that role, huh, Fielding?" Michael slapped a hand on the glass table. "We have a difference of opinion on that score. The twins are mine."

"Don't be ridiculous." Kipp's chest expanded a few inches. "I hate bringing this up with a lady present, old man. Your ex-wife was pretty outspoken about the infrequency of your lovemaking."

Michael's face went suddenly florid. "It so happens, pal, we were intimate the day I left for Norway. January fourth. You're welcome to calculate that out."

Kipp seemed shaken by Michael's announcement. "I—I…that's the day before we, ah, that is…when Lacy and I first slept together. I think you're lying, Cameron. Lacy said she had to schedule an appointment with you to make love."

"Think what you want. Lacy's forte was high drama. I guess I always knew she was impulsive. I'm only just realizing *how* impulsive."

Faith slumped down hard in her chair. She blinked up at them, stomach roiling. "So what you're, uh, both saying is that it's a mystery as to who fathered the twins?"

Neither man acknowledged Faith's conclusion.

Kipp checked his watch for about the third time in five minutes. "I have to get back to New York. I don't have any more time to argue. Here's the bottom line. There's a boy upstairs in the nursery with Fielding genes. Because of that, he's entitled to a legacy. I won't go into everything that entails. Suffice it to say he'll be well taken care of. You two will be hearing from my attorney. That's a promise."

Faith and Michael watched in silence as he stalked out.

"Two can play his game," Michael said, his expression thunderous. "I don't care how many damned Roman numerals he has after his name. Fielding will be hearing from my lawyer, too. Meanwhile, I'm going up to visit the babies. I don't advise trying to stop me, Faith." Giving her only seconds to respond, he, too, stormed out.

Faith's shoulders slumped. "Oh, Lacy," she murmured. "What kind of mess have you left me with this time?"

Sighing, she regained enough composure to pick up the phone and call the duty nurse in charge of the premie ward. "My sister's ex-husband has asked to visit the twins, Eileen. I'm willing to extend him that courtesy today, but make sure everyone on the duty roster knows Lacy left custody papers on file. If Michael or anyone else wants to see the babies from here on out, staff will have to call me for authorization. Is that clear?" When she was certain the charge nurse understood, Faith rang off.

Stopping at the reception area, she thanked Dr. Peterson's secretary for the use of his office. After that, she went upstairs to her own ward, post-surgical. Faith wanted to see the babies again after Michael left. Somehow, she couldn't shake the feeling that he presented a threat.

Her mind not on work, she nevertheless emptied her mailbox. It was full. Among the usual junk was a notice to stop at the finance office and discuss Lacy's hospital bill. Faith stared at the statement. She had a tidy savings account. She'd expected to use it to stock a nursery; she'd also figured it would allow her to take six months or so off work. Last night when she couldn't sleep, she made lists of what the babies would need. Planning for two of everything ate up money fast. To say nothing of the fact that the cost of funerals had skyrocketed since she'd arranged her mother's.

Closing her eyes, Faith rubbed her forehead. It hadn't entered her mind that she'd owe for Lacy's care. But then, what company would insure her sister? Even if she had a policy, it probably excluded her preexisting condition. Faith placed this new worry at the bottom of her stack. The next envelope she opened was almost as distressing. The babies needed names before the state could issue birth certificates.

Faith picked up a pen. Abigail was easy. That had been Lacy's wish. *Abigail Dawn.* It was a middle name denoting hope, and the two went well together, Faith thought. *Hyatt.* She wrote the last name in block letters. Writing it felt good. Like thumbing her nose at Kipp Fielding III and his father.

The form for Lacy's son remained mockingly blank. Faith made a list of names she thought sounded strong. Nicholas kept floating to the top. "Nicholas it shall be," she murmured, then chewed on the eraser while she searched her list for an acceptable middle name. *John.* A solid biblical name. Also, it'd been Faith and Lacy's grandfather's. Faith remembered him as a soft-spoken man with twinkling eyes.

Once that chore was complete, she dispatched her remaining mail quickly. A glance at her watch suggested she'd wasted enough time; Michael should be long gone from the nursery. She dropped off the birth certificate forms in the outgoing mail on her way to visit the twins.

By now she knew the routine and proceeded to don

sterile gear before she entered the nursery. Tying the last set of strings on her mask, Faith pushed open the door to the premie ward. And froze. A fully gowned and masked Michael Cameron sat in Faith's usual chair. He had a baby lying along each of his forearms, their little heads cradled in the palms of his big hands. Both pairs of baby eyes were wide-open. Faith was near enough to see their mouths working. Oh, they looked like perfect little dolls.

Fuzzy dark hair spilled from beneath Nicholas's blue stocking cap. Abigail's wispy curls glinted pale gold in the artificial light.

Faith's gaze shifted to Michael's face. Her stomach knotted and her knees felt watery. There was no mistaking the tears that tracked down his cheeks. An involuntary protest rose in Faith's throat, blocking the breath she tried desperately to suck into her lungs. She didn't *want* to empathize with Lacy's ex. Throwing out a hand, she clutched the privacy screen to keep from falling.

Michael heard the sound. His rapt gaze left the twins. ''Faith.'' He said her name softly. ''I know I've been here beyond the time you set, but...but they're incredible. I've never been so humbled. Since Lacy risked everything for them I really hope that somehow she knows how perfect they are.''

Faith watched him transfer his attention to a tiny hand that had worked free of its gown and felt the blood drain from her face.

With one gloved finger, he captured the baby's waving fist. ''Fielding said they're labeled Babies A and B Hyatt. I stopped in finance to pay Lacy's bill and discovered she'd never legally changed her name after the divorce. Officially the babies are Camerons. As they

should be," he said sternly, his eyes lifting in time to
witness Faith's retreat. Michael called her to come back,
to no avail.

Hands over her ears, Faith stumbled into the hall. She
needed to get home and call Lacy's lawyer. Maybe the
custody papers, which plainly stated Lacy wanted the
babies to go by the name of Hyatt, were flawed. She
took the time, however, to detour by the nursing station
to retrieve the birth certificate forms she'd filled out
incorrectly.

What was in a name, anyway? Michael had admitted
the divorce was final. And she certainly hadn't *asked*
him to pay Lacy's hospital bill. Maybe he was being
thoughtful. Then again, he might have an ulterior mo-
tive. At any rate, Faith felt disloyal to Lacy as she
crossed out Hyatt on the forms and wrote Cameron. As
she dropped her gown, mask and bootees in the laundry,
she mentally rearranged her budget to include attorney's
fees. If Fielding and Cameron expected her to fade quietly into the woodwork, they'd better think again. She
intended to be a devoted mom to her sister's babies.
The kind she'd never had time to be for Lacy. She'd
been too young then and stretched too thin in caring for
their ailing mother. Still, the thought of so many lawyers getting involved made Faith almost sick to her
stomach.

CHAPTER THREE

ATTENDING LACY'S FUNERAL was even harder than Faith had imagined. She was touched by the number of people from the hospital who came out of respect for her. Likewise, by the number of Lacy's old friends from high school and college who'd shown up. Faith made a mental note to catch Abigail Moore after the service so that she could tell her about her namesake.

A few acquaintances had sent flowers and cards. Including Kipp Fielding III. His was an ostentatious arrangement of red and white roses. They dwarfed Michael's small white basket of violets. The violets brought tears to Faith's eyes; they were Lacy's favorite flower and Michael must have gone to a great deal of trouble to find a florist to provide them at this time of year.

More surprising than his thoughtful gesture, however, was seeing the man himself walk into the chapel. He paused at a back row and greeted two couples who'd arrived earlier. People Faith had never met. Now it was obvious they'd known Lacy through Michael.

He didn't tarry long with his friends. Head bent, he walked slowly down the center aisle and knelt in front of the closed casket. Faith had thought her tears were all cried out until she watched his jaw ripple with emotion several times before he leaned forward to kiss the oak-grained lid. There was a decided sheen to his eyes when he rose. Or maybe she was watching him through her own tears.

She couldn't think of a thing to say when he sank onto the bench beside her. Even if she'd thought of something, she didn't trust her voice not to break.

"I swung past the apartment to pick you up," he murmured. "You'd already gone. You must not have listened to the messages on your answering machine. The last one I left said I'd booked a car service for us. I know you don't own a vehicle."

Faith clasped and unclasped her hands. The truth was, she *had* listened to the message. But Lacy's lawyer ordered her to have as little contact as possible with either of the two men. The attorney, David Reed, had been quite adamant, in fact.

Fortunately, Faith was saved from answering Michael when the minister stepped up to the pulpit. She'd asked Reverend Wilson to keep the service short in deference to the people who had taken time off work. However, his opening prayer droned on and on.

Ending at last, the minister segued into a poem by Helen Steiner Rice. The words celebrated life, and Lacy had been particularly fond of them. Anyone who'd ever received a note from her would recognize the piece, as she'd had it reprinted on the front of her monogrammed note cards.

Next, a singer—a woman Faith had selected from a generic pool on file at the funeral home—had half the people in the chapel sniffing and wiping their eyes with her rendition of "The Rose." Faith chose the song because Lacy had worn out two CD copies of it. Too bad if anyone thought the lyrics inappropriate for a funeral. Faith wanted the service to epitomize Lacy's life.

Her own cheeks remained wet as the minister delivered a tribute she'd written yesterday. The words hadn't come easily, but Faith wanted people to know that her sister wasn't shallow and vain, as some might remember her from high school and college. For one thing, Lacy had artistic talents. Before her debilitating illness, she'd dreamed of becoming an interior designer. If the media chose to cover the funeral, Faith also wanted them to report how selfless Lacy had been, giving her life in exchange for healthy babies. But it was all she could do to listen to the eulogy. The tears coursed down her cheeks and plopped on the lapels of her new navy suit.

Before Reverend Wilson brought the service to a close, Michael turned to Faith and whispered, ''May I say a few words?''

''Of c-course,'' she stammered. When he stood, she was shocked to discover her right hand had been tightly entwined in his. Faith immediately pulled away, but she missed the warmth of his hand as Michael stepped to the pulpit and faced the small gathering.

''Lacy Ellen Hyatt Cameron passed through our lives at warp speed,'' he began in an unsteady voice. ''Her sojourn with us was much too brief.'' He paused to clear his throat, and Faith saw his fingers tremble. She lowered her gaze to the floor and sucked her upper lip between her teeth, biting down hard to hold off a new bout of tears.

However, Michael didn't dwell on Lacy's death. He invited everyone to remember the woman who'd lived life full-tilt. ''The Lacy we all knew brightened a room just by being in it. She hated sitting still. She loved to go and do. She loved to argue and debate.'' His voice cracked a little, but a semblance of a smile curved his lips as he suggested she was probably even now testing

St. Peter's mettle. "It's that Lacy who'll live on in my heart and I hope in yours as well."

People were dabbing at their eyes as he sat down again. Faith felt as if a weight had been lifted. She'd blotted away her tears while the minister offered a final prayer. "Thank you, Michael," she managed to say once everyone began to mill about. "Lacy kept things to herself this last year. I…we…stopped communicating." Faith licked a salty tear off her upper lip while twisting a tissue into bits. "If I hadn't been so wrapped up in work, I keep thinking she might have confided in me more. I'm afraid I gave up too easily, trying to reach her at the beach house. When she didn't return my calls, I…" Faith didn't finish the statement.

"I'm more at fault than you are, Faith," Michael said, his hazel eyes dark and troubled. "I let our lawyers act as go-betweens after she filed for divorce. I should have sat down with her when I returned from Norway. I can't tell you how sorry I am that she ended up hating me."

"I'm sure she didn't feel that strongly, Michael."

"Then how come Fielding believes I'm a first-class SOB?"

"On the phone, Lacy seemed happy enough at Christmas. She didn't give the slightest indication you two would be splitting up in January."

"When you called, she put on a convincing act. She was pretty upset with me for missing most of the major holiday parties we'd received invitations to. Every passing day, she seemed to feel more resentful of the time I devoted to my patients. I didn't know how to bridge the chasm between us."

"I'm sorry, Michael." Faith stood and bent down to pick up her purse. She started to walk away, then turned back. "Don't be too hard on yourself. Lacy's craving for attention goes back to her childhood. To when our entire household centered on our mother's poor health. At the same time, it terrified Lacy to think her illness might somehow force her to become dependent on others—like our mom had been. Looking back, I believe Lacy assumed the transplant would make her one-hundred percent good-as-new."

Michael tugged at his lower lip. "Which explains why she became so terribly hostile toward follow-up care. I wish you'd said something sooner, Faith. You've answered my biggest question. I never understood how Lacy could act so cavalier about the second chance she'd been given. I'm a doctor, for God's sake. You'd think I'd have picked up on her feelings."

Faith touched his arm. "You were too close to the problem. It dawned on me gradually, after you two had left Boston."

"We were married for five years. How could I completely miss what bothered her so much?" he asked with a snag in his voice. "Kipp got the picture, didn't he?"

"It's a little late for recriminations. Kipp treated her so shabbily he's hardly in a position to judge you." Removing her hand from Michael's arm, Faith backed away. "Uh, Michael, I have to go. The funeral director just signaled that it's time for me to get in the family car to make the trip to the cemetery."

"You're doing that alone? I'd planned to ride with friends." He waved toward the back of the chapel. "I'll keep you company if you'd prefer."

"No. Please don't change your arrangements. Someone from the funeral home will accompany me. Right now, I need a minute to decide which flowers go to the cemetery and which I want sent to the hospital to brighten our waiting rooms.''

"All right," he said, frowning. He let her go, yet didn't join his friends until the director approached Faith and the two left the room.

THE ASSEMBLY AT THE GRAVESIDE was smaller than the gathering at the chapel. As there wasn't to be a formal reception, friends took the time to speak with Faith before claiming seats beneath a shade tent. She was so caught up in talking to Abigail Moore, relating Lacy's desire to name her daughter Abby, Faith didn't realize Michael had arrived and had slipped into the seat beside her. Or not until he exhaled sharply.

Abigail sobbed. "I'm so surprised and…and humbled. Lacy phoned me once after she'd moved back to Boston. Just to talk, she said. I suggested meeting for lunch, but she put me off. I never knew she was pregnant, Faith. I feel as if I let her down. Call me when you take the babies home. I'd love to visit."

Faith nodded and pressed Abby's hand. She winced when Michael leaned over and hissed in her ear. "I was under the impression Dr. Finegold lost Lacy during the delivery. When did she name the twins?"

"Before she went up for her C-section. Lacy gave me custody, remember. And she wasn't aware that she carried twins. It's common for women to name their babies, Michael. Abby was what Lacy had called her child. I chose Nicholas," Faith said, injecting a challenge in her voice.

Michael's brows puckered. He probably would have said more if the minister hadn't asked them to stand for a prayer. Relieved, Faith tore her gaze from Michael's flinty eyes. Bending her head, she willed her bucking heart to slow. David Reed had specifically warned her not to provoke either Michael or Kipp Fielding III. He said to refer them to him for answers to any and all questions concerning the babies.

She shouldn't have let Michael's earlier vulnerability reach her. Well, it wouldn't happen again. He and Kipp were her enemies. She'd do well to remember that.

Faith was first in the circle of mourners to lay a carnation atop Lacy's casket. An attendant had provided each person with a flower. The director sidled up to Faith as she stepped out from under the awning, asking if she preferred to mingle a bit or return to town. "Town, please," she said with a tremor. "I'll come back tomorrow for some private time with my sister."

The short walk to the waiting car proved to be the hardest part of the entire ordeal for Faith. Her knees wobbled like the front wheel of a novice bike rider. She would have stumbled and maybe even fallen if the director hadn't had a firm grip on her elbow. The shaky feeling kept her from turning back for a last look. Not that she would have had a clear picture anyway. Once she was sitting in the car, her nose pressed to the side window, the lovely hillside with its spreading elms and soft carpet of green all ran together. There was such finality attached to the ritual of leaving the cemetery. Up to now it had been easy to pretend that Lacy was only a phone call away. Watching the blur of row after row of headstones stripped away the fantasy, underlined the truth. Her only sister was gone, and there were too many things left unsaid between them.

On the ride back to town, Faith went through half a box of tissues the director had thoughtfully provided.

It was barely noon when the black car pulled up outside her apartment. So little time, Faith thought frantically—it took so little time to cut you forever from the sphere of a loved one.

The long afternoon that lay ahead seemed interminable as she stepped out of the car into the sunlight. And once she'd changed clothes, she found she didn't want to be confined with her thoughts. She could go mad worrying about what Michael and Kipp might be plotting with regard to Lacy's babies. Yet, if she stayed here, Michael could call or show up unexpectedly and further debate her right to name the babies. He hadn't seemed happy with the names she'd chosen.

She considered going to the hospital nursery. There she could hold part of Lacy close, thus assuring herself and the babies that she'd protect them from the men who'd taken such a recent interest in fatherhood. Though in a worst-case scenario, Faith knew one of the two men was the children's biological parent. She might be more willing to face up to that fact if the loss of the twins' mother wasn't so terribly real just now.

On the spur of the moment, Faith grabbed her purse and left the building, deciding to wander aimlessly downtown; she'd visit the twins later. She had no particular destination in mind—until she found herself in front of a major department store. Then she remembered the list of items needed to set up a nursery for the babies. Why not shop now? After all, David Reed, Lacy's lawyer, had told her to outfit a room. He said a judge would certainly take her readiness to provide the babies with a home as a positive sign if it came to a court battle. In her heart, Faith feared it would come to that. What she didn't want to think about was which of the three combatants would win such a fight. Kipp Fielding III, Michael Cameron...or her.

"Be optimistic," she muttered under her breath as she hurried into the store.

Upstairs, the baby department, with its array of pastels and primary colors, infused warmth back into Faith's cold limbs. Buying for Lacy's babies was going to be fun. Faith so rarely shopped for fun. In her mother's stead, she had learned at an early age to weigh price against serviceable value. To be frugal. It was a practice she adhered to when buying for herself. She was determined to give Lacy's babies all the things she'd never been able to give Lacy. That included lavishing them with her undivided attention. She'd been so young, so totally inadequate as a surrogate parent to her sister. Things were different now. Her life was different.

As she wandered through the baby furniture, Faith chose cribs and dressers with clean, classic lines. Beautiful wood that would endure. Crib bedding was another matter. Faith tried to imagine what Lacy would have wanted for her children. Lacy's taste in clothing and furnishings, had tended toward flashy colors while Faith gravitated toward softer shades. She thought about her apartment done in ivory, gray and mauve, and deliberately purchased two wild circus quilts richly patterned in blocks of green, yellow, orange and blue.

The saleslady steered her toward matching crib sheets, bumper pads and a diaper stacker. Next, she added large clown decals for the wall. She'd already decided to paint the nursery walls four different primary colors. She might even pick up paint on the way home and begin the project this evening.

Toys. Faith spotted them across the aisle. She headed straight for a large plush monkey with a funny face. How foolish, she thought, squeezing its soft body. The stuffed animal was bigger than either of the twins. It'd be far more practical to buy a nice mobile or a couple of small rattles. But she couldn't make herself let go of the monkey. It remained hooked on her arm as she reached for an equally impractical giraffe. Faith had to stand on tiptoe to grab the giraffe from the top shelf. In so doing, she dislodged a pile of bears.

"Goodness!" Bears of all sizes tumbled onto the other side of the display.

"Hey!" Faith heard a faint, gruff protest. She dashed around the corner and almost bowled over a man covering his head with both arms to ward off raining bears.

It took Faith a moment to realize she knew that profile. "Michael? What are you doing here?"

"Uh, hello, Faith." Michael shifted two small teddies to his left hand, and began to pick up the larger ones spilled across the carpet—a move that placed him in direct visual alignment with Faith's trim ankles. Hands unexpectedly clumsy, Michael dropped the bears he was collecting. His mouth felt dry as cotton. Lord, what was the matter with him?

Faith's attention focused on the two bears Michael kept separate. One was pink and the other blue, both washable terry cloth. They matched two soft receiving blankets draped over the crook of his elbow.

Several silent minutes passed before Michael realized he was the only one righting the bears. Faith's gaze remained fixed on his intended purchases.

"I stopped off at the nursery after the funeral," he explained, halting his task long enough to meet her eyes. "A nurse, Teri I think was her name, said premies respond to having the type of blanket they'll be wrapped in at home laid over their isolettes. She also suggested tucking small toys inside. Along with frequent holding, she said, that gives premature babies a sense of well-being.''

A sharp pain sliced through Faith's stomach. Her first reaction was to wonder why Michael hadn't gone straight back to New York where he belonged after the funeral. Her second was more an overwhelming sense of fear than a clear thought. A fear that this situation was cartwheeling out of her control.

''You don't have any idea what type of blankets Abigail and Nicholas will have when they go home,'' she said tartly. ''I'm outfitting their nursery. Not in pink or blue. Lacy liked wild colors. Bright colors.'' She said it almost desperately.

Michael's face appeared so crestfallen, she almost regretted her outburst. Or she did until it struck her that he was going behind her back to gain entry into the nursery, despite her request. No doubt he'd used his status as an eminent surgeon to inveigle his way in.

Faith's voice dropped. ''Go home, Michael. Don't make me get a restraining order against you. I spoke with Lacy's lawyer last night. He said she was very much of sound mind when she came to his office to draw up those custody papers. He further said that if you or Kipp Fielding want visiting privileges, you'll have to request approval through Family Court. Any questions you have are to be directed to him. His name is David Reed. You'll find him in the phone book.''

''Why would you drag Lacy's good name through court? Look at her recent behavior. The doorman at our apartment knows she left me that night in January in a fit of anger. From there she had a torrid affair with a married man. Then she ran off without telling anyone and hid out. *Think,* Faith. She deliberately went off her lifesaving medications.''

Faith heard only the warning that overlaid his apparent concern. Pain exploded in her chest. She should have suspected Michael was being nice at the funeral to put himself in a good light. Now she could believe this steely-jawed man with the hard eyes had driven her sister away. "And you're lily-white?" she said angrily. "Lacy left you because you were obsessed with work. Somehow I doubt a judge will find it *her* fault that Kipp pretended to be single. No one knows better than you, Michael, that Lacy's anti-rejection drugs were experimental. Who'd fault her for not wanting to jeopardize her unborn child?"

"I see. You and Lacy's lawyer have it all figured out, don't you, Faith? Well, I wouldn't spend a lot of money furnishing that nursery if I were you." Michael drew himself up to his full six-foot-three height. "Courts have been more favorable to fathers over the last few years, especially if they have the means to provide for their kids. I have the means several times over. And the desire. Tell that to your David Reed."

Faith watched him stride down the aisle. She felt as if she'd been trampled by an elephant. Michael stopped to pay for his purchases, chatting easily with the saleswoman as she rang them up. He appeared impervious to the fact that he'd left Faith shattered and it struck her how little effect her words had had on him. Michael Cameron intended to apply the same tenacity that had made him a world-famous surgeon to overturning her guardianship of Lacy's babies.

He obviously didn't realize she could be tenacious, too. More determined than ever to outfit the nursery as Lacy would want, Faith finished her shopping and requested everything be delivered. Leaving, she visited a paint store. And lugged the heavy cans up to her third-floor apartment. Then she put all other plans on hold while she ran to the hospital to visit the babies. She needed to touch them. To hold them.

Faith cuddled Abigail first, and then Nicholas. "You're going to love the room I'm fixing for you," she told them both as they gazed at her with unfocused eyes.

The pediatrician came in while she was there. He unwrapped the babies and checked them over thoroughly. "They're gaining like champs," he said over their chorusing squalls. "Two more weeks at this rate and you'll be able to take them home."

"So soon? That's wonderful news! The nurses seemed to think they'd have to stay here much longer." Faith couldn't contain a happy smile.

"If they'd lost a lot of weight, that would have been true. Nicholas only lost an ounce and Abigail two. The way they're chowing down, unless something unforeseen crops up, my guess is they'll both top five pounds soon. Dr. Finegold mentioned your predicament, Faith. For what it's worth, I'll be glad to put in a good word for you. The babies may be stable, but caring for premie multiples can be tricky. I like knowing they'll be under the care of a trained nurse."

"I appreciate your vote of confidence, Dr. Sampson. I'm planning to take at least six months off from work. A year if I can swing it financially. Our administrator said he'd hold a position open as long as possible. Otherwise, I'll use our on-site day care. I've already placed my name on the waiting list. Gwen in E.R., said the day care has openings from time to time."

"If you're able to stay home six months, that's great, Faith. A year would be icing on the cake. After I examine the twins next week, I'll give you a call. I should be able to give you their actual release date then."

"Thank you," Faith murmured. She watched him cuddle Abigail while she diapered Nicholas. She felt all thumbs and hoped he didn't hold that against her. She hadn't diapered a baby since Lacy was little. "I'll get the hang of this soon," she promised.

Sampson laughed. "I have no doubt you will. Call my office and ask my receptionist to put you in touch with a parents-of-multiples support group. They have a newsletter and meetings where other parents of twins, triplets and upward exchange information. My other advice is to lay in a mountain of diapers. You won't believe how many you'll go through in a day."

"Diapers." Faith snapped her fingers. "I went shopping today and bought out the store. Even paint for the nursery walls. How could I have forgotten diapers?"

The physician handed her Abigail and gave a wry glance at the wet spot on the front of his lab coat. "Breaks of the trade," he said as Faith apologized for leaving him holding a near-naked baby so long.

"Always remember to diaper Nicholas first. Or he'll decorate those newly painted walls."

"They aren't painted yet. As soon as I leave here, I'm going home to do that. Two weeks," she mused happily, giving each baby a kiss before she tucked them back into their warm cocoons.

By dinnertime that evening, Faith's muscles ached so badly she could hardly stand up straight. The result of her labors pleased her, however. The walls looked cheery, complementing the soft gray carpet and white ceiling. She liked the room.

It suited her to keep busy and to restrict her thoughts to the subject of the babies. So after eating a light dinner, she went to work recovering the cushions on a comfortable rocking chair—the only piece of furniture she'd saved from the old house. The chair had belonged to her mother. Faith remembered how on good days her mom would sit by a sunny window and rock the infant Lacy. As the cushions cut from jungle-print chintz took shape, Faith imagined herself rocking Nicholas and Abigail to sleep.

It was an image that remained with her until she received a phone call from David Reed the next day. "Faith, could you come down to my office, please? I've got faxes from Kipp Fielding's legal team, and also from Michael Cameron's attorney. I want you to see what we're up against. We need to plan our strategy."

"What strategy?" she asked weakly. "Lacy signed custody of the children over to me, as you know. I agreed to raise, clothe and feed them. What other strategy do we need?" She heard his sigh and the creak of his chair.

"I know you're not naive, Faith. I explained during our first phone consultation how messy custody fights can get. On top of that, this case is quite unusual."

"How so?" she asked, although she knew more or less what he'd say.

"Normally it's a matter of determining visitation rights for a noncustodial parent. Occasionally Family Court has to intervene for grandparents. But your case has two men claiming to be the twins' father, and an aunt—you—to whom the biological mom assigned full custody. To say nothing of a very influential grandpa. Fielding Junior made a fortune on Wall Street. It looks as if he's prepared to use it to guarantee himself a grandson."

Faith's legs wouldn't hold her. She fell into a chair. "So are you saying it's hopeless?"

"No. Oh, my, no. Your position in the triangle is equal to the others at this point. Old man Fielding may have New York judges in his pocket, but his clout won't be half as great in Boston. I've cleared an hour on my calendar at one o'clock. It would be in your best interests to meet with me, I think."

"Of course," Faith barely had time to say she'd be there before he hung up. Her nerves were completely jangled. She could practically see Reed rubbing his hands together. He'd struck her as something of a barracuda. Maybe that was good. She hoped it was. And hoped he was clever enough to solve the matter in her favor, preferably within two weeks.

Faith showered and dressed with care, then left for her appointment. After all, if she expected the man to represent her enthusiastically, it would help if she made a good impression. She hoped his fees would be manageable—another thing that worried her. They hadn't discussed what he charged. Faith had a fair savings account, but she'd need it to allow her to stay home with the twins.

Broad-winged bats beat up a storm in Faith's stomach as she walked downtown to the building where Reed's offices were housed. Passing a corner café, it dawned on Faith that she'd skipped lunch. She didn't think she could eat a bite, but she certainly hoped her stomach didn't growl at an inopportune time during their session.

"You're prompt," said a matronly receptionist when Faith checked in. "Mr. Reed likes that in a new client. Just let me ring his office and let him know you've arrived. Can I get you a cup of coffee or tea, Ms. Hyatt?"

"No, nothing, thanks," Faith murmured, hoping she was the only one who knew her hands were shaking so hard she'd spill a beverage. As she'd only seen one other lawyer in her life, when she needed power of attorney to take charge of her father's welfare, she didn't know what to expect of this so-called strategy visit.

"Come in, come in, Ms. Hyatt," boomed a jolly voice.

Faith leaped out of the chair she'd taken in the corner of the waiting room. No wonder he sounded so jolly. David Reed resembled Santa Claus. Though dressed in conservative blue rather than a red suit, he was round and sported white hair and a full beard.

"You don't look a thing like your sister," he said, clasping Faith's cold hand.

"No," she murmured, "I don't."

He merely nodded, indicating she should take a chair near his desk as he closed his office door. "Well, I hope you're more solid than you look. This fight could be long and nasty."

Faith's heart sank. "I...I assumed the court would uphold my sister's wishes."

Reed steepled pudgy fingers. A fair-sized diamond winked in the sunlight streaming through a window that overlooked Boston Common. "Your sister was less than forthright with me, Faith. May I call you Faith?"

"Please do. How, uh, in what way did Lacy lie to you?"

"For one thing, she led me to believe the baby's father was dead. Oh, she didn't come right out and offer to produce a death certificate, but she implied as much. She never said a word about being divorced. In essence, Lacy let me think the money she willed you and her unborn child had come to her through an inheritance."

"I didn't know she'd left any money. She never said anything. We hardly had time to cover the custody papers, which, to be truthful, I signed quickly to ease her mind. I never expected her to d-di-die."

"I believe you, Faith," Reed said, bouncing his fingers together again. "I hope the judge will. Either of the other two legal counsels could imply you want custody only for the money."

Faith gasped. "Surely not! I'd planned to care for the babies out of my own savings. I doubt that whatever Michael settled on Lacy was a huge amount."

"The living trust your sister set up is approximately half a mil. You, if made custodian, have access to the interest until the babies turn twenty-one. Add to that proceeds from the sale of a beach house. Another seven hundred and fifty thousand."

Faith tried to keep her jaw from dropping but didn't succeed.

"I see you had no idea," David said. "I wish I'd gotten your reaction on video. Now you understand my concern. The Fielding team will surely make an issue of the money. And I've got no doubt that Dr. Cameron knows how much his ex-wife was worth."

Clasping her hands tightly, Faith brought them up under her chin. "I don't want Lacy's money, Mr. Reed. Is there a way to put it completely in trust for the twins?"

"There is. But you might not want to be so hasty. If your aim is to win full custody of those infants, it could get costly."

"Of course that's my goal. As I explained, I have three bedrooms. I rented a larger place, assuming my dad would stay with me after he sold his house. In fact, he's living in an assisted-care facility, so I have lots of space. I've already turned one bedroom into a nursery,'' she said passionately. "I can't believe either Michael or Kipp will offer the twins as much love and attention as I'm prepared to give."

"Maybe not," David said bluntly. "But one of them is the natural father. That's why I wanted to talk to you face-to-face, Faith. Fielding's team has demanded that the court order DNA testing. It takes four to six weeks after they give the go-ahead—and they will," he added. "The test will establish paternity beyond any doubt. If we dig in and fight after that, we'll be contesting a bona fide parent. I'm not saying we couldn't win, considering the mother didn't think highly of either Cameron or Fielding. It does mean that preparing our case will require a lot of expensive hours. I'll need a full-time legal researcher and a legal secretary assigned exclusively to this." He paused. "To be honest, the case intrigues me. Hell, I foresee it being a tremendous boost to my practice."

For the longest time, Faith chewed the inside of her mouth and stared out the window. "I only want what's best for Nicholas and Abigail," she finally said, her voice barely above a whisper.

"I realize it's a monumental decision. Maybe you'd like to go home and sleep on it. Those men both have the best counsel money can buy. I want you one-hundred-percent committed before we jump into a dog-fight."

Faith refocused and looked into his serious blue eyes. "I am committed," she said. "You just hit on the whole point. Kipp Fielding has money coming out his ears and a Roman numeral after his name. Oh, he wants Nicholas all right. To carry on his prestigious family name. He doesn't give a damn about Abigail. Michael has money, too. But my sister divorced him because he was never home. He's a world-famous doctor, who's completely consumed by his work. Lacy thought I'd be the best person outside of herself to raise her child, er…children. Unless the court can show something colossal to make me change my mind, I'm going to fight. I don't need to sleep on it. If holding on to custody takes every penny of my portion of Lacy's estate—so be it.''

Her impassioned speech set the wheels in motion. All the way to Lacy's apartment, where—as she'd promised Reed—she'd handle the disbursement of her sister's belongings, Faith prayed she was doing the right thing for the babies. Unfortunately, she couldn't shake the image of the tears Michael had shed when he held the twins. A court fight would turn Michael against her. He'd most likely end up hating her. But she'd promised her only sister—and she'd lost her heart to those babies. What did it matter that she'd lost her heart to Michael years ago? That was then. This was now.

CHAPTER FOUR

THROUGHOUT THE REMAINDER of the week, Faith dashed about town in search of the items left on her list. As she entered each store, she looked over her shoulder to see if Michael skulked nearby. After the third day had passed without incident, and since he hadn't popped in at the hospital, she began to relax and enjoy her shopping sprees.

She bought a double stroller that did everything but talk. Before setting out to buy one, Faith hadn't had any idea how many types were on the market. The one she selected was blue canvas awash with white daisies. It included sunroofs and a basket large enough to hold a sack or two of groceries plus a big diaper bag. Perfect for walks in the park. There was mosquito netting to drape over both infants during nice weather and clear plastic that zipped on to make the interior cozy if the weather turned blustery. The whole thing folded easily to fit into the trunk of a car.

Pleased by that purchase, Faith then bought what the clerk referred to as "a diaper system." The microfiber bag had waterproof linings and pullout changing pads and removable totes.

The clerk insisted Faith needed two infant carriers. Those were in the event she had to take the babies in a cab—to their appointments with Dr. Sampson, for instance. Faith wondered if the fact that she didn't own a car could be counted against her at the hearing. But if she purchased one, the men's lawyers could say she was spending Lacy's money on personal pleasures. Not to mention she'd have to take driving lessons.

In the end, Faith elected to drop the problem in David Reed's lap. Let him argue that she'd lived in Boston for thirty-four years without owning a car. If the judge thought she needed one to be a good mom, the expense wouldn't be her decision.

As her purchases arrived at her apartment, Faith assembled cribs and a changing table. She added two small chests of drawers and saw the room shrink. Later, when the twins were older, she'd give one of them the third bedroom. Right now, they needed to be together.

"MY APARTMENT IS BEGINNING to resemble a baby store," Faith confided to Gwen one afternoon when she stopped at the hospital to have lunch with her friend.

"It must be costing you a mint to buy all that stuff new. Babies don't know if you buy their equipment at thrift stores and garage sales."

Faith wrinkled her nose. "True, but Michael Cameron and Kipp Fielding III will." She pushed her nose up with one thumb to imply snobbery.

"You poor thing. I'll bet you wish you'd recorded your conversation with Lacy. From what you told me, she didn't want her babies raised by either of those jerks."

"It all happened so fast, Gwen. I was worried about Lacy overtaxing herself. Because of that, it's probably just as well there were no witnesses. At that point I didn't want to sign any custody agreement. It sounded too much like Lacy was giving up. But I can only imagine how our conversation would come across in court."

"Yeah," her friend agreed glumly. "I still think you need to be lining up potential witnesses. Hey, didn't Sue and Vince from the crash cart team hear your sister make you promise to raise her kid? The day after Finegold lost her, the cafeteria was full of wild rumors. Some were valid, I'm sure."

"Were Sue and Vince on the team?" Faith rubbed at the frown creasing her forehead. "That tells you how rattled I was, Gwen. Much of that night is lost to me."

"Let me hunt them up and find out, okay? You have a heavy enough load. Just ask your lawyer if you need character witnesses waiting in the wings."

"All right. I have two appointments with him before our hearing next Thursday. Reed is coaching me on when to speak and when to keep my mouth shut."

"Is David Reed as good as the lawyers coming down from New York?"

Faith picked at her salad. "I don't have the vaguest idea. I'm sure Michael has someone successful representing him. That's the way he is. And Fielding's father is a big shot. David said we could figure his whole team are top legal eagles. Even if David turns out to be lousy, I'm stuck with him. I'll have to trust that Lacy knew he was good when she engaged him. I do know he wants to win."

"Well, that's a plus. Hey, you've hardly touched your lunch. I hate to bug out on you, but my time is up. Shall I see if Trish can get away to keep you company?"

"No." Faith rose and picked up her tray. "I really have a lot I should be doing. And I'm visiting Nick and Abby while I'm here."

"Stop in E.R. before you leave. If it's slow, maybe we can grab a cup of coffee."

"Maybe. I still have high chairs on my list and a few other things."

"Your infant carriers will double as high chairs until the kids are four or five months old. Two high chairs! Gad. Is there room in your kitchen?"

Faith envisioned scrunching two high chairs next to her table. "What are you suggesting? That I find a house? Even if I had time to look, which I don't, it'd undoubtedly be farther from work, and more expensive. My being able to take at least a six-month leave of absence is based on the rent I'm paying now. I'm determined to not touch the money Lacy left, except to pay attorney's fees."

"I know. And if the babies were yours, you'd make do. I panicked, thinking how you described Michael's apartment. You said it was huge."

"And elegant. And Kipp Fielding's home, from the way he described it, is a mansion."

"Don't you worry." Gwen gave Faith a hug as they walked down the hall. "A house isn't what makes a home. Love makes a home."

"You're right, Gwen. There's so much stuff coming at me, I lose sight of the most important thing. Michael will either have to find a wife or hire a nanny. Kipp has a wife, but no one's heard a peep from her. Lacy said they were separated at the time of the affair. Who knows if the woman's anxious to be a stepmother?"

"See? Beside them, you look like a candidate for mother of the year. You took care of your mom and raised Lacy. You can bet your boots Michael Cameron won't take six months off work."

"Everything you say sounds logical, Gwen. I'm afraid to get my hopes up too high, though. Courts have a way of deciding kids need two parents. Believe me, if there was a man I even remotely liked who liked me back, I'd propose to him.'' She shook her head. ''Three contenders. And frankly, none of us can offer the twins an ideal home.''

''Quit being so hard on yourself. It's not like every natural parent who brings a kid into the world has a flawless setup. I hate to break it to you, girl, but nobody's perfect.''

''I have noticed that.'' Faith smiled. ''Gwen, did you ever lie awake wondering if you had what it took to be a good mom? What if the judge decides I didn't do such a hot job of raising Lacy?''

''For heaven's sake! You were a kid raising a kid. Now you're an adult. But to answer your question— yes. Parenting is a scary proposition. Unfortunately, nobody's designed a test to see if anyone has the know-how to do the job. While you're buying things, pick up a practical book on parenting. Read as much as you can before you bring the twins home. Speaking as a mother of four, I guarantee you won't have time later.''

''What a good suggestion! I hadn't thought of buying a book. Oh, I'm so glad you had time to join me for lunch today.''

Gwen laughed. ''Off to the nursery with you. Before the shine on my halo tarnishes. And don't mention this discussion to my kids. They'll blow my cover. They think I'm the most inept mom in the world. Not to mention the meanest.''

Faith still had a smile on her face when she stepped off the elevator outside the premie ward. Her smile faded the minute she donned her gown and stepped through the door and saw Michael holding one of the twins.

"I thought you'd gone back to New York," she said, scrabbling for balance.

"I did for a few days. The judge assigned to our case suggested Fielding and I have our blood for the DNA testing drawn here at Good Shepherd."

"Oh." Faith saw he was holding Abigail. She lifted Nicholas to her shoulder, where he promptly spit up, then started to cry. "Poor baby," she murmured as she rubbed a hand over his back.

"Teri said he's been spitting up after feedings the past couple of days. She said it's nothing to worry about, just that he eats too fast. What do you think?"

Faith blinked at Michael in confusion. "Teri is a trained neonatal nurse. I would assume she knows what she's talking about."

He lowered his voice. "She's a kid. I doubt she's much more than twenty."

"Hmm. At twenty-eight you were performing heart transplants. Age has nothing to do with credentials. But if you'd like, I'll read his chart. See what nurses on the other shifts noted. Does he act sick?" She kissed the baby's cheek, swayed with him tucked against her breast, and was rewarded with a sleepy yawn. "If he had a fever, they'd separate him from the other babies. I'm sure it's nothing, as Teri said."

"If you're confident, then so am I." Michael let Abigail grip his gloved finger. The baby claimed his full attention, and he and Faith drifted into silence.

She roused after Nicholas fell asleep, walked to his crib and laid him carefully down. After rearranging the blankets, she tiptoed back to peer at Abby over Michael's shoulder. "Why would the judge make you guys come to Boston to have blood drawn when you have perfectly competent labs in New York?" The question had bothered her ever since Michael had explained why he'd returned to Boston.

He cleared his throat. "I don't know if I should tell you. My lawyer says we're adversaries, Faith."

Flushing, she stuttered, "S-sorry. I shouldn't have pried."

"Aw, hell, let our lawyers be adversaries. That's what we pay them for. The legal experts said if Kipp and I came here to have our blood drawn at the hospital where you work, your attorney would be less likely to claim contamination or mishandling."

"I suppose David might do that. I would never have thought of such a thing, but lawyers don't think like normal people. I mean, like lay people," she said when Michael threw back his head and gave a rollicking laugh. It was a laugh that grabbed hold of Faith and sent an uncertain longing deep inside. A longing that, even in panic, made her wish she and Michael Cameron were anything but adversaries. Struggling against the unwanted emotions, she turned her back.

"I'm not laughing at you, Faith," Michael said, sobering quickly. "Your statement was a slip of the tongue, but so very true. Everyone makes jokes about lawyers, and yet we willingly toss our hearts at their feet and shell out big bucks, hoping they can fix whatever's gone wrong in our lives."

"What if they can't fix things in our case?" Facing Michael again, Faith was gripped by such apprehension she barely got the words out.

"Oh, they'll rule in favor of someone. One of us three." Michael, too, sounded cheerless. He crooked the back of his index finger and brushed it lightly over Abigail's soft, translucent skin. "The trouble is, there'll be only one winner. Two of us will lose. That's the sad fact. I've seen lawyers and courts in action, and I've seen that it's often the person with the craftiest, most glib-tongued attorney who takes home all the marbles."

Faith saw how gently Michael stroked Abby's cheek. Despite Gwen's encouragement, Faith suddenly felt on unstable ground again. "Has something else happened, Michael? You sound so…cynical."

He tore his gaze from the baby and studied her somberly.

His demeanor prompted Faith to blurt, "I'm afraid Fielding will come off looking better to the judge. Aren't you? He has a stay-at-home wife, and a huge house with a huge yard. To say nothing of a rich papa backing him one-hundred percent."

"My apartment has twenty-four-hour-a-day security," Michael returned, as if in self-defense. "The rooms are big and airy. There's a nice neighborhood park nearby, and good schools less than a block away. My parents aren't super-rich, but I guarantee they'll dote on their grandchildren. They're currently running a free medical clinic for street kids in Sao Paulo, Brazil, but if I need them to strengthen my position in this case, they'll fly home at a moment's notice."

"Is that a polite way of telling me that my position is the shakiest? My apartment is dinky compared to yours. I suppose you've told your lawyer that I'm also the caretaker of my dad."

Abigail began to fuss and Michael shifted her to his shoulder. "Apparently, you have a low opinion of me, Faith. I don't know, maybe from your perspective I deserve it. Lord knows, I screwed up my marriage to your sister. This is different. Lacy might have made a conscious decision to cut me out of her life, but the babies aren't in a position to do that. Until they're old enough to pass judgment on my ability to be a parent, they ought to live with me. They're as much a part of me as they are of Lacy. Dammit, Faith, surely you understand what I'm saying. You struggled to keep your family together for years. Lacy told me about the many times you and your mom staved off social workers who would have removed you girls from the household.''

''That's right, Michael. Children belong in a loving environment. My mother was ill, but she loved us. And Dad loved her. Yes, it was tough, but we weren't raised by strangers or nannies. Lacy made no bones about how much your work took you away from home.''

Rising, Michael swayed gently to quiet the baby. ''This is an argument better saved for the hearing. It's easy to see that neither one of us is going to change the other's mind. All we're doing is creating tension. I'd hoped we could be sensible.'' He studied Faith as he rocked, missing the woman he remembered. The old Faith looked at all sides of an issue and never jumped to conclusions. Lacy had a short fuse and a hot temper. Not Faith. At least, she never used to.

''That's some statement coming from the man who stomped off in a huff last week in the toy department.''

''I admit you hit a raw nerve that day. At the moment, though, our arguing has upset Abigail, which I'm sure is the last thing either of us wants.''

''You're right. How long are you going to be in town? Perhaps we should set a schedule for visiting the twins so we don't show up here at the same time.''

''I'm sorry it's come to that, Faith.'' Honest regret darkened Michael's eyes. ''No matter how the DNA shakes out, you are always going to be the children's aunt. Let Fielding act like an uncivil ass. I'd like it if you and I kept an open line of communication.''

"Has Kipp been uncivil?" Faith frowned.

"To me. In the lab. And after he had his blood drawn, he stepped into my cubicle and informed me we'd do all our talking through our lawyers. Which reminds me. Has Reed called you regarding the Fielding's lawyers' latest brief?"

Faith shook her head. "I haven't talked to David today. I have an appointment to see him this afternoon. Tell me. I hate surprises."

"Lon Maxwell, my attorney, faxed me a copy of a complaint Kipp's team filed. They want to restrict our visits to the babies. Apparently Fielding has a boat race in Key West. He'll be gone for the next two weeks. The gist of the brief—Kipp claims it's unfair that we get to spend time with the twins when he can't."

"So the babies are supposed to be deprived of cuddling because he's off sailing?" Faith said explosively. "That's dumb. What's wrong with his wife? Or his father? Couldn't *they* visit?"

Michael placed the now-sleeping Abigail in her bed. He pulled the stocking cap over the ruff of light hair curling around her ears. Absently he set the pink terry-cloth bear in the corner nearest her head. "Don't get mad at me, Faith," Michael cautioned quietly as he followed her into an anteroom where they both shed their masks, gowns and gloves. "If the auburn-haired ice queen who was with Fielding downstairs is his wife Shelby, I get the distinct impression that nothing about this situation pleases her."

"Really? Didn't he tell us Shelby was dying to adopt a child? Even Lacy said Kipp and his wife reconciled in order to try a new fertility method. That sounds as if she really wants a baby."

"Maybe so. I could be reading her wrong. If she's

undergone a lot of fertility tests, it's possible that being in the lab is what she found distasteful.''

As the two walked to the elevators, Faith stopped suddenly and grabbed Michael's arm. ''Say you didn't read her wrong. If confronting her husband's infidelity is what's bothering her, why is she sticking with the jerk? I mean…they weren't even divorced, and he was screwing around.''

Michael gave a short laugh. ''I'm only guessing, but the Fielding fortune might be old Kipp's trump card. The lady wore more gold than they found in Cleopatra's tomb. You know the type. She breathed money. Suit looked like a million. Italian shoes. Fingernails that have never seen a chip.''

The elevator arrived and they stepped inside. Because they were alone, Faith broached something that still disturbed her. ''David told me this custody settlement could end up costing all of us a lot of money if it drags on.''

''That's the main reason I hate to see you take a leave of absence, Faith.'' Michael ran a compassionate gaze over her face. ''DNA is going to prove that one of us— either Kipp or me—is the twins' biological father. I can't help but think those results will be the deciding factor. Real dad gets the twins. Case over. That leaves you the poorer for having shelled out your savings to Reed.''

Faith glanced at her watch. ''Do you have time for a cup of coffee? I've got an hour before my appointment with David. There's something I'd like to discuss with you—somewhere other than the hospital cafeteria. I don't want to contribute any more to the rumor mill.''

''I had a list of things to do, but sure,'' he said, peeling the cuff back over his watch. He hesitated to mention his appointment with a furniture rental firm. He'd intended to tell her about taking a six-month lease on a unit next door to her, until Lon Maxwell cautioned him to think of Faith, as well as Kipp, as the enemy. Well, she'd find out soon enough. He'd seen the rental sign the day of the funeral, when he'd stopped by her place. The location was convenient, and he'd thought being neighbors would help maintain good relations with Faith. At Lon's strongly worded suggestion, he'd tried to find other accommodations nearby. There was next to nothing available. Nothing suitable.

"Is the bagel place three blocks over still in business?" he asked, avoiding explanations of private matters. "I came in fasting for the blood test. I could use a bite to eat."

"It's still there. And on my way to Reed's office. I'll buy my own. Okay?"

Resting a hand on her back, Michael guided Faith out of the elevator and toward the hospital's front entrance. "In some ways you haven't changed in six years, Faith. Still prickly as a cactus when it comes to letting a man do anything for you."

"What do you mean?" Her steps faltered.

"Come on," he scoffed. "Don't tell me you don't have a clue how many poor residents' hearts you broke with that *I can take care of myself* attitude. I know the common belief is that interns and residents don't have two dimes to rub together, but we had our pride. Any one of us could have bought you pie and coffee in the cafeteria. Or pizza and a beer if you'd ever gone to Tony Bruchetto's when you were asked. It doesn't take too many turndowns for guys to get the picture."

"Oh? And what picture is that?"

"Back then, we all thought you were a snooty Boston

blueblood. Or that you had your sights set on one of the senior M.D.s. Like Dr. Rubin. Did it break your heart when he married that socialite? I forget her name.''

Faith drew back in shock. "Dr. Rubin? You mean Steffan Rubin?''

"The very same. You followed him around O.R. like a lovesick puppy.''

"I did no such thing! Dr. Rubin was one of the few surgeons who didn't eat first-year nurses for breakfast. I followed him around because I could learn more from him than from anyone else. The other docs had me cowering in my shoes. Besides, your crowd went to Bruchetto's after the late shift. Mom needed me at home. She was really, really sick. By then the hospice team cared for her while I worked. But she always fretted until I got home and took over. Anyway, it wasn't as if you lacked female companionship, Michael. I was probably the only nurse at Good Shepherd who didn't pay you homage on those evenings at Bruchetto's.''

Michael grabbed for the door to the restaurant as another couple came out. He missed and the door shut in Faith's face. Apologizing profusely, he opened it again and ushered her inside. "Surely, you don't mean you left the hospital after working a full shift and then nursed your mother all night?'' Michael's shocked gaze said he hadn't known.

"It didn't kill me. Anyway, it's all in the past. My schedule wasn't any worse than yours when you were building your practice. I know, because Lacy used to call and talk my ear off on the nights you stayed with a new transplant patient.''

"She did? I don't recall our telephone bills reflecting that.'' He stared at the board listing coffees and choices of bagel toppings without really seeing them. His mind reeled, back to the year he'd all but turned handsprings in O.R. trying to make an impression on Faith Hyatt. All these years he'd thought she'd brushed him off for no good reason.

"Lacy reversed the charges." Faith chuckled at the way Michael's head snapped up. She gave her order for an iced coffee, paid for it and carried it to a table at the back of the room. Idly. She swirled the ice in her drink. Instead of drinking, she plotted how to introduce the topic of Lacy's estate disbursement, which was what she needed to tell Michael. He seemed to think she hurt for money. In the interest of fairness, she thought he ought to know that in a way, she'd be using his own money against him.

"Why am I just now hearing that you subsidized my wife after we moved to New York? I swear I never stinted on household expenses. Lacy had money. I hope she didn't insinuate otherwise."

"Honestly, Michael. It's no big deal. Lacy said you put her on a strict budget. I was impressed, since I'd never been able to tell her no. Besides, if you must know, I welcomed her calls. I was lonely. Losing Mom and then having to place Dad in managed care so soon after you and Lacy moved to New York was hard. You guys assumed I had Daddy for company. In fact, I was more like his nurse. I did everything I knew to combat his depression. Nothing worked. Lacy said I had to place him in managed care. Eventually I had to agree that was best."

They sat in silence for a moment. Both concentrated on their drinks, and Michael his food. Faith spoke first. "I didn't ask you here to rehash the past. In addition to preparing custody papers in my name, Lacy made me her sole beneficiary.''

''That's good.'' Michael set his bagel aside and touched the napkin to his lips. He glanced over his shoulder to see what Faith found so puzzling. Or was it something he'd said?

''Do you mean that?'' she murmured, her eyes shifting to meet his.

''Of course. Why wouldn't I?''

''The bulk of Lacy's estate came from your divorce settlement. Including a tidy sum from the proposed sale of your beach house.'' Faith shredded her napkin, waiting for him to tell her that, under the circumstances, he would contest Lacy's will.

Instead he smiled gently. ''So? Lacy didn't work. Where else would she have gotten money to live on?''

She let her lashes lift slowly until their eyes met. ''I'll use my portion to fight you and Kipp for custody of the twins. You said I should step aside and not waste my savings. But I'll spend every dime Lacy left to carry out her wishes. The last thing she said to me was 'take care of my baby.' Don't forget she didn't know there were two.''

''I see.'' Michael pushed his plate aside and downed the rest of his coffee. ''I guess we'll each do what we have to do, Faith,'' he said in an understanding voice.

''Then you really aren't mad about the money? I thought you'd be furious, but I didn't think it was fair not to tell you. Better you contest the will now, before I spend any of it and have to pay you back out of my savings.''

''It was Lacy's money to do with as she pleased. We were partners in marriage, Faith. She apparently had qualms about a lot of issues in our marriage, but lack of money wasn't one. I'm truly sorry for everything that went wrong between us. Sorry I didn't try harder.'' He dug in his pocket and tossed a couple of bucks on the table for a tip. Michael didn't know what more he could add to his apology. Frankly, he didn't know why he even felt a need to apologize. The more he thought about what had gone wrong in his marriage, the more he decided it was as much Lacy's fault for not understanding the nature of his job as it was his for failing to see how deep her unhappiness went. He didn't want to think that he might have married the wrong sister.

A part of Faith's brain knew Michael had risen and pushed back his chair. She concentrated on the last of the melting ice in her drink. She was sorry his marriage hadn't worked out. Or rather she was and she wasn't. And that uncharitable wedge of ambivalence left her feeling like a traitor—or worse. Lacy would probably still be alive if she and Michael hadn't divorced. Still, she couldn't help wondering how differently all their lives would have played out if she hadn't been so shy when she first met Michael. Today she'd learned quite by accident that he'd known she was alive back then. Surprisingly, he'd noticed other men's interest in her, too. And in spite of all the time that had passed, he remembered she'd been absent from the crowd that frequented Bruchetto's.

If... Faith never finished the thought. She had been too shy and too bogged down with work to flirt the way other nurses did. It was far too late to wish she'd been more like Lacy so that Michael might have fallen in love with her rather than her sister. Might-have-beens were futile. Faith would die of embarrassment if Michael ever learned of her wayward daydreams.

''Are you going to stay and finish that watered-down

coffee?'' Michael asked, forcing Faith to look up at him.

"Yes. David's office is only a short walk from here. Don't let me keep you. I know you have things to do.''

"Yeah, but I'm not sure this is a part of town where a woman should walk alone anymore. The neighborhood used to be safe, but a lot can change in five or six years.''

"You're right about that,'' she said. "But not in this particular neighborhood. Thanks for worrying though. I can't remember the last time anyone did,'' she added almost to herself.

Michael thrust his hands into his pockets. "I suppose that's, uh, because you're so damned self-sufficient, Faith. Well, you take care, you hear?''

Her heart beat fast at his words. She was tempted to turn and watch him weave his way through the wrought-iron tables. Instead, she wrapped both hands around her glass and tried to hit the straw with her shaky lips.

Faith waited until she was sure Michael would have hailed a cab or disappeared in whatever other manner he chose. Luckily the street was clear except for a couple of teens, weighted down with backpacks, trudging home from school. She fell into step behind the boys and listened to their banal chatter as she followed them for three blocks. They turned left at the corner where she turned right to go to David's office.

On the ground floor of his building, she spotted a rest room. Faith stopped to comb her hair and freshen her pale pink lipstick. Frowning into the mirror, she tried to see herself the way a man like Michael would see her. Her unwieldy brown hair curled in Shirley Temple fashion. Or it would if she didn't keep it short. Her more generous friends said the cut made her look like Audrey Hepburn. Ha!

Critically Faith decided her brown eyes were boring. Lacy's eyes had shone a flawless sky-blue. Faith hoped both Abigail and Nicholas inherited their mother's eye color.

Chiding herself for letting her mind wander, Faith tucked her comb back in her purse and took a minute to straighten her blouse and smooth the lapels of her suit. At least she had good metabolism. She'd been wearing a consistent size seven since high school. That certainly helped in the wardrobe department. Snatching her purse off the mirror shelf, Faith pushed open the door and hurried across the lobby to catch an elevator heading up to David's floor.

"Hello, Ms. Hyatt." She'd been there so often this past week, the receptionist knew Faith on sight. "Mr. Reed just buzzed out to see if you'd arrived yet. Help yourself to coffee or tea while I let him know you're here."

Smiling, Faith shook her head. "I just finished some before I came. I'll read a magazine until he's ready. If he's started something else, tell him I don't mind waiting."

The receptionist hung up the phone and beckoned Faith. "He sounds anxious to see you. Please, go right in. You know the way."

As Faith reached for the doorknob, David flung his door open. "I'm glad you're a little early," he said. "Come in. Sit down. It's crunch time, Faith. It seems Kipp Fielding has to go out of town for a few weeks. His team convinced the judge to advance the preliminary hearing."

"Advance it? To when?" Faith hovered over the

edge of the chair David had pulled out. She neither stood nor sat.

"Relax." He placed a beefy hand on Faith's shoulder and eased her into the chair. "We're to meet in Judge Brown's chambers at ten tomorrow. Fielding and his wife are in town because he had blood drawn at Good Shepherd. They're staying the night. Don't look so horrified. Sooner is better. This way, we'll get some rules established up front."

"Is Dr. Cameron going to be there, too?" Faith asked. If Michael had known that the meeting had been moved up, why hadn't he said anything? He hadn't heard yet, she decided. He would have shared that information with her.

"The court clerk said Dr. Cameron is also in Boston. She spoke with his counsel. Maxwell said advancing the date wouldn't pose a problem."

Faith twisted the topaz birthstone ring she wore on the middle finger of her right hand. She wore her mom's wedding band on the ring finger of the same hand. She gripped it now as if it were her talisman. "I saw Dr. Cameron at the hospital today. He said Fielding's lawyers objected to our visiting the babies while Kipp's away in Florida."

David thumbed through a stack of papers on his desk. "I'd intended to talk with you today about drafting a response. If you want to object, we'll need to file before four o'clock. That will force the judge to deal with the issue tomorrow. Otherwise, I'm afraid the judge might give in to Fielding's request, at least until results of the DNA come back."

"That's absurd! Of course I want to object. Don't these people know babies need to be held and rocked? Infants who are left on their own fail to thrive. Some stop eating. Even the good eaters can end up with developmental problems.''

''Good, good,'' Reed said, scribbling as fast as he could on a legal pad. ''I'll have the firm's paralegal look up some specific cases to quote. I thought it was a silly point for Fielding's team to insist on. It's not as if you or Cameron asked to remove the twins from the hospital.''

Faith glanced guiltily away, then back. ''I thought you said I'd have no problem taking Nick and Abby home when the doctor releases them.''

David fiddled with his pencil. ''I didn't expect the case to heat up so fast.''

''I'm ready to bring them home,'' Faith said. ''I mean, I've outfitted a nursery like we discussed. Dr. Sampson, the twins' pediatrician, said he might let them go home as early as next week.''

''Next week? That changes things.'' David snapped his pencil in half. He raked one hand through his hair. ''And the first hearing's tomorrow. I counted on having more time to prepare our presentation, Faith. I haven't hired the extra legal assistant or the secretary I mentioned we'd need.''

Faith slipped out of her suit jacket and rolled up her sleeves. ''I'm a good typist, David. And I'm a good organizer. I've also pulled back-to-back shifts in my time, so I can run on a lot of caffeine and a little sleep.''

He studied her helplessly, massaging his jaw.

''I made a promise to my sister. I said I'd be there for her child. And you promised me you'd work hard and win this case. I'm holding you to that promise.''

''I did do that,'' he agreed. ''All right.'' He slapped a broad palm down on his desk. ''By damn, what are we waiting for?''

"Nothing. I'm ready when you are." Faith hoped he couldn't hear how her heart nearly hammered out of her chest. In all her life, she'd never made waves. But this newfound assertiveness felt good. Pretty darned good, in fact.

CHAPTER FIVE

AT FOUR IN THE MORNING Faith yawned her goodbye to David Reed and a legal secretary named Lisa and climbed into a cab leaving the law offices. Reed had pulled Lisa from a temporary pool, then decided to keep her on for the duration of what he'd labeled the Baby A & B Hyatt-Cameron case. The young woman, wife of a sailor who was on a submarine somewhere in the Mediterranean, had performed admirably and without any complaint about the hours.

Before their long night ended, Faith developed a grudging respect for her lawyer. David had dates and cases stored in his head from twenty years back. He assigned Faith the job of finding specific cases in his firm's law library, which she did, one at a time, carting the heavy tomes to him when she'd found each reference. He, in turn, plowed through the legalese and scribbled out the portions of the text he wished to use at the hearing.

Lisa Dorn organized and typed his copious—and by Faith's estimation—almost illegible notes. The points David chose to emphasize were typed on legal forms, then copied and sent by night courier to the opposing teams. According to David, in cases of this nature, the winning side was often the one that followed each and every rule to the letter.

Faith was exhausted at the close of the ordeal, but

she felt she knew where David was headed. The test cases he intended to present had all been won. He'd decided to use quotes from ten in all. In each instance, a grandparent or other family member had been awarded custody over a biological parent.

Of course, Faith thought, as she let herself into her dark and silent apartment, Michael's and Kipp's attorneys had probably spent the night at precisely the same chore. Only, Michael's team would cite cases where a divorced spouse had won. Kipp's lawyers might have the hardest job. David said that until the DNA came back, Kipp had the weaker case. They had only his word and hearsay evidence from a very ill Lacy that the couple had engaged in an intimate affair. David said he expected Kipp's team to present signed affidavits from friends or staff at the country club who'd seen the couple together. It was still secondhand evidence. Reed doubted very much that anyone other than Kipp could swear to the intimacy part.

If Shelby Fielding attended the hearing, it seemed less likely Kipp III would want his and Lacy's activities explored at any great length. Or maybe that didn't matter to him. Faith had heard of open marriages, in which both partners conducted affairs. She'd hate for Lacy's babies to be raised in such an atmosphere.

As she tossed and turned in bed, Faith wished she could drop off to sleep. She'd set her alarm for eight-thirty. It was now six o'clock. Two and a half hours of rest would be better than none at all. Then it occurred to her that a single mother of new twins would undoubtedly have sleepless nights, staying up till dawn with sick or colicky infants. Maybe the judge would be impressed to learn that Faith could function on little sleep.

She finally drifted off. And dreamed of the hearing. A clerk escorted her into a dark, damp dungeon. The judge sat in a throne chair, higher than anyone else in the room. His eyes were empty red holes. When he spoke, tongues of fire licked out over the tables.

Michael looked coolly handsome in a blue suit, white shirt and striped tie. Kipp had on white pants, a navy jacket trimmed in gold braid and brass buttons. Though Faith had never seen Kipp's wife, Michael had described her. Shelby sat regally at Kipp's side. The elder Fielding chewed on a huge cigar and looked exactly like Edward G. Robinson.

In her dream Faith wore her nursing shoes and wrinkled white stockings, hideously unattractive with an apple-green suit that had once belonged to her mother.

Kipp sneered. Shelby smirked, and Michael laughed. The judge whammed an alarmingly gigantic gavel and roared for silence. That was when Faith noticed that the table she'd been assigned was empty. At Michael's and Kipp's sides, lawyers busily sorted stacks of well-prepared documents. David had left her to face the mess alone.

Gasping and panting, Faith shot bolt upright in bed. The clock said six-twenty.

Not wanting to risk a return to the same awful dream, Faith turned on the light and climbed out of bed. As she gathered a towel and clothes to put on after showering, she thought she heard water running in the apartment next door. She pressed an ear to the wall and listened. Nothing. Obviously she was hearing things.

"Another figment of your overactive imagination." The next-door apartment had been vacant for six months. Eccentric old Mrs. Coleman who'd lived there had everyone in the building except Faith convinced she

was a witch. The woman had looked the part and ha-
bitually said some strange things. Rumors circulated
about odd lights and secretive activity in the dead of
night. Faith had never seen or heard anything out of the
ordinary. However, there was no denying the unit had
developed a stigma that made it virtually unrentable.
Rumors of that nature had a way of spreading to potential tenants.

Every time she saw the building manager, Mr. Kin-
ney complained about a perfectly good apartment going
to waste. Faith thought to herself how fortuitous it was
that at least she wouldn't have to worry about a next-
door neighbor annoyed by crying babies.

And Nick and Abby did have fine sets of lungs each,
she acknowledged around a smile as she spun the
shower knobs and stepped beneath a fast, hot spray.

She felt much better after the shower. And more alert.
The pale pink suit she'd bought lifted her spirits another
notch. It was completely unlike the ghastly outfit she'd
worn in her dream. A softly gored skirt gave the ensem-
ble a feminine touch, as did the classic tucked-in blouse.
Faith rarely took time to apply makeup. Today she wore
a thin gloss of pink lipstick and a touch of mauve eye
shadow. The clerk at the cosmetic counter said Faith's
eyes were her best feature and had convinced her to
enhance them a little. Enhancement couldn't hurt on this
all-important occasion, when she wanted to influence
the people deciding the fate of Lacy's twins.

Still, she was nervous. She tried not to think what
would happen if the judge refused to consider her claim
on the babies. To fight a queasy stomach, she carried a
glass of milk into the nursery and sat there until the
bright, cheery surroundings worked their magic and
brought her a measure of serenity.

By the time her stomach stopped feeling jittery, she had only twenty minutes to reach the courthouse. So, for the second day in a row, she splurged on a cab.

As in her nightmare, a clerk did lead her to the judge's chambers. There the resemblance ended. Not only didn't Judge Brown sit on a throne and breathe fire, she was a regal-looking African American woman. David Reed had arrived ahead of her, and seeing him there, sorting through a briefcase full of papers, dissolved the last uncomfortable knot in Faith's stomach.

Michael stood when she approached the horseshoe-shaped table. "You look nice," he said, sliding a hand the length of his tie. He wore a summer-weight khaki suit, not blue. His shirt was pale yellow and his tie was covered with comic turtles. The tie elicited a grin from Faith.

"You like it?" he asked with a smile that deepened the laugh lines around his eyes and mouth. "It was a gift from the last kid I transplanted. A girl in Norway. She's an incredible artist. She drew the turtles freehand and silk-screened them on this material. I think she has a promising future." Growing suddenly sober, he let the tie drop. "Six months ago she was knocking at death's door. You'll probably say this is hokey, but when the tie came in the mail last week, I got this insane notion that it's a lucky charm." Michael lifted one shoulder in an elegant shrug.

"There's nothing hokey about talismans, Michael." Faith opened her purse and fished out a framed piece of glass in which was embedded a four-leaf clover.

Seeming to relax, Michael unbuttoned his jacket and perched on the edge of Faith's table. He flagged an eyebrow toward the left side of the room. "Do you suppose old Kipp is carrying a rabbit's foot?"

She peered around him at the huddle of immaculately dressed people surrounding Kipp, and a pretty woman she assumed was his wife. "I'd say he's relying on the Roman numerals after his name." Unlike in her dream, Kipp wasn't wearing yachting clothes. If his silk designer suit didn't have "Made in Italy" stitched on the label, Faith would eat his conservative navy tie. Mrs. Fielding was pretty much the way Faith had pictured her, up to and including the frosty pursing of her lips. But Faith couldn't have been more wrong about Kipp's father. The man, who could have been anywhere from fifty to sixty, was in total command over there. Fit, tan and blond, dressed in what was obviously a hand-tailored suit, he was clearly accustomed to being the center of attention.

Faith disliked Kipp Fielding Jr. on sight. He had cold blue eyes and a shark's smile.

As if Michael read her mind, he murmured, "I'd do anything to keep that bastard from renaming Nicholas and branding him with that damned number four."

A crew of maintenance workers entering the room through a side door kept Faith from responding. Talk stopped as the men set a small table and a comfortable-looking leather chair at the center of the horseshoe for the judge. The clerk who'd led Faith to the room took her place behind a steno-typewriter.

Judge Brown smiled at the men. "Thank you, gentlemen, for your help. This is a somewhat larger group than I'd expected." Her interested gaze touched on everyone at the table before she opened her briefcase and removed a spiral-bound notebook. Two more people entered the room. A man and a woman. Both wore plain, dark suits. They claimed the empty seats next to David.

"Who are they?" Michael asked Faith in an undertone. "Have you hired a full legal team—like Fielding?"

"I've never seen them before. They're obviously acquainted with the judge." Which was true as the trio exchanged pleasantries.

"In the interest of time," the judge said briskly as she settled in the leather chair and steepled graceful fingers. "I propose we get right down to business." She waved a hand in the direction of the newcomers. "Even though this meeting will be conducted as a hearing, I've taken the liberty of including two senior legal advisors from Family Services. Daniel Burgess and Barbara Lang. In the event this should evolve into a trial, Mr. Burgess and Ms. Lang will represent the minor children on behalf of the state of Massachusetts."

Faith felt her stomach go into spin cycle. Had she been naive, thinking they'd walk out of here today with a settlement? Apparently. Michael caught her eye. He, too, appeared surprised and uneasy.

None of the lawyers scattered around the table, however, seemed taken aback by the announcement. One by one they nodded and jotted notes on their legal pads.

Judge Brown relaxed in her chair. "Shall we continue introductions? In the Fielding camp, Kipp Fielding III, the plaintiff. He's flanked on either side by his wife, Shelby, and his father, Kipp Jr. Their legal team, Bob and Keith Schlegel and Nancy Matz of Schlegel, Schlegel and Matz are from New York City."

There was a faint rustling around the table as everyone eased forward to get a look at the competition.

Judge Brown shuffled her notes. "Plaintiff number two, Michael Cameron, M.D. He's represented by Lon Maxwell, who also practices in New York. Plaintiff three, Ms. Faith Hyatt. She's retained David Reed, who is a partner in the local firm of Masterson, Reed and Jacoby. Now that we have preliminaries out of the way, ladies and gentlemen, we'll begin hearing from each of you in the matter of custody for twins of the deceased, Lacy Hyatt Cameron. I'll recognize one counselor at a time. I trust the main concern of everyone in this room is the well-being of the two minors. I assure you that I will not make any hasty decisions regarding their welfare. Whether we need one meeting or ten, we'll reconvene until I'm satisfied we're doing what's right for the children.''

She sent a withering gaze around the table. Someone in a dark suit entered the office with a glass pitcher and poured water into the empty glasses that sat in front of each person, including the judge. When that had been accomplished and he'd shut the door again, the judge resumed. ''Bob Schlegel filed the first formal request with regard to this case. Mr. Maxwell and Mr. Reed have both responded on behalf of their clients. So I'll ask Bob if he has anything further to add.''

The white-haired member of the Fielding team cleared his throat. ''Your Honor. Mr. and Mrs. Fielding have read the rebuttals. Their position hasn't changed. Mr. Kipp Fielding III is committed to a summer and fall sailing schedule. He's an important member of the U.S. sailing team. He is, of course, also an officer in his father's stock brokerage firm. My client is willing to leave his place on the sailing team at the end of this season. However, he can hardly be expected to let the other team members down.''

''I don't believe anyone has asked him to quit the team,'' the judge said. ''Dr. Cameron merely suggests that Mrs. Fielding assume her husband's visiting privileges until he returns. Ms. Hyatt's counter-brief indicates essentially the same.''

There was a scraping together of the chairs at the Fielding end of the horseshoe. Faith wished she had a clearer view of the proceedings, but she sat in a curve that excluded her from seeing either Kipp or Shelby's face.

The younger Schlegel broke out of the huddle. ''Shelby Fielding is undergoing complicated fertility treatments in New York. I'm sure in this enlightened day and age, I don't have to spell out the delicacy of the procedures. I think it's sufficient to say the success or failure of the process depends in part on the patient's optimal physical and mental condition. We contend the two-hour commute from New York City to Boston would place undue stress on Mrs. Fielding.''

Lon Maxwell voiced what sprang to Faith's mind. ''Judge Brown, I'd like to ask the esteemed Counselor Schlegel how that compares to the stress of caring for infant twins. I hate to be indelicate, but if Mrs. Fielding's fertility quest is successful, she could be dealing with three children under one year of age. Or possibly more.''

David Reed drew attention to himself by leaning back and gesturing widely with one arm. ''Mr. Maxwell has brought up an excellent point, Judge. I'm sure my client would be interested in seeing statistics relative to known numbers of multiples born to mothers who'd undergone fertility treatment. I've read it's a high percentage.''

All three of the Fielding lawyers scowled. Judge Brown prodded them to answer. ''What about that, Counselors? Have you and your client discussed what would happen in the event Shelby Fielding conceives twins or triplets?''

Again the group conferred. Michael nudged Faith. *An interesting concept,* he mouthed silently.

She chewed the inside of her cheek. For the first time she was glad Lacy had found David Reed. He'd certainly thrown the Fielding camp, as the judge had called it, a major curve. Kipp's father's eyebrows waved wildly at the team members.

At last Bob Schlegel rallied. "Your Honor, may we suggest that Counselors Maxwell and Reed are trying to cross a bridge before we come to it? Mrs. Fielding hasn't yet conceived. Perhaps our colleagues are trying to steer us away from the question at hand. That of fair play."

"Nothing of the kind," David broke in gruffly. "You may not be aware that I had the privilege of serving Lacy Hyatt Cameron at the time she took ill. I assure you the Fieldings' fertility issue was very much on her mind when she directed me to draft her custody papers. You see, young Kipp told her he was returning to his wife because she'd found a new fertility method to try."

Faith frowned. *She* had told David that. He'd said Lacy had implied Kipp was dead. She didn't want David lying on her behalf.

"So then Lacy Cameron admitted Kipp fathered her babies," argued the last member of the Fielding legal team. Nancy Matz sounded very pleased she'd picked up on that.

Lon Maxwell twirled his pen. "Seems to me none of the topics under discussion make a lick of sense until we get the results of the DNA tests done on my client and young Fielding."

The judge nodded. "I agree."

"About damn time," snapped the eldest Fielding.

"Dad," Kipp muttered.

Clearly not happy with the elder Fielding's outburst, Judge Brown opened a watch that hung on a gold chain around her neck. "I have to preside in court in half an hour. Up to this point, we've made little progress, although that's fairly standard for a first meeting. I must say Mr. Maxwell has a point. It's senseless to proceed until the DNA results are in. I'd be happy to set a tentative date for…say, six weeks down the line. Or we could wait until the lab has the report and schedule a meeting then."

Lon Maxwell closed the folder he'd been working from. "I vote we wait for the results. My client said the technician told him it could be from four to six weeks."

The Schlegels spoke in unison. "Affirmative." Then Keith Schlegel folded his hands across his pudgy stomach. "I take it we agree that no one visits the babies until our client returns from his trip?"

David Reed all but bounded from his chair. "I'll agree to no such thing! Didn't any of you read the testimony from Dr. Hal Sampson that I enclosed in my rebuttal? Sampson is the pediatrician attending the twins. The babies are up to weight, and he plans to let them go home from the hospital next week."

"Home to where?" chorused Lon Maxwell and all of Fielding's counselors.

"Home with Ms. Hyatt," David growled. "I believe she is the legal custodian, at least until the matter of paternity is settled."

Furor erupted around the table. Judge Brown didn't have a gavel, but she did rap her knuckles on her table until order resumed. "Granted, Mr. Reed, you did properly file custody papers for Lacy Cameron. I'd remind you, however, I can still make the twins wards of the court.'' She nodded at the couple seated to David's right.

"That's correct,'' Daniel Burgess, said, all the while bobbing his head. "Barbara and I can request they be placed in a neutral foster home until such time as the DNA results come in and another hearing is arranged.''

Faith cried out. She hardly realized she'd grabbed Michael's arm. He, too, lost his color and swallowed repeatedly before covering her hand with his.

Reed rubbed his chin several times before he spoke. "I'm not disputing your power to place the children elsewhere, Judge. I guess I assumed you'd grant my client temporary custody, since we all agreed at the beginning of today's hearing that the welfare of the twins is our top priority. Ms. Hyatt, the babies' aunt by blood, has set up a nursery in her apartment to accommodate the youngsters. She's arranged for time off from her job as a nurse. No matter what the DNA proves, she will continue to play a role in Nicholas and Abigail's lives.'' He gave an eloquent shrug.

Keith Schlegel narrowed his eyes. "Judge Brown. I contend Reed is playing us all for fools. My client would have set up a nursery if he'd been aware the babies were so close to being released.''

Michael didn't wait for his attorney to speak for him. "Your client might have known that if he'd bothered to visit the twins. I've seen Faith interacting with the babies. She loves them, and they already know her. I have no objection to placing the babies in her care temporarily.''

Again there was a moment of disruption in the room. Then, as expected, the senior Fielding convened his team. They all talked separately and at once. Faith tried not to be anxious, but her stomach rolled like a ship on the high seas. She wanted Lacy's babies permanently and refused to dwell on the word *temporary*. Right now, she prayed they wouldn't fight her taking Nick and Abby home from the hospital. She'd dreamed of seeing them sleeping peacefully in their new cribs. Even if they were torn from her during a later battle, they deserved to spend their first months, with family rather than a foster family—strangers who couldn't possibly love them as much as she did.

Michael squeezed her fingers and gave her a lopsided smile. "Relax," he murmured. "Fielding and his cronies might not want to let you take the kids. But it's clear Kipp and Shelby aren't ready to give them a home."

"I don't know," she whispered back. "With their resources, how long would it take for them to buy out a baby store and install an au pair in their mansion?"

"Do you really think the judge would go for that? She doesn't strike me as a woman who misses much. I may be wrong, but I had the feeling she wondered why, if they were truly excited about taking the twins, Shelby Fielding was still going through with fertility treatments."

"Hmm. I can't help feeling sorry for Shelby. Not too many women would welcome a husband's illegitimate offspring with open arms."

"Oh? Wouldn't you if you loved the man?"

Faith frowned. "Do you doubt there's love between them?" She sighed. "Poor Nick and Abby. They'll still probably go to live with Kipp after the results of the DNA come back."

"Thanks a lot." Michael stiffened in his chair. "Those are *my* babies. Trust me—I can feel they're my own flesh and blood when I hold them."

She pursed her lips. "I know what Lacy believed. She thought her baby was Kipp's."

David shushed them as Bob Schlegel's deep voice rang out. "My client will approve Ms. Hyatt acting as foster parent. He does request that she bring the children to see his father and Mrs. Fielding at least once a week during the time he's away. And another thing," the man concluded, cutting through Faith's protesting gasp, "we object to Ms. Hyatt having named the children. Please stipulate that she refrain from using those names while they're in her care."

David Reed snorted. "My client doesn't own a car. She relies on walking to get to her appointments around town. Before Schlegel suggests she use public transit, may I remind him we're talking about two premature babies? Dragging them back and forth to New York City on a packed commuter train is inviting exposure to all kinds of viruses and germs."

The judge glanced from one lawyer to the other. "Mr. Schlegel, that request does seem a bit excessive. As we've already established it unfeasible for Mrs. Fielding to travel, I'm granting Ms. Hyatt the same privilege—she can keep the babies at home. I will allow the grandfather visiting rights, provided he calls and arranges a convenient time with Ms. Hyatt and doesn't just barge in without notice."

Kipp Jr. didn't look too pleased. Clearly he was a man unused to having people thwart him.

"About the matter of the names, Your Honor..." One of the Schlegels reintroduced his earlier objection.

David jumped in before Judge Brown had a chance to answer. "It's a small matter to request a legal change of name if and when the DNA proves Mr. Fielding III is the natural father. My client was simply following her sister's wishes in naming her daughter. Lacy, you understand, did not know she was having twins. Anyway, at this age, what's in a kid's name?''

Faith felt the argument between the men swirl around her. David hadn't said anything she hadn't said herself. Only now, she'd begun to think of these babies as Nick and Abby. She doubted she'd ever be able to call them anything else. There was David maintaining babies couldn't possibly identify the sound of a name at such a young age. She'd be a fool to refute him in this crowd. But not for a minute did she believe that what he'd said was true. The names fit the twins. And from the moment she'd begun calling them by name, they seemed to respond. It hadn't just been her imagination. It truly hadn't.

Nancy Matz made herself heard above the heated discussion among the male attorneys. ''Gentlemen, perhaps we could settle on a written agreement from Ms. Hyatt. One stating she won't contest a name change at the time paternity is determined.''

David bent his head toward Faith. ''If you don't want them reneging on allowing you to take the twins home, let them have their way on this. They're assuming you won't press your custody suit once paternity is established. It suits me to let them labor under false impressions. Why give them more time to prepare a defense?''

''All right,'' she said slowly. ''I suppose I also have to agree to let Kipp's father visit.''

''Yes. Be happy we won a major victory without really having to get in the trenches and fight dirty. I never expected either of the men to agree so readily to your guardianship.''

''Temporary guardianship,'' Faith said with distaste. David Reed closed his folder. ''Haven't you heard that possession is nine-tenths of the law? It applies to custody as well as material objects. Unless you strongly object, I'm about to make a truly magnanimous gesture on your part.''

''Wh-what?'' Faith stammered.

''We'll invite Dan Burgess and Barbara Lang to make an appointment to visit you. My thinking here is they'll see what a natural mom you are. It couldn't hurt if they recommended leaving the babies in your care, in the event that we have to take off the gloves and fight Fielding.''

Something about his glee at the prospect of a down-and-dirty fight didn't sit well with Faith. He'd prepared her the other night, of course. But she'd hoped against hope that it wouldn't come to a bitter court confrontation. It was probably naive of her to dream anyone with rightful access to these babies would voluntarily step aside. Her sigh could be heard throughout the room.

David bounced the tips of his fingers together as he talked. ''Ms. Hyatt will sign a waiver with regard to names. I'll have it notarized. She welcomes scheduled visits from Kipp's father. We'll include her address when we forward the waiver. Also…'' He dragged out the word until he had everyone's attention. ''Ms. Hyatt extends invitations to Dr. Cameron and to Mr. Burgess and Ms. Lang. That ought to be quite agreeable to all parties, don't you think, Judge?''

As Michael had said, Judge Brown was nobody's fool. She stared intently at Faith until she almost blurted out that it had been Reed's idea, not hers. Seconds before Faith could disgrace herself, the judge picked up her pen and made a few notations on her pad.

''I believe we've answered all immediate questions,'' she said at length. ''I see we're out of time.'' She checked her watch again. "Unless some unforeseen problem arises, we won't reconvene as a group until the DNA results come in."

The judge stood and gathered her belongings. Everyone in the room rose and waited quietly while she moved around the horseshoe and shook each hand in turn. "My son has twin boys," she murmured as she clasped Faith's fingers in her cool hand. "I wonder if you know how much work you've let yourself in for." Giving a small laugh, she released Faith's clammy fingers. "Twins are a lot more than twice the work of a single child, believe me. My husband and I went to help our son and daughter-in-law when the boys were born. It took four adults running around the clock to take care of those little tadpoles. I've never been so exhausted in my life."

Faith gave a sickly smile. Judge Brown had hit on the elusive uneasiness that had haunted Faith, but which, so far, she'd successfully held at bay. Competent as she was at her job, when it came right down to it, she was afraid she didn't have what it took to be an adequate mother. Because, in the back of her mind, she'd never believed that she'd handled raising Lacy well.

"Faith?"

She came crashing back to earth. Judge Brown and her clerk had both left the chamber; Kipp's entourage were packed up and scuttling out, too. "Sorry, Michael. I must have, um, spaced out for a minute."

"Looked that way," he teased. "What I said was that the hearing wasn't nearly as bloody as I expected."

"Bloody? I, ah, no. It was quite civil, wasn't it?"

"I suppose this was luck," he mused, loosening the knot on his tie. "Once we get the results of the DNA,

I assume the two of us left in the fray will be more inclined to duke it out with no holds barred.''

"Is that your way of warning me to not expect you to be so nice the next time around?'' she asked. ''By the way, Michael, if you hope to be taken seriously, don't wear that tie again. Those silly turtles would make anyone want to laugh. But perhaps you missed the look on Judge Brown's face when she stopped to shake your hand.''

"I saw. If you ask me, she said to herself, now that Cameron guy is human.''

"Was there doubt?'' Faith said dryly.

"Some people think doctors are a stuffy lot.''

"Really? Well, other people consider them playboys. Surgeons especially have a bad reputation in the family market.''

"Well, if *that* isn't a generality, I don't know what is. I didn't end my marriage. Lacy left me.''

"Mmm. So she said. Because you were never around. How will that play in a future courtroom drama, I wonder?''

The smile lingering on Michael's lips winked out. He studied her cool features a moment, then abruptly dismissed himself. Stepping around her, he struck up a conversation with David Reed, and the two walked out chatting amiably.

Faith was left alone to ponder how her exchange with Michael had gone awry. Sadly, she'd never known how to hold his interest. Not that it mattered now. What *did* matter was that she'd fulfilled her promise to Lacy, if only temporarily.

CHAPTER SIX

FAITH STEPPED INTO the sunshine outside the courthouse and experienced a shift in her attitude. Why had she snapped at Michael? After all, she'd successfully leaped one hurdle today. Only time would tell what lay ahead. Worrying in advance about something over which she had no control was of no earthly good, to her *or* the babies. DNA would make one man or the other her foe. Faith frankly doubted any custody battle was ever pretty. Michael had said once before that it would go easier on everyone if the plaintiffs remained civil to each other. She wanted to stay on good terms with him. It suddenly dawned on her—what if Lacy had been wrong, and Michael *had* fathered the children? Faith saw Michael relying on her, needing her help as the twins' aunt.

While contemplating Michael in the role of dad, Faith was beset by an urgent need to visit the twins. On its heels came a desire to detour past the cemetery. That was probably the better choice, since she hadn't asked Michael if he planned to visit the babies. He'd probably gone straight there from the hearing. It was likely he'd go back to New York now and resume his surgical practice until the test results became available. After snapping at him, the least she could do was allow him extra time at the hospital.

Too used to pinching pennies, Faith caught a bus to

the cemetery instead of taking a cab. In spite of the
lovely day, a chill enveloped her when she passed between the wrought-iron angels that served as gate sen-
tinels.

Once she'd found the plot of new-turned ground,
Faith wished she'd stopped at a florist's to pick up a
fresh bouquet. The last of the funeral flowers had turned
brown. This was a perpetual-care cemetery. Why hadn't
someone thrown them away? And where was the stone
she'd ordered?

As thoughts tumbled disjointedly through her mind,
staving off memories of Lacy, Faith recalled the man at
the quarry where she'd ordered the rosy headstone saying it'd take three to four weeks. She sank to her knees
in the warm, fragrant grass, and idly crushed brown
flower petals between fidgety fingers.

"Lacy," she murmured past the lump in her throat.
"Today we made some progress toward fulfilling your
wish. It's not final, you understand. The judge can still
take the babies away from me. Oh, God, Lacy. I hope
you knew what you were doing, handing them over to
me."

Faith scattered the next handful of petals. She
brushed at a curling edge of grass. How long would it
take for this bare earth, whose shape reminded her far
too much of the casket, to fill in completely with grass?

Darn, she'd promised herself she wouldn't cry today.
The tears fell anyway. "Lacy," Faith sniffled, "I wish
you could see Abigail and Nick. They're beautiful. Perfect. I'm telling you this so you'll know your sacrifice
wasn't in vain."

A discreet cough sounded nearby. Faith straightened
swiftly and smoothed the heels of her hands over her
wet cheeks. "Michael," she gasped, blinking up into a

stabbing shaft of sunlight. "Wha-what are you doing here?"

Going down on one knee, he placed a cemetery-approved cone vase near the site of the crumbling brown bouquet. Dewy violets bobbed among a profusion of white daisies in his new floral offering. "Seems we were of like minds Faith. Forgive me, please. I didn't mean to intrude." Rising agilely, Michael extended her a hand.

Even with his help, Faith was slow to climb to her feet. His flowers were so lovely, she paused to remove the last of the dead ones. An awkward silence fell between them. Both gazed down at the pitifully small plot of ground.

"I came out here," Faith said at last, "because I thought you'd be at the hospital visiting the babies."

"When I walked to the parking garage with Reed, he stated plainly enough that I need to make appointments to see the twins—just like the Fieldings. The way you and I parted, I didn't think you'd be too inclined to grant me visitation privileges today."

Faith raised the hand filled with flower stalks to shield her eyes from the sun as she stared into Michael's face. "About the way I bit your head off earlier—I, well, I'd like to apologize. I can't imagine what made me act like a shrew. Nerves, maybe."

"I'm not blaming you, Faith. The hearing was nerve-racking for everyone."

"It's not knowing how it'll all turn out that makes things so tough. Realistically, I know the custody can go any way. It only makes sense for each of us to spend time getting to know the babies. I won't impede visits by you or the Fieldings."

Michael smiled. "I knew you'd do the right thing,

Faith.'' He wanted to hug her. But he let his half-raised arms drop. It wasn't smart to touch her. Especially not here, standing next to Lacy's grave. Lord help him, he wanted to hold her and comfort her....

''Yes, well, the parenting book I've started reading says children benefit emotionally and socially from active, early involvement by fathers,'' Faith was saying.

''I believe I *am* the father and I want to be a good one,'' Michael said forthrightly. ''I understand your reservations, Faith. And you were right about my profession taking its toll on family life. Do you by chance know of a bootee camp for dads?'' he said teasingly, as much to relieve his own tension.

It was on the tip of Faith's tongue to say she didn't want to be having this conversation where Lacy could hear them. Of course, that was stupid. It was just that Michael stood so tall, so broad-shouldered, so alive that he made her feel weak in the knees. She couldn't help reacting to his disarming grin. The more he brought out these ambivalent feelings inside her, the more she clamped down on speaking candidly to him. As a result, she said nothing at all.

Sensing he'd put her off again, Michael groped for something to say. ''If you're finished here, I can give you a lift back to town.''

She mulled over his invitation. ''I planned to stop at the hospital, first,'' she finally told him. ''It's really better if we stagger our visits, Michael.''

''As you wish,'' he said stiffly. ''I'll be more than happy to drop you off at Good Shepherd and time my visit with the six-o'clock feeding. Feeding them is—'' He broke off, restrained his excitement. ''I get a kick out of it,'' he said softly.

Faith recognized the change in his expression and

deeply regretted that her relationship with Lacy had caused this wall to go up between them. But some realities would never change. She was Lacy's big sister, and he was Lacy's ex-husband. The fact that Faith had once had a terrible crush on him and the fact that he was now single only added to the discomfort she felt around him. She probably ought to feel shame for allowing such yearnings while standing beside her sister's grave.

"Good Lord, Faith," Michael exploded. "A ride into town is no big deal. I wish you'd quit looking at me like I'm the Boston Strangler."

"Thank you for the offer," she said meekly. "I accept." It wouldn't do to divulge even the slightest hint of the thoughts running through her head.

"You have the most revealing eyes of any woman I've ever known," he said as they turned and strolled toward the gate. "No wonder you never joined any of the residents' poker games. You would've lost your shirt."

Feeling the tension slide away, Faith laughed. "At last the truth. You guys *did* play strip poker in the basement dead-record room. And you claimed not to understand why no nurse ever agreed to meet you there."

"Ha! Was that the story you heard? You remember Donna Murphy?"

"Vaguely." Faith frowned. "A busty redhead."

"Yeah." Michael grinned mischievously. "She had freckles…well, never mind where she had freckles. Those were the good old days." He felt less on edge talking about the days before he married Lacy. Removing his suit jacket, Michael tossed it into the back seat of his dark green BMW. After unlocking the passenger door for Faith, he rolled up the sleeves of his dress shirt and slid behind the steering wheel.

Michael had dark hair on his arms, but only a dusting above the knuckles of his beautifully shaped surgeon's fingers. Faith recalled the knots that had formed in the pit of her stomach every time she'd been assigned to his surgical team. Something as simple as watching him scrub had completely entranced her. Even now as he looped one elegant wrist over the wheel and turned to back out of his parking spot, her mouth felt dust-dry.

"I wonder whatever happened to Donna," she said for the sake of keeping the conversation alive. "Now that I think about it, she was a terrible nurse. A walking disaster on the wards."

Once he'd eased into traffic, Michael glanced at Faith. "She married Daryl Sawyer."

"Daryl Saw—? That little bald guy with Coke-bottle glasses? Proctologist, right?"

"Right. Except Donna married Daryl's father."

Faith's mouth flopped open. "Isn't he some hotshot plastic surgeon in Hollywood? I saw him on a talk show touting a newfangled kind of laser liposuction."

"That's him. I met him at a surgical convention in Athens. Donna had been liposucked everywhere except—" He abruptly dropped his hand back to the wheel from where he'd cupped it six or so inches out from his chest. "She looked okay," he said lamely.

"Men! Why are you all obsessed with breasts?"

Michael's gaze ran over Faith's compact frame. She still wore the pink suit he'd nearly drooled on at the hearing. In Michael's opinion, small breasts looked pretty damned good. Faith had always looked damned good. He coughed—choked really—and berated himself for allowing his thoughts to wander.

"You can let me out here," she informed him, stabbing a finger at the south entrance of Good Shepherd Hospital. It was the opposite end of the building from the nursery, but Faith wanted to disappear from beneath Michael's scrutiny. He made her feel self-conscious in a way she hadn't felt in…at least six years. Self-conscious and plain. Unfeminine. She'd never resorted to stuffing her bra, although in high school she'd certainly been tempted. Now friends purported to envy the rapid metabolism that kept her trim. At least the women did. Faith knew men like Michael probably found her too boyish looking.

"You want out here?" Michael jerked his attention back from checking out his former sister-in-law. He felt a stirring below his belt—and an immediate sense of guilt. He should definitely not be thinking what he was thinking. Like how his hands could probably span her waist. Or how he'd like to unbutton that blouse and find out if she wore cotton or silk underneath. She obviously didn't know, but men were obsessed by the mystery surrounding any woman they found interesting. Especially the parts she kept hidden—and not just the physical either. Michael recalled a time he'd been very interested in Faith Hyatt. Before he met Lacy. Back then, Lacy made him feel ten feet tall, while Faith had made it very clear that she needed no one but herself.

"Ah, hell," he muttered, swinging the car in next to the curb. "You want to hike a mile to the nursery, be my guest." Yanking on the emergency brake, he vaulted from the car, circled the hood and jerked open her door.

If Faith had any doubts about coming up short in his perusal, they were obliterated by his actions. "Thanks for the lift," she mumbled.

Did he expect a more effusive show of gratitude? she wondered as she hurried through the revolving glass door. Faith saw Michael reflected in the glass, still leaning on the open passenger door. He seemed to be staring blankly after her, although she was too far away to see the expression in his eyes.

Damn Michael Cameron for making her lose the modicum of self-esteem she'd worked so many years to build. "And whose fault is that?" she asked under her breath while pacing in front of the elevator. "You get within fifteen feet of him and you let your mind turn to alphabet soup," she scolded herself, walking into a thankfully empty elevator. Then she laughed and rotated her tense shoulders. "Maybe he knows. Maybe he hopes someone'll see you talking to yourself. Then he and Lon Maxwell can declare you incompetent to take care of the babies."

Faith was careful to lock her thoughts inside once the elevator door slid open and she stepped out onto the busy ward. She exchanged greetings with several staff members and waved to others as she traversed the halls on her way to the nursery.

A familiar figure stood at the viewing window. Faith's steps slowed, but Kipp Fielding III had caught a glimpse of her reflection. He studied her somberly.

Craning her neck, Faith glanced into the waiting room where she supposed Shelby and his father must be sitting. The room was empty.

"Are you alone?" she asked, realizing the question was inane.

His face didn't change as he shoved his hands into his pockets and gave a brief nod.

"I supposed you'd be back in New York by now,

packing for your trip to Florida, or whatever it is sailors do before sailing off into the sunset.''

"Shelby complained of feeling ill after we left the hearing. We checked into a hotel, which allows her to rest awhile. I leave for Florida on Sunday.''

"Ah. Then your dad's staying with Shelby?''

"No. He went back to New York. I, uh, tried phoning you.'' Incredibly blond eyelashes swooped down to shutter very blue eyes. He chewed nervously on his lower lip.

Something about his lost expression troubled Faith. "Would you like to take a closer look at Nicholas and Abigail?'' she asked gently.

The curtain over his eyes lifted, revealing an eager light. Almost as if afraid to concur, he spread his hands. "I know you don't have any reason to like me, Faith. But it's important to me that you understand. I, uh, Lacy wasn't just a one-night stand.'' He cleared his throat and looked everywhere but at Faith. The tips of his ears turned red as he went on. "We connected…like two shipwrecked souls.''

"You don't have to explain. What's done is done.''

"I want you to know. Lacy said she was on the pill. I took her at her word. Cameron thinks I'm an idiot for not making more of her scar. I did notice. She brushed off my concern, saying she'd been in a car accident.''

"I see,'' Faith said. But she didn't—unless Michael was right and Lacy had systematically planned to get pregnant. If Lacy had arbitrarily picked Kipp to father the child she was determined to have, her plan had backfired when she'd fallen in love with him. Faith didn't think Lacy's tears for this man were an act. "Although your lives crossed for whatever reason, you both harbored secrets. Neither of you was really free to make a new commitment.''

''Hindsight is always clearest,'' he said, sighing heavily.

''Yes, and now there are two more lives that'll forever be disrupted. Do you love your wife?'' Faith asked abruptly.

If a swift, affirmative reply was what Faith was after, she didn't get it. Kipp rocked back on his heels and stared through the window at the rows of bassinets. Faith had almost given up on getting an answer when he finally spoke. ''Our fathers were business associates before Shelby or I were born. Our marriage was preordained from the cradle.'' He shivered. ''It would be impossible for me not to love Shel. She was raised to be the perfect mate for me. Included in the life plan she was handed was a requirement that she produce the next Fielding heir.''

''I see,'' Faith murmured. This time she *did* see. The perfect mate didn't feel perfect when she failed to conceive. Judging by her brief peek at Shelby Fielding, Faith would say it was probably the first failure the woman had ever experienced. She had no doubt that in Shelby's privileged circle, only success was accepted. ''I've had control of my own life for so many years, I can't imagine what jumping to someone else's command would be like,'' Faith said. ''Your wife must be a nervous wreck if both sets of parents are demanding she have a baby.''

''Her parents and my mother were killed when their yacht sank in the Mediterranean. If anything, that made my father more insistent. It was on the anniversary of their deaths that Shelby left me.''

''I want Lacy's babies to grow up in a happy, normal

household. I told Michael, and I'll tell you. I'm going to do everything in my power to keep them.''

"I'd already deduced that. But I'm warning you. If the DNA tests prove they're mine, you won't have a prayer of retaining custody.''

"So we're back to square one. Pity. I was beginning to like you.''

"Does this mean you'll refuse to let me visit the babies today?''

"Not at all. Michael pointed out that I'd be wise to remain agreeable. He reminded me that no matter who the father is, I'll always be the twins' aunt.''

This time Kipp's acknowledgment was curt. While Faith directed the nursing supervisor to provide him with sterile clothing for his visit, she elected not to go in with him. She had learned her lesson watching Michael interact with the babies. Faith didn't think she could stand it if Kipp fell under their spell as Michael had.

Faith hung out with a few pals in the nurses' lounge until Kipp left. As it turned out, waiting wasn't all bad. She'd no more than slipped on her sterile gear when Dr. Sampson walked in.

"By Jove," he announced, beaming at Faith. "These tots have done so well, I'm going to let you take them home on Monday.''

Faith could only grin foolishly as the nursery staff gathered around, hugging her happily.

Word spread through the hospital with the speed of light. Faith's friend, Gwen, showed up with several nurses from the floor where Faith had worked. They pried her away from the babies and hustled her back to the lounge. "This is short notice," Gwen exclaimed, waving a can of soda once everyone had quieted down.

"Cicely and I want to give you a baby shower. How about Saturday evening, Faith? At your apartment? Tacky, we know, but that way none of us will have do a whirlwind housecleaning. Besides, it'll make things easier on you. You won't have to cart so much loot home on foot or in a cab. With twins, people naturally buy double of everything. Oh, and in case I didn't mention it, we're providing refreshments. All you have to do, little mama, is relax and enjoy."

"A shower." Faith had never dared hope she'd ever be the recipient of a shower, neither the wedding or the baby variety. "That's too cool, you guys. But—but maybe you'd better not go to all that trouble," she said with a tremor in her voice. "At the hearing today, it was decided my custody is only temporary. The decision won't be made until the men's DNA tests come back."

"Fiddlesticks. We don't care, do we, ladies?" Gwen said, and she squeezed Faith's arm.

Megan, a young nurse from Faith's ward, piped up. "Faith's pretty brave, taking on two babies at once. She deserves a real blowout. You'd better party hearty, pal," she said to Faith. "From what my friends who have singletons tell me, get-togethers are few and far between afterward. And that's with only one baby."

"Singletons. Aren't you clever," Gwen teased. "What do you call twins or triplets?"

Megan rolled her eyes. "Twins are twingles. Moms of triplets have no time to think up cutesy synonyms."

"I'll take singletons, thank you." Cicely pretended to shudder. "Actually, erase that statement. Don't give me any more. Three of them run me ragged. Add to that a full-time job and a spoiled husband." She wrinkled her nose.

"Amen to that." Gwen grimaced. "Faith has it made on two counts. She's taking a leave from work and she doesn't have a husband making demands on her."

"Lucky lady," someone in the back row was heard to say.

"Oh, you guys," Megan chided. "I, for one, want a husband when I have kids. Don't try to tell me any of you want to be single. Cice, how many times have you had to work overtime? I've heard you call Dan and ask him to pick up the kids from school or from the sitter. Plus, he starts dinner. Why can't you give the man credit?"

Gwen looked sheepish. "My Jerry is a sweetie. He's a wonderful dad. You're right, Megan. It's a bad habit a lot of working women fall into—complaining about their spouses. Some women have to do it all—cook, clean, work outside the home *and* have total care of the kids. They're the only ones who should gripe. Sorry."

Faith observed the pensive, or perhaps guilty, expressions on the faces of her friends. Everything they'd said had started her thinking about her situation. Eventually she'd have to return to work. Maybe sooner rather than later, depending on how much she'd have to pay in attorney's fees. It was entirely possible that she might have to hire a mother's helper. The very thing she'd objected to in Michael's situation. Sadly she wondered if Kipp and Shelby, for all their faults, might not be able to offer the babies greater stability. Her own life seemed bleaker for not having a husband with whom to share the joys and trials of parenting.

"Hey, Faith." Gwen snapped her fingers in front of Faith's blank face. "I asked if seven-thirty on Saturday is good for you? That way, the people who work the eleven-to-seven can attend."

"Any time is fine with me. I'm the one living the easy life, remember?"

"Like Megan said, enjoy it while you can." Cicely tapped her watch and made shooing motions toward the door. "Back to the salt mines, ladies. Two minutes, and our break is over."

They said goodbye to Faith. Soon she was left alone with her thoughts. For all the household chores she'd done while growing up, her dad had shopped for groceries and often cooked dinner, even though he'd frequently worked overtime and come home tired. In the mornings, her mother used to brush and curl both girls' hair. There had been times their mom had barely been able to breathe, but she'd pitched in whenever she could.

A lot of women today raised children on their own, Faith argued as she shed her gown, mask and paper bootees. She was, after all, fit and capable. There was no reason she shouldn't manage beautifully.

As she stepped inside an empty elevator and turned to press the first-floor button, Faith saw Michael walk out of the adjacent elevator. He was surrounded by people who carried flowers, presents and a balloon bouquet. The balloons were pink and white. They must be on their way to visit a new mother who'd had a baby girl.

Michael split off from the crowd and angled toward the nursery. The door to Faith's elevator slid closed, blocking him from sight. She probably should have gotten out and told him the news about the twins being released on Monday. No, she decided. Let the nursing supervisor inform him and Kipp. Faith didn't feel like discussing visitations with either of them quite yet. By Monday, Michael would be back in New York and Kipp off to his boat race; she'd be able to start establishing a routine without any interference. After the shower on Saturday, she'd have time to wash and dry any clothing and sheets and blankets she might receive as gifts, and she could finish preparing the nursery. With luck, she'd be granted an entire week to spend alone with the babies.

Was privacy what she really wanted? Or would she rather have a happy marriage like Gwen's? For six years, every time Faith pictured herself married, the man in her fantasy could pass for Michael Cameron's twin.

SATURDAY, GWEN AND CICELY arrived at five to begin decorating for the shower. They brought several bottles of champagne, as well as the makings for punch. Abigail Moore, Lacy's friend, arrived next. She said she'd stopped by the hospital nursery to see the twins and they were gorgeous.

Cicely popped the cork on the first bottle and poured each one of them a glass. "To Nicky, Abby and Faith." She held her glass aloft.

"Before you toast us, come see what I've done in the babies' room," Faith begged. Taking Gwen's hand, she dragged her down the hall. Abigail followed.

"Gad! It belongs in *House Beautiful*. Isn't that monkey adorable?" Ab snatched him up and laughed at the funny face.

Gwen leaned over her shoulder. "He looks a lot like Dr. Peterson, but don't tell anyone I said so."

"You nuts." Faith grabbed the monkey away and propped him up next to the giraffe again. "You two are the baby experts. Is there anything I need that I've forgotten to buy?"

Gwen made a slow circuit of the room. "Cribs,

changing table, diaper stacker, chest of drawers, mobiles, toys and a comfy rocking chair.''

Following at her heels, Abigail named a few things Gwen had missed. ''Night-light, wedge pillows to keep them on their backs, diaper pail and baby wipes. I don't see a bathtub.''

Faith choked on her sip of champagne. ''How could I have forgotten about bathing them? Lord, how do I go about handling two?''

''One at a time,'' Gwen said, tongue in cheek. ''Remember from nursing school how slippery babies can be?''

''Don't even mention it,'' Faith gasped. ''Come back into the kitchen. I'll add a bathtub to my shopping list. Darn, I thought I had everything covered.''

''Maybe someone'll give you a bathtub as a shower gift,'' Cicely said, pausing at the kitchen counter to top up their glasses.

''Well, if they do,'' Faith said, ''I'll take it off my list. Are you two driving? If so, you'd better back off on the bubbly.''

Gwen deliberately drained her glass, smacking her lips afterward. ''Jerry's picking us up. He offered. Told me to live it up. He knows what a god-awful week it's been at work.''

''Why don't you leave E.R. and come back to the ward,'' Cicely suggested between blowing up pink and blue balloons.

''Yeah,'' Faith agreed. ''Peterson's going to fill my slot temporarily. It'd give you a break from E.R. for six months or so. A year if I can swing it financially.''

''The post-surg ward is stress of a different kind, that's all. There's a lot more lifting than there is in E.R.

After having four kids and tossing patients around for so many years, my vertebrae are giving out.''

"Have you seen an orthopedist?" Faith asked.

Gwen screwed up her face and reached for the champagne bottle again. "Fred Morrison. Until he started talking fusion. It's either that or he wants to prescribe a heavy-duty painkiller that knocks me on my butt. I can't take them and work. And I have to work—we need the money. Jerry has a good job, but he doesn't make enough to put four kids through college."

While Faith made sympathetic noises, Cicely stood up, leaned over the kitchen counter and peered around the kitchen. "Is something wrong?" Faith asked.

"Just checking to see if you had something burning in the oven. Don't you smell it?"

The other two sniffed around. Gwen finally shook her head. "I think the champagne must have dulled my senses."

"I do smell something, but I'm sure it's not in here." Faith opened the bakery box one of the women had brought. It was a beautifully decorated cake. A stork carrying two babies, one blanketed in pink and the other in blue, had been outlined on the icing. Bottles and bootees dotted the rest of the cake. "How wonderful!" There was a loud knock at her door, and she hurried to answer it.

A whole troop of women stood clustered in the hallway. Faith stepped aside to let them in, and several others got off the elevator and ran down the hall.

"Pee-ew," said the last woman through the door, holding her nose. "Your neighbor's really stinking up the hallway. A pathetic bachelor or a newlywed, I'll bet."

"Neighbor?" Faith stared at Betty, who worked in

admissions. "The only other apartment on this floor has been vacant for six months."

"Hmm," Betty drawled. "Then I'd say a hungry burglar broke in."

Faith continued to stand in the hall as the others swarmed into her living room and piled their gifts next to the couch. "I'd better call the manager," she said at last. "I don't see any smoke, but there's definitely a burning odor out here."

She excused herself and made the call. She didn't talk long. With the women all yakking at once, she could barely hear the manager's explanation.

"What did he say?" Gwen asked, slicing a hand through the air to silence the noisy group.

"Apparently he did rent the unit. To a single guy. He said not to worry about anything unless the smoke alarm goes off."

"So you have a new neighbor. Why are you frowning, Faith? Maybe he'll be gorgeous, straight and looking for a girlfriend."

Faith shrugged. "I hope he won't complain every time the babies cry. They're bound to," she said. "It takes time to change two kids and heat their bottles."

"I didn't stop to think," Betty said from the seat she'd found for herself on the floor next to the mountain of gifts. "Bachelors tend to throw wild, noisy parties."

"I wish no one had rented the place," Faith grumbled. "I hope this isn't a bad omen."

"Quit worrying." Gwen tore sheets of paper out of a preprinted pad of baby shower word games. "Now come and play."

"Hey, between changing diapers and feeding babies, maybe you can teach the guy how to cook," Cicely said, prodding Faith with the eraser of her pencil.

That garnered a laugh from everyone in the room. The festive mood continued when Gwen hauled out glasses and poured champagne all around. Soon, everyone was having such a good time the next-door neighbor was forgotten.

By the time the party ended and Faith saw her friends out, she'd accumulated not only the missing bathtub, but a thermometer, two musical swings, more stuffed animals and enough darling outfits to last the babies for a year.

Instead of going to bed, Faith stayed up and wrote a lengthy thank-you for each gift. Gwen had convinced Faith she'd never have time later.

She heard the floor creak next door, and considered popping over to introduce herself. But taking the initiative with a man wasn't something she did easily. While she deliberated, she heard his outer door slam.

Faith glanced at her kitchen clock. One o'clock. Either her neighbor was planning to close the bars, or he worked odd shifts like she had.

Stifling a yawn, Faith sealed the last envelope and shut off her lights. She went to bed, leaving the questions about her neighbor unanswered.

CHAPTER SEVEN

SUNDAY, FAITH CRAWLED OUT of bed, snapped on the bathroom light and groaned as she caught sight of the disheveled image in the mirror. "Champagne, ugh." She popped two aspirins. "Never again."

She felt better after showering. In the process of dressing to visit her dad, she contemplated future visits when she'd be taking the twins. Most residents at the home loved babies. With any luck, her dad would show some interest, too.

Faith hummed to herself as she left her apartment. Motherhood—even temporary motherhood—was going to be such a joy. It was hard to imagine ever complaining about it, even in fun as her friends had done at the shower. Young though she'd been when she assumed care of Lacy, every new phase her sister entered had delighted Faith. Well, not the teen years, but looking back, Faith decided her problems had stemmed as much from all the responsibilities she'd had to juggle: her college classes, caring for her mom, who was quite ill by then, managing the household and mothering a young woman who didn't want to be mothered.

Even after those rough years, Faith had envisioned getting married someday and having children of her own. That likelihood now seemed remote. Not too many men would want to take on raising twins—if she succeeded in gaining custody. And if she didn't, she'd still be involved in the babies' lives. Michael might be the exception. And he'd never mentioned wanting a wife.

The attendant at the front desk told Faith her father was having a bad day. She found it to be true. He was entrenched in the past and confused Faith with her aunt Lorraine. Faith gave up after an hour of watching him flip from show to show on his small TV.

Depressed, Faith didn't take him out to lunch as she normally tried to do. Instead, she left word to have his doctor call her at home to review her dad's medication. If they didn't do something, he'd never experience the joy of knowing his grandchildren.

Having jogged back to her apartment, Faith changed into sweats and took several baskets of laundry down to the basement, where the communal washers and dryers were. It wasn't until her third trip that it struck her she'd have to do this several times a week with two babies. Did she bundle them into infant carriers and cart them up and down the stairs? How could she do that *and* carry laundry? And what if one or other baby fell ill?

A washer and dryer in her own apartment was probably the best solution. But how could she fit them into her already overcrowded place? Dashing upstairs with a basket of things that needed folding, Faith ran into movers struggling to get a tan leather couch through her elusive neighbor's door.

She craned her neck to catch a glimpse of the man as she passed, but saw only two more brawny movers.

Back in her apartment, she noticed the message light blinking on her telephone. Figuring it was her dad's doctor, she hooked the laundry basket over one hip and paused to play the message.

''Faith, it's Michael. I would have called Friday after

I visited the twins, but I had business to take care of in New York.''

''Good,'' she muttered aloud. At least, now he and Kipp were both out of her hair. Except that wasn't the end of Michael's message.

''While I was at the hospital, Trish told me the twins are being released tomorrow. I was on the road before it dawned on me that you don't have my cell number. It's the easiest way to reach me.'' He rattled the number off fast. Faith had to search for a pen and back up the message so she could write it down. Although why she'd need to call him she couldn't fathom. As if he'd leave in the middle of a consultation and race to Boston to hold her hand.

In the next breath, he said, ''If you need anything, anything at all, Faith, call me. I'll move heaven and earth to help. That's the God's truth. Um, I've rambled on long enough and we're both busy. See you soon. G'bye.''

For a moment she pictured them as a team. ''Yeah, sure,'' she snorted, placing her index finger on the button to erase his message. As if she'd ever call on him.

Still, she couldn't help dwelling on his words. His offer *sounded* sincere. Had Michael done the same to Lacy? Reassured her, then not been around to follow through when she needed him?

It was how doctors were. Faith could have told Lacy that. Or maybe not back then. At the time Lacy fell in love with Michael, Faith had only worked at the hospital a year. She'd viewed doctors as kings among men, and Michael Cameron had worn a jeweled crown.

Then he'd married her little sister. And work had become just that. A place to go every day. Something to keep her mind occupied so she'd forget the doctor who'd brightened her life.

Boy, she hated all these windows opening into the past. She ought to be telling herself that Dr. Cameron was only one man in a vast ocean of men. She should flush him out of her mind.

Faith dumped the clean baby clothes on her bed and sat beside them, covering her face with both hands. The bald truth was, she'd never stopped pining for Michael. Whenever Lacy invited her to visit, she used to worry that somehow her sister would guess. Had she ever had an inkling? Surely not.

Hopping up, Faith went into the bathroom and rinsed her hot face in cold water. Studying her dripping reflection with coolly assessing eyes, she knew she'd done the right thing in hiding her infatuation from Lacy. Really, she'd had no choice. But that attraction, that *wanting* had never gone away.

When it came to fighting Michael for the babies, didn't her feelings make her a bit of a fraud? She yearned for him, yearned to share the joy of these babies with him. In court, she might be forced to state, or at least imply, the opposite.

Oh, she was a fraud. It hurt to admit it. The truth was, if it turned out Michael and not Kipp had fathered the twins, she might have to rethink her stand in the custody fight. But never in ten million years could Faith tell him why.

For the remainder of the day, as she raced back and forth finishing the laundry, Faith delivered convincing pep talks to herself. Kipp was her nemesis. After all, Lacy had been sure he'd gotten her pregnant. Or pretty sure. Faith didn't find it hard to think about fighting Kipp Fielding III for custody.

All night she struggled with her conscience, but she couldn't have slept, anyway. Her new neighbor spent the night bumping around, hanging pictures or who knew what.

Bleary-eyed, she showered and heard water running next door. At least the man was an early riser. The chorus before six-o'clock feedings shouldn't upset him.

Faith puttered until nine, when she called a cab to take her to the hospital.

Wrestling a double stroller, an oversize diaper bag weighed down with diapers, blankets, bottles and baby clothing, plus her purse, down the elevator and out the door left Faith panting.

"Looks like you brought the whole nursery and forgot the baby," the cabby said as he helped her fold and tuck the stroller into the cab's trunk.

"Everybody's a comedian," she said, rolling her eyes.

"Hey, you look like you could use a laugh."

"Oh, great. I look that bad?"

He grinned and slammed the back door. "Where to?"

"Good Shepherd Hospital. Without a scenic tour."

The man yanked on the bill of his ball cap and glanced furtively at her in the rearview mirror. "Sorry about the jokes. You shoulda said you had sick kids."

Faith opened her mouth to explain. She closed it again and stared out the window at the passing scenery. She was too weary from lack of sleep to go into the convoluted details with a man she'd never see again. "Thanks," she mumbled.

She tipped him well, as he'd gone to the trouble of opening and stabilizing her not-so-portable stroller. All it took was a flick of the wrist, the salesclerk had guaranteed Faith. Ha! The darn thing required a degree in mechanical engineering to set it up and break it down for travel.

"I'll wait if you want, or come back and pick you up," the man offered as he pocketed the money Faith thrust into his hand.

She squinted up. "It's such a gorgeous day, I'll walk home with the twins. But thank you, anyway."

"Twins! You poor woman." He shook his head. "Good luck," he muttered as he climbed back in the cab.

What she needed luck with was manipulating the side-by-side stroller through the hospital's revolving glass door. She wriggled it in, all right, but the diaper bag got caught in the section behind her. A teenager on his way out gave the door a hefty shove, nearly ripping Faith's arm off. An old man came to her assistance. He saw what was happening and yanked the stroller into the lobby so she could go around again and join up with the dangling bag.

"Phew," she exclaimed, once she'd made the circuit. "*Thank* you."

"You okay, missy? I was afraid we'd need a doctor to amputate your arm."

"Nothing so drastic. I'll soon get the hang of maneuvering this contraption." Thanking him again, she hurried down the hall, only to face a similar problem at the elevators. Faith eventually arrived at the nursery, flushed and more than a little disheveled.

The first person she laid eyes on was Michael Cameron. Arms crossed, he lounged negligently in the doorway of the nursing office. His walnut hair appeared newly cut. He wore brown loafers, tan slacks and a pale gold T-shirt that molded itself to his wide chest. If he'd worn boots instead of loafers, Faith would have said he belonged on a motorcycle—in a *GQ* ad.

Compared to Michael, Faith felt frumpy. Her blouse had come untucked from her walking shorts and a lock of hair had fallen over one eye. She blew it aside in exasperation. "What are you doing here? Yesterday, when you phoned, I thought you were in New York."

"I was. Now I'm here. To help settle the babies in their new home."

If Dr. Sampson hadn't stepped off the elevator then and ambled over with a wide smile, Faith would have exploded at Michael. He'd all but accused her of incompetence, for heaven's sake!

"Anxious to get them home, are you, Faith?" Dr. Sampson reached into a closet and helped himself to a clean lab coat. "I hope you realize you can't bring the kids back, and there are no trade-ins on new models."

"He's such a tease," the nursing supervisor said, holding open the door to let Faith, Michael and the doctor into the examining room, where she'd already wheeled the two isolettes. "As if anyone would let these precious babies go," she crooned. Then, when the couple's situation seemed to dawn on her, she made a strangled sound.

Faith had put her foot in her mouth a few times herself in front of patients or their families. She commiserated. "Honestly, Eileen, I don't know how you can bear to let *any* of them go. It's a good thing I work the post-op ward instead of here."

The nurse gave her a grateful smile. "We hang on to a little piece of each one."

When Michael looked puzzled, she pointed behind him to a corkboard wall of photos. "Most parents send us one of the newborn pictures. Oh, say, hasn't anyone provided you with information on the hospital photographs?''

Faith and Michael shook their heads.

"After Dr. Sampson formally releases you, and after the babies are dressed to go home, a photographer comes to the mom's room and takes the pictures. Wait, you don't have a room. Three-ten is empty. Use it.''

"This dynamic duo is all yours,'' Dr. Sampson announced. He handed the nurse the twins' charts, squeezed Faith's arm and shook Michael's hand. "I'll leave instructions at the nursing station about when to bring them to the office for checkups, along with sample packs of formula.'' Winking, he strode off, calling over his shoulder, "Now you can get back to the important task of having their pictures taken.''

"I wish I'd known about this earlier,'' Faith said as she began dressing Abigail. "I just gave all my cash to the cabdriver. Shoot, and I used all my film at the shower the other night or I'd take a roll at home.''

Michael dug out his wallet. "I have money, Faith.''

She clamped her teeth over her bottom lip. Only yesterday she'd sworn she wouldn't accept help of any kind from Michael Cameron. Here she was, breaking the pledge already.

"It's a nominal sitting fee,'' Eileen assured them. "That entitles you to one free eight-by-ten portrait. You're not obligated to order any. Everyone does, though,'' she said conspiratorially. "Some of them are ghastly, but there's something special about that first photo.''

"Take the money, Faith.'' Michael tossed forty dollars on the examining table. "I'd say no strings attached, but I'm going to want copies of the pictures.''

"Of course. I'll insist on repaying you half the sitting fee."

He threw up his hands. "A few lousy bucks. It's no big damned deal."

"Don't swear around the babies, please," Faith said primly.

Michael smoothed a hand over his hair. "I don't make a habit of swearing. But sometimes you can be so exasperating."

Fortunately, before Faith could reply, another nurse opened the door and stuck her head inside. "Do you have one of the babies ready to do the oxygen saturation test in your car seats?"

Faith moved Abigail to one side of the table and covered her with a receiving blanket. She laid out Nicholas's new romper. "I'm taking the twins home in a stroller. We're walking," she said.

"It's a hospital rule. Babies aren't released until their car seats are checked and properly adjusted," the young nurse insisted.

"That's going to be difficult. I don't own a car," Faith told her.

"I came to drive you home." Michael picked up Abigail, who'd begun to fuss.

"Well, I'm walking." Faith pursed her lips. She was having difficulty snapping Nick's romper.

"You can't walk everywhere," Michael argued. "Stay here and get the pictures taken. I'll go buy car seats. Tell me where to find them."

"I have two infant carriers at home. The clerk in the baby department said they'd double as car seats for the next few months. I plan to buckle them into the back seat of cabs when we go for doctor's appointments."

"Those will do." The nurse sounded relieved. "We're required to run the tests."

"Good grief." Faith folded a blanket around Nick. "Are you saying I got that double stroller down here for nothing?" She didn't know why, but tears pricked at the back of her eyes. She'd wanted this day to be perfect.

Michael noticed her mounting frustration. He rubbed a hand along her tense back. "Give me your apartment key and tell me where to find the carriers. It won't take me fifteen minutes to make the round trip. Go have the pictures done before the kids start to squall. We'll decide after the test whether to walk home using the stroller or to pack it in the truck and take the car."

Faith nodded. She didn't trust herself to speak. If she got weepy over something as trivial as this, Michael would have good reason to think she couldn't cope with two babies. It must be because she hadn't slept well for the past two nights. After a decent night's rest, she'd bounce back to her old self.

Nicholas didn't like the photographer's bright lights. Abigail had fallen asleep again, and the woman taking the pictures wanted her to open her eyes. Nick flailed his arms and bellowed so loudly Eileen rushed into the room to see what was wrong.

"I don't have all morning," the photographer said irritably. "These babies weren't on my schedule. I have half a dozen others lined up and waiting."

"Maybe a few sips from a bottle will calm this young man," Eileen suggested. She turned to the photographer. "Why don't you shoot the Benton pictures in 312? That'll give Faith time to settle Nicky."

"All right." Wadding her background sheet, the photographer picked up her portable lights and took off.

"Is it time for Nicholas to eat?" Faith asked anxiously when the woman was gone. "According to the schedule Dr. Sampson gave me, Nicholas ate at ten and isn't due for another feeding until twelve."

"I imagine a taste will suffice. This is generally his nap time. All this activity is new for them." Eileen bustled out; she returned a minute later with a two-ounce bottle. Reporters from three newspapers followed her and barged in to interview Faith and take pictures.

Faith refused to allow the use of flashes, but she didn't know how Abigail could sleep through their noisy questions. Ignoring them, she paced the floor and patted Nick's back. He wasn't about to be appeased. At least, not until she took the bottle from Eileen and popped the nipple in the baby's mouth. His little chest rose and fell a few times, but he latched right on. "Excuse us." She closed the door, shoving the reporters out.

Eileen scooped up Abigail. "Dr. Cameron is back with the car carriers. The Oximotor test takes ten to fifteen minutes. I'll get this one started."

Michael came into the room just as Nick sucked the bottle dry and began to fuss again. He issued a few terse answers to the press crowded around the door, then asked what was wrong with Nick.

"I think he's still hungry. That two-ounce bottle only whetted his appetite."

"So feed him more," Michael said, relieving Faith of the bottle so she could burp the baby.

"It's not his scheduled feeding. Eileen thought a taste would do."

"Isn't the new method to feed on demand?"

"Well, he's demanding, all right," Faith acknowledged, feeling the beginning of a headache. "I hate to ask, but could you go to the nursing station and get another of those sample bottles?''

"Don't hate to ask, Faith," Michael said solemnly. "I want to help. As a matter of fact, I'll feed him if you'd like to go see what's happening with Abby. Eileen disappeared with her through those double doors at the end of the hall.''

Faith swayed from side to side, still holding the baby. Would she be shirking her responsibilities if she left Michael to quiet Nick?

"Would you rather I checked on Abigail? I thought you might like to see what they're doing to test the infant carriers.'' Michael didn't want to step on Faith's toes, but he intended to share in the going-home process. She might as well resign herself to that fact.

"I'll have someone bring you a bottle." Faith handed over the squirming Nicholas. She ducked the press and ran right into the photographer. "Could you go on to the next family?" Faith asked. "They're running a test on Abigail, and Nicholas is still hungry.''

The woman checked her watch. "Mrs. Cameron, you've already thrown my entire schedule off. I'm due at another hospital at one o'clock. I'll give you ten minutes. If you're not ready then, you'll have to do without pictures.''

Something in Faith snapped. "First, I'm not Mrs. Cameron. I'm Ms. Hyatt. Second, I'm sure other studios have left portfolios with our hospital administrator. Are you quite sure your company can afford to lose the repeat business of so many new mothers? I'm on staff here. And we have the largest birthing center in the city.''

"Sorry," the woman mumbled, shamefaced. "Take whatever time you need. I'll call ahead and explain my delay. A lot of new moms eat lunch before they go home. I'm sure it won't present a problem."

"Do that." Faith pushed through the double doors and heard Abigail wailing. And why not? They had her cinched in the infant carrier, which was strapped to a machine rocking her forward and back and alternately bouncing her up and down.

Eileen sprinted into the room. She ripped open a plastic packet and stuck a clear pacifier in Abby's mouth.

"Oh, I hadn't planned on using pacifiers," Faith told her.

Eileen laughed. "All new moms say that, honey. My advice with twins is to stop on the way home and buy a couple of sets. See, it quiets them right down."

"I know, but..." Faith didn't go on. Already she felt as though she was treading water. She'd read the parenting book from cover to cover and had come away with such good intentions. It seemed that in the space of an hour, they'd broken all the rules.

Faith felt her energy—or what remained of it—drain out. Maybe she would let Michael drive them home. He could help her cart all the stuff they'd collected up to her apartment. She hadn't realized the hospital gave care packages to new babies. Knit caps, bootees, diapers and formula, to mention only a few things. If Eileen added anything else, there wouldn't be room for the babies.

"This kid slurped down another full two ounces, which I had to go get," Michael informed Faith when she carried Abigail back into the room. "You'd better ask Dr. Sampson if you can increase the amount of his formula at each feeding."

"Sorry." Faith rubbed at the lines that creased her forehead. "It's probably due to all the excitement. I told you this isn't even Nick's regular time to eat. Anyway, Dr. Sampson has gone. I saw him get on the elevator. The good news is the reporters went, too.''

Michael started to say something, but just then the woman taking the pictures knocked at the open door. ''Good, good,'' she said, quickly setting up her equipment again. ''They finally seem content. Do you want their pictures taken together, separately or both?''

''Together,'' Faith decided aloud at the same time Michael said, ''Separately.''

The photographer arched an eyebrow.

''It occurred to me they'll both want an album some- day,'' Michael said, pulling Faith aside.

''I should have thought of that.'' It upset her that Michael seemed to have a better grasp on parenting than she did. ''Someone gave me two baby books at the shower. One for each.''

''In any case,'' the photographer put in, even though no one had consulted her, ''Twins should be treated as individuals, Mrs. Cam—Ms. Hyatt. Although it's not so much a problem with a boy and a girl.''

''Why's she so confused about your last name, Faith?'' Michael muttered.

''She thought we were married.''

Michael arranged the sleepy Nicholas on the back- ground sheet as the idea burned into his brain. *Married to Faith*. An idea he'd entertained six years ago. Ob- viously not one that had ever occurred to Faith, judging by the way she was giving the photographer the evil eye.

''She made a natural mistake,'' he growled. ''No sense trying to explain. It's no one's business.''

''My thoughts, exactly. Okay,'' she said in a louder

voice, turning to the woman. "We've decided on separate shots."

It took quite a lot of coaxing to film both children with their eyes open. After the woman had handed Faith a receipt for the money and left with the completed address forms, the clock had pushed past one. Nicholas still hadn't had his car carrier examination. Then Abby woke up crying.

"She's wet," announced Michael. "Probably hungry, too. I'll take care of both of those problems if you'll round someone up to give Nick that test."

"I'm sorry for tying up your day, Michael. I didn't realize checking them out would be this involved. When we release patients from the surgical floor, we plop them in a wheelchair and someone escorts them out to a waiting car."

Michael grinned. "This reminds me more of buying a car. You have to work up through five levels of sales pitches and get all the gizmos explained before you can drive it out of the dealership."

"I've never bought a car. Now I doubt I ever will," she said, and sighed, heading out to the nursing station.

"What'll it be?" Michael asked her at two o'clock when they were finally released to leave. "So, are we walking or taking the car?"

"In view of all the junk we've collected," Faith said, "it makes more sense to take the car. Unless you're anxious to go home to New York. By three, traffic out of town gets wicked, or so I'm told."

Michael gazed into her wide brown eyes for a moment, debating with himself as to whether he should forget Lon Maxwell's instructions and tell Faith about the apartment he'd rented—next to hers. He apparently debated too long.

"Never mind," Faith said, bending to arrange the cartons of formula in the stroller's basket. "Transportation is my responsibility. I might as well figure out now how to lug stuff home. I'll be grocery shopping by stroller. This will be good practice."

"I know you want to be independent, Faith. But I told you I want to help."

Faith glanced up, expecting to see some version of I-told-you-so reflected in his eyes. She saw only compassion. It affected her empty stomach more than she cared to let him see. "Then quit standing around, and load this stuff in your trunk while I take Nick for his test. According to Eileen, someone on staff still has to bring the babies and me out in a wheelchair. That should give you time to put the infant carriers in your back seat. Eileen also said someone on staff has to check that they're properly installed."

"Right. You bet." Michael made short work of packing the stroller and taking off. Half an hour later, he stood at the curb jingling the car keys in his hand as a nurse wheeled Faith out, a blanketed baby cradled in each arm. Her small-boned face glowed with pleasure. Michael wasn't prepared for the longing that struck suddenly, without warning. She looked so *right* holding the twins. It forced him to take stock of all that was missing in his life.

Faith looked up then and saw him. She smiled hesitantly. Suddenly it felt too much like she was being wheeled out to meet a loving husband. Why had she ever agreed to let him drive them home?

Michael saw the light fade from her large, expressive eyes. This was a tender, momentous occasion. One usually shared by husband and wife. Michael didn't know what was going through Faith's head, but knowing her, she was probably thinking about Lacy. About how if things had been different and he hadn't been such a jerk, he'd be meeting Lacy here right now. He didn't know how to tell her there hadn't been that kind of tenderness between him and Lacy for a long time before she decided to divorce him. No man liked to face the fact that he'd made a wrong choice. Since this wasn't the time or place to discuss it, Michael offered Faith what he hoped was a friendly smile. A smile of reassurance.

She struggled to stand, still seeming uncomfortable. "Here," Michael blurted. "Give me Nicholas. I'll go around to the other side and strap him in. You handle Abby."

It was this working in tandem with Michael that threw Faith off balance. She was awfully afraid she could get used to having him around to rely on. But he wasn't going to be around. He was going to drop her off at her apartment and head back to his busy clinic. As he should. He had obligations and patients needing his attention. Lacy's babies were her responsibility.

"Have you got her fastened tight?" Michael suddenly said directly over Faith's left shoulder. She jumped and struck her head on the car's door casing. Bright lights flashed behind her eyes, stunning her for a moment.

"Hey." Michael guided her gently to the curb. "Are you all right?" he asked as he massaged the top of her head. He even dropped a kiss on the spot.

"I'm fine." Although she didn't sound it. "We need to hurry and get to the apartment. Abby's starting to cry louder. She didn't have a bottle when Nicholas did."

Unhappy at losing this moment of connection, Michael held the passenger door open for Faith, then closed her inside. It took less than five minutes to travel the five blocks to her apartment. He wished the ride had been longer even though Abigail was screaming her head off well before they parked.

Faith whisked the babies up to her apartment and went straight to the nursery. Michael finished carrying everything in from the car.

"What can I do?" he asked, pausing to look around at the decor of the nursery as he pocketed his car keys.

"Do?" Faith had placed Nick in the crib. He sprawled there contentedly. She was in the process of changing Abby's diaper. "Oh. You can let yourself out. As soon as I wash, I'll fix Abigail a bottle. My door locks automatically. I hope you have an uneventful trip back to the Big Apple, Michael."

He opened his mouth and promptly closed it again as Lon's objections replayed inside his head. Kipp and Faith were his opponents. He'd been warned about getting too chummy. Yanking the string on one of the crib mobiles, Michael listened to the first tinkling strains of Brahms "Lullaby" before muttering, "You have my cell number if you need me." He'd planned to fix lunch, but something in Faith's frosty manner changed his mind.

"Um, yes. I wrote the number down. But don't worry. We'll be fine."

Michael ran a finger softly down each baby's cheek, then waved to Faith and left.

She sat in the rocker and fed Abigail. When the musical mobile ran out, she leaned back and enjoyed the silence. This was what she'd envisioned. Their lives were going to be perfect, after all.

Only not for long. Faith had no sooner settled Abby in her crib than Nick woke up bellowing. A dry diaper didn't satisfy him. It was way too soon for him to eat again. He spit out the pacifier Eileen had included in the packet and kicked and wailed nonstop. In a matter of minutes, paradise had turned to chaos.

Finally, hours later, Faith rocked the fussy boy back to sleep. The babies were reacting to new surroundings, she told herself. Bigger cribs. Both of them—all three of them—would eventually adjust.

By midnight, Faith was dead on her feet. The babies' schedules were completely off. Nothing coincided. They were supposed to eat at the same time. She'd bought a special pillow to hook around her middle in order to feed them simultaneously, but neither baby would take a bottle while lying on it.

Dawn broke and Faith had yet to sleep a wink. She stood tensely at the window and promised herself she'd get them on track today. How hard could it be?

As the second evening rolled around, she was near tears. She hadn't found time to shower or eat more than a few bites. One or the other of the twins seemed to cry constantly. Faith didn't know if she could survive another night without sleep. But, of course she could. Other single mothers did.

At one in the morning, she thought she'd succeeded. Both babies had closed their eyes. Suddenly Nick stiffened his legs and let out a bloodcurdling cry. She walked the floor with him. His cries woke Abigail. As the nursery clock edged up on two, Faith joined their chorus of tears. She'd consulted her book but found no firm answers.

She was making her hundredth revolution around the small room when someone pounded on her front door. "Oh, no," she sobbed. "We've awakened our neighbor."

Faith's arms ached from holding both babies for so

long. It wasn't easy shifting either so that she could unlock and open the door the length of the chain.

"Please, I'm sorry," she said into the dim hallway. "I have new twins," she explained. "One's very fussy. I'm planning to phone the doctor as soon as I—the office is open."

"When in hell were you going to call me?" growled a familiar voice on the other side of the door.

"Michael?" Swabbing at her tears, Faith loosened the chain and let it fall. She swallowed back more than tears. The man was barefoot and bare-chested. His formfitting, ratty jeans were zipped but not buttoned. His eyes were heavy-lidded, and his face bore a two-day stubble that made him look dangerous. Sexy and dangerous.

"Wh-what are you doing here dressed like that?" Faith squeaked as he herded her back into the room and kicked the door shut.

"For two days I've been sitting next door listening to these infants cry, waiting for you to call. Which you refused to do—but I'm not letting my babies down to accommodate your stubbornness."

"Next door! You're living next door?"

"Yes. How long since you've slept? Hand me those two. You hit the sack."

Faith jerked back, pulling the babies right out of his hands. "I'm not letting you have them! I know why you're doing this, Michael. To make me look bad."

"Give me a break. I don't have to do that. You already look like hell." With that, he wrenched the babies away from her. Stripping them out of their blankets, he draped two sweating little bodies over each of his broad shoulders. Like magic, after a few snuffles and shudders, the infants snuggled their faces into his neck and both fell asleep.

Faith's shaking legs gave out and she collapsed onto the couch. A part of her muzzy brain wanted to kiss Michael for the blessed silence. Another part wished for the energy to boot his sneaky, sexy body straight back to New York. Before managing to do either, she toppled to the side, snoring softly.

Her last puzzled thought before she fell asleep was, *Michael's living next door. What does that mean?*

CHAPTER EIGHT

FAITH OPENED ONE EYE. She didn't know where she was for a moment. Sunbeams danced in lacy patterns across the wall she faced. Her living room wall, she decided as other familiar objects fell slowly into place. Memories of the twins came crashing back, shooting her upright. Faith shed the afghan that had been covering her.

Dry-mouthed and gritty-eyed, she brushed a hand over the blouse and shorts she'd worn for two days. Or was it longer?

The apartment was silent. Frighteningly so. Faith went dizzy from sitting up too abruptly. Suddenly she remembered a scene from the previous night. Michael hammering at her door, then barging in looking like a *Playgirl* centerfold. He'd taken the two crying babies from her arms.

Had he kidnapped them? A sense of panic overwhelmed her. Michael was a cornerstone of the establishment, so the very idea seemed far-fetched. But every day the newspaper was filled with stories of nice guys doing the unthinkable.

Afraid to see what awaited her in the nursery, Faith prepared herself for the worst. Her heart beat erratically and her stomach churned as she stumbled down the hall and, with badly shaking hands, pushed open the door that stood ajar.

What she saw was the last thing she'd expected. Michael seated in her mother's rocker, a baby lying comfortably in each arm. They were sucking contentedly on bottles held in the long, elegant fingers he'd curved around their little faces.

"How do you do that?" Faith inquired softly. "I've tried and tried. My arms simply don't reach."

His gaze seemed to warm her as it flowed from the top of her tousled head all the way down to her bare feet. "Good afternoon, sleepyhead. I've got to admit it took me two night feedings, breakfast and midmorning snack to finally get the hang of doubling up like this."

"Afternoon?" Her bottom jaw went slack. "I slept that long?"

"I passed a cup of coffee under your nose this morning, after I bathed the kids and had a shower. You didn't twitch a muscle. I figured you needed the rest. They slept well once I placed them in the same crib. Hal Sampson said it might make them feel more secure."

"You bathed the babies?" she parroted dumbly, realizing that Michael had shaved and changed clothes. Now he wore a shirt and gray slacks instead of jeans and…nothing. Thank goodness. Faith felt faint at the memory of how he'd looked last night. Or maybe she just needed sustenance. As a nurse she'd seen plenty of naked chests. Other bare parts of a man's anatomy, too. None had ever affected her with the jolt she'd received last night.

"These two are on the verge of sleep," he murmured. "Why don't you hop in the shower? While you're doing that, I'll see what I can round up for lunch."

Crossing her arms over her breasts, Faith propped a hip against the door. "I'll go when you tell me what's behind this sudden spurt of domestic benevolence."

"That was a mouthful."

"You're stalling," she accused him. "You wouldn't move into the apartment next door unless it served your purposes. And why, by the way, didn't you tell me earlier? You'd better have a darn good explanation."

"Won't you feel more like having this discussion when you're clean and fresh?"

"I feel fine. Greatly rejuvenated after—what? Ten hours of sleep?"

"Um, about that." He gently tugged an empty bottle from Nicholas's mouth and tossed it into the crib. Rocking forward, he tipped the baby up and patted his back until the little guy burped. Climbing to his feet, Michael settled the boy in his crib, still holding Abigail. He then returned to his seat and transferred Abigail's bottle to his free hand. "This little squirt would sooner sleep than eat. I think we should keep prodding her and get them back on some kind of schedule, don't you agree?"

Faith gaped. Of course she did. Erratic schedules were the reason she'd gone without sleep. She'd been in the process of either changing or feeding one baby or the other for a full twenty-four hours. "Let's back up. You're right. I will be able to handle this discussion better after a shower." Vigorously massaging her temples, Faith left the room. Not until she stood naked under a hot spray did she allow herself to think about what might be going on with Michael. Last night he'd dropped the bomb about being her neighbor. A neighbor who'd moved in last week. Which meant his precipitous appearance last night had not been spur-of-the-moment. He'd been behind the wall, waiting like a vulture for her to screw up.

And why had he acted so secretive about moving into her building?

Already sputtering, she stuck her head beneath the

spray. The water might be hot, but Faith's blood ran cold. Even when he was a resident, others on staff had insisted Dr. Cameron mapped out and followed a detailed agenda. Back then, his aim had been to become the number-one cardiopulmonary surgeon. A person didn't have to be too bright to figure out what his goal was now, why he'd barged into her home like this. Michael had his sights set on fatherhood. What Faith found hard to reconcile was that he knew the babies might not be his. Why, then, was he willing to waste his time? This was the man Lacy had complained never took a day off. The man who rarely took an evening away from patients.

Guilt was the obvious answer, Faith decided as she grabbed a towel and dried off. Or at least part of the answer. He felt remorse for not trying harder to keep Lacy from following through with the divorce. There was always the possibility that he was spying on her, looking for ways to damage her position in the custody case. Although it hurt to think he'd be so sneaky... Forewarned now, she vowed to be alert.

A shower and clean clothes refreshed her. Facing Michael didn't seem quite so daunting as it had earlier. He was a man dedicated to saving lives. A load of guilt drove him to act out of character. It shouldn't be too hard to offer absolution and send him back to New York.

After peeking in at the sleeping babies, Faith partially closed the nursery door and followed the smell of food to the kitchen. She had only to see the bowls of creamy tomato soup and the thick turkey sandwiches to admit she was starved.

''Yum.'' She sniffed the air.

Michael pulled out one of the kitchen chairs. ''Better

hurry and eat before the soup gets cold. What took you so long?''

"I washed my hair. It took time to blow it dry."

His gaze wandered to her short, curly locks. "I guess you were quick, at that. Lacy used to spend an hour to dry her hair."

"Because hers was so thick," Faith said, after taking her seat and letting him slide her closer to the table. "When Lacy was little, I burned out more dryer motors making sure her hair was completely dry before she went to bed. Mother was of the era that believed going to bed with a wet head insured pneumonia."

"Was Lacy as bald as Abigail when she was really little?"

Faith bristled. "Abigail isn't bald. It's just that her hair is so fine and blond, it's hard to see. Nick doesn't have any more. His is a smidgen darker, that's all."

"More than a smidgen. But in the child development book I bought, it says that's not unusual. Especially in fraternal twins."

"You bought a book." Faith's eyes snapped up from their concentration on her soup.

"Don't act so surprised. You gave me the idea."

"What if the twins don't turn out to be yours?"

He stared at her the entire time he finished chewing the bite of sandwich he'd taken. Then he swallowed. "Is it my imagination, Faith, or are you hoping they aren't?"

She fumbled for words. "I started thinking, feeling sorry really, for the patients you're letting down by being here. Say the DNA takes six weeks. How many lives could you save in that period of time?"

His eyes grew wary. "What gives, Faith? Lacy was

the one who resorted to flattery to get her way. Not you. You've always been honest, direct."

Ashamed, Faith stirred a spoon around and around in her soup.

"Come on, just say what you're thinking."

"All right," she blazed. "Your patients have always been your number-one priority. What's changed?"

"What makes you think something's changed? Doesn't a man deserve a break from work once in a while?"

She smiled crookedly. "Now who's being slippery? You've hardly taken a weekend off in the six years I've known you. Suddenly a vacation? Admit you were spying on me, Michael. That's why you moved into my building, isn't it?"

"No, I wasn't, and no, I didn't. Priorities can change." He frowned as he bit into his sandwich.

"Have yours? Or is this penance because the first time you called Lacy's bluff, something bad happened?"

Michael choked. "Well, that's direct enough," he said when he was finally able to speak. They both sat there, eyes connected and smoldering for what seemed like an eternity. Michael gave in first. He expelled the breath he'd been holding and got up to stare out of the kitchen window. "There's no one thing at the bottom of my decision to take a break. Yes, I'd felt my marriage hitting the rocks, and I found myself powerless to stop it. Then to learn Lacy had died..." He lifted both shoulders and let them fall again. "It's more than that, though. Something...moved inside me the first day I held the twins. I—I can't begin to explain."

"You don't have to," Faith said meekly. "The same thing happened to me."

"My book refers to the spell as *twin shock*." Michael returned to the table and sat again to earnestly make his case.

"Everyone gravitates toward twins."

"Yes, but the author was referring to parents. A… a…special connection."

"Then how do you account for the fact that I felt it? I know you experienced a sense of bonding, Michael, so you're convinced they're yours. But wouldn't you rather keep your distance until the tests come back, and save yourself a broken heart?" Faith suddenly sat straighter. "Unless men don't suffer broken hearts."

"Of course we do. What do you think? That we're made of iron?" He glared at her. "You've certainly developed a rotten attitude toward men."

She had the grace to avert her eyes, because quite the opposite was true. At least, when it came to Michael. Since the first moment she'd set eyes on him, the attraction had been there. Heaven knows she'd done her best to resist it. To tell herself it didn't exist. Apparently to no avail.

"I'm staying here until the tests come back," he said, when it appeared Faith wasn't going to answer him. "My book also says raising multiples is physically and emotionally demanding on both parents, and I've discovered how true *that* is. After your first couple of days going it alone, can you truthfully say you don't need my help?"

Faith didn't have to think long or hard. Neither did she wish to sound too eager. She slowly counted out fifteen seconds. "I can see the value of having a second pair of hands, Michael. If your mind is made up, I suppose we can split some duties. We need to set down rules, though."

"Rules?" Michael didn't think he liked the sound of "setting rules." Fortunately, one of the twins—Nick, he thought—awoke with a wail. Michael bounded to his feet. "I'll go. You've barely touched your lunch. Rule number one should be that we keep up our strength. So eat." Dust bunnies flew in his wake.

Faith planted both elbows on the table and rested her chin in her hands. She hadn't had time recently to get the housework under control. Scrubbing floors was about the best way she knew to combat irritation. Was that what she felt at having Michael underfoot? Or was it more like sexual frustration?

She didn't want to examine the question too closely. Getting up, she stomped to the microwave and reheated her soup. She promptly burned her tongue, causing her to mutter something unladylike under her breath. "It's going to be a long month."

Michael stuck his head into the kitchen alcove. "Nick has wet through everything. He needs changing from the inside out. Which chest of drawers is his?"

Faith pushed her bowl away and started to get up.

"Hey, sit still and finish your lunch. I'm capable of handling this."

After their baths, Michael must have put them back in the same outfits they'd been wearing. "I'm full anyway," she said. "If we're going to share baby duty, you need to know my system. By the way, does this sharing include us both doing laundry?"

He looked startled. "Laundry is a mystery to me. I send out everything I wear." He always had, even as a resident. His colleagues had teased him unmercifully.

"Everything? Didn't Lacy do laundry?"

"Hers, I suppose. Or maybe not." It flustered him to realize he didn't know.

"Well, here the washers and dryers are in the basement. The other day I thought I should buy a set. Then I couldn't decide where I'd put them."

"I think there's a washer and dryer in my apartment. That'll be much closer."

"Yes, but you aren't going to live there forever, Michael. I need to make arrangements for the long term."

"Now who's second-guessing the court decision?"

Faith wore a sheepish look when she walked into the nursery. "I believe in the power of positive thinking."

"For you, but not for me?"

"I thought we weren't going to argue about this, Michael."

"We did say that. I can't help it, though. It bothers me that you refuse to take me seriously. What do I have to do to convince you I want the twins?"

"This is Nick's dresser," she said, stopping to pull clean sleepers from a drawer. "I stacked crib sheets, blankets and receiving blankets on shelves in the closet. Diapers to refill the stackers are in there, too. The pink packages are Abby's, the turquoise ones are Nick's."

"His and her diapers?"

"It has to do with anatomy, Doctor. Nick's have more padding in front, Abigail's are thicker toward the back."

"Oh. Yeah, I can see that makes sense."

Michael watched the deft way Faith handled Abigail, who had opened her eyes and started to mewl. "I'll confess it's my fault Nick is soaked through. This morning I grabbed the first diaper at hand. Now I see it has little pink animals on the front band and not blue."

"You get a gold star for trying," Faith said. "Say, did I ever thank you for letting me sleep? And, um, thanks for covering me up."

He shrugged. "I tried to wake you and send you to bed. That couch didn't look all that comfortable. But you were dead to the world."

"Saturday night was the baby shower. Everyone stayed late. I was excited about bringing the twins home, and didn't sleep Sunday, either. Monday night their schedules were way off. By last night, I'd gone through my reserves."

"So all that laughter and music I heard until the wee hours on Saturday night was a baby shower?"

"What did you think?" Faith whirled to confront him.

"Frankly, I didn't know what to think. I checked the hall several times, but never saw anyone come or go. I'd never pegged you as a party girl, but the later it got and the noisier it became, I decided you'd changed. Next morning, when I saw you hauling all those champagne bottles down to the Dumpster, I was sure you had."

"You were spying on me!"

"Not intentionally. I glanced out my bedroom window and you happened to be standing by the trash bin."

Faith bounced Abigail on her shoulder. The nursery had shrunk after she'd installed furniture. Now with two adults trying to change two babies, it seemed smaller yet. Every time she bumped into Michael or he brushed past her to deposit a wet diaper in the shiny chrome can, she felt self-conscious. "I have things under control now, Michael. Feel free to go back to your apartment."

He sucked the side of his cheek between his teeth and clamped down to keep from reacting to her brush-off. "What's on your agenda today?"

"Nothing. Why? I'm on leave from work, you know."

"After the babies' next feeding, let's sit down and draw up a schedule. Loose, of course, because babies aren't predictable. We ought to be able to set up some sort of daily planner around their general feeding times."

"After what you said at the hospital, Michael, I decided to let them eat when they wanted to. I'll catch up on household chores while they sleep. Or I can do that whenever you feed them. I know you won't want to hang around all day, every day."

"There's where you're wrong, Faith. I do want to. I want us to share fifty-fifty."

"But...but...but..." she sputtered, her eyes clouding.

"What's the matter, Faith? Do I make you uncomfortable? I certainly don't mean to."

"It's not that," she hastened to say. She didn't want him analyzing and eventually figuring out why he made her nervous. After only a few short hours in his company, Faith was awfully afraid she could get very used to having Michael around. And what would happen to her heart when he up and left, as was inevitable? It had taken her years to get over his marrying Lacy. Faith hated to think what it would be like if he took off after she'd come to depend on him—and on his help with the twins.

"What *is* bugging you, then?"

"I've lived in this apartment house for a long time. I...don't want the residents getting the wrong idea." Faith latched on to the first thought that made sense.

"I hate to be obtuse, but what wrong idea?"

"With regards to our re...lation...sh-ship."

"If anyone read yesterday's paper or saw the TV news, they'll know our relationship." Not that Michael himself hadn't sat next door a number of days indulging in some pretty explicit fantasies.

"What do you mean?"

"I'll bring over a copy of yesterday's paper," he said. "The reporters seem hyped about the custody case. I don't recall them taking our pictures when we picked up the kids. But there we were, together on the front page. They even had a shot of Kipp at the helm of his yacht, and his wife walking into a New York fertility clinic."

"Why?" Faith gasped.

"It's sensationalism," he said bitterly. "Prominent surgeon's ex-wife dies in childbirth. Her sister and the son of a prominent Wall Street millionaire fight the doctor for custody of the deceased mother's twins."

"Millionaire? I had no idea," Faith exclaimed, looking a little sick.

"Lon Maxwell phoned last night. From now on, he wants us to say 'no comment' to any questions. I think he's overreacting. By now, we're yesterday's news. To clear the air between us, Faith—Lon's the one who insisted I not tell you or Kipp that I'd be spending time in Boston. Lon would have a fit if he knew I rented a place next door to you."

"He's not alone," she grumbled. "But back to the news article—I want the reporters to leave us alone. I'll phone David and ask his opinion on how to stop their intrusions."

"You might want to do that now, while the babies are quiet. I can't get over how alert they are. They're already turning toward us when we speak."

"Tomorrow they'll be two months old. According to

my baby book, they'll be playing patty-cake by the time the DNA tests are back and their future is settled."

Michael's expression softened. "I'm not thinking that far ahead. I'm taking one day at a time."

The look of love he focused on the twins brought a rush to Faith's heart. Mumbling an excuse to leave, she hurried out to call her attorney.

BY THE END OF THE SECOND WEEK, it appeared Michael's assessment was more accurate than Lon Maxwell's. At first, any time they took the babies out for walks, it caused a stir. Faith even had to escape a reporter when she made her weekly visit to see her father. The first week, news teams hung around outside the apartment. Then, little by little, as both Faith and Michael refused to speak, the reporters lost interest.

By the middle of the third week, Faith had begun to relax. She and Michael had fallen into a comfortable routine. They shared chores during the day. He cooked as many meals as she did. She'd throw laundry into the washer and Michael would put it in the dryer, or vice versa. Though they spent their days together, every night after the eleven-o'clock feeding, he returned to his apartment. He joined a health club and went there every morning, delaying his arrival at Faith's until after she'd dressed for the day.

She found herself wishing for more. No matter how sternly she chastised herself for thinking foolish thoughts, her feelings for Michael didn't go away. Far from it.

She loved to watch him with the babies. She'd initially assumed he'd gravitate toward Nick—masculine bonding or some such thing. After all, Kipp and his father certainly showed a preference. But Michael divided his time equally. He seemed as delighted over Abigail's blowing bubbles as he did when Nick latched onto his finger and cooed. Faith teased him when he came home from the store with frilly dresses for Abby. Not that she didn't splurge on the babies, but she tended to favor practical cotton outfits.

Faith's phone rang early one morning near the end of the third week, while she was home alone. The call threw the first wrench into her idyllic days with Michael and the babies. Kipp Fielding III was on the line.

"I'm home from Florida," he announced without preamble. "Dad and Shelby have been too busy to visit the twins. We're driving down to Boston today. Should be there by eleven. I'd like directions to your apartment."

Taken completely off guard, Faith stammered out her address. Then after they'd said goodbye, she began to fume. The judge had said to phone ahead and request a convenient time. Kipp hadn't even asked if she had other plans. And he hadn't asked how the babies were, which struck her as odd, considering how silent the Fieldings had been.

In the next instant, Faith panicked. She hadn't vacuumed in two days. The apartment wasn't dirty, but it was cluttered. She had a tendency to leave packages of diapers in every room. It was easier than always running to the changing table.

She looked quite harried and disheveled when Michael let himself into the apartment half an hour later than usual.

"Where have you been?" Faith demanded in such a shrewish tone that he swallowed the catchy tune he'd been whistling.

"Working out. Same as I've done every morning. I

stayed later than usual—ran into an old friend." He paused. "Faith, is something wrong?"

She shoved a stack of medical journals he'd brought over to read into his hands. "Do you have any other stuff here that's obviously yours?" she asked, opening the door and literally pushing him into the hall.

"A coffee cup in the kitchen, and a couple of shirts in the guest bedroom. I put them in the closet because I never know when Abby's going to spit up or I'm going to be slow with a diaper and Nick's going to pee all over me. What's this about, Faith?"

"The Fieldings are coming," she said, sounding a bit hysterical.

Michael tipped back his head and laughed. "Sorry," he said when she glared at him, hands on hips. "Reminded me of that old movie, *The Russians Are Coming, The Russians Are Coming.* Why are you so worried?"

"I'm not worried about Kipp and Shelby, although Kipp's father is intimidating. It's more that I don't think they'd be overjoyed to find us consorting. In a manner of speaking," she said, blushing wildly when Michael arched a brow and stared at her in a slightly mocking fashion.

"You know what I mean," she snapped, throwing up her hands.

"I don't. So spell it out, please."

"Have you forgotten that Kipp's team of attorneys filed a complaint over the two of us having greater access to the babies? You said yourself that Lon cautioned you to hide the fact you'd moved to Boston."

"I know he did. But the judge decided old man Fielding and Shelby could visit as often as they wished.

Which, by the way, I haven't seen them doing. Not even once.''

"Please don't be difficult, Michael. You've had three weeks of nearly twelve-hour days with the twins. It can't hurt to let Kipp and his family have one day. They'll probably only spend a few hours. I'll call you the minute they leave. I promise.''

Her dark eyes seemed so genuinely distressed, Michael wasn't able to refuse her. He bent to kiss her forehead. "Okay.''

Faith jerked back as if she'd been burned. "Wh-why did you do that?''

"You still act as if my primary goal in life is to cause you trouble. I just want to convince you that my motives are pure.'' He grinned, but then his expression grew more serious. "I can't see any reason I should disappear while the third party in this case decides to exercise his court-mandated rights. But because it matters to you, Faith, I'll stay out of sight. What will you say, though, if Kipp asks how many times I've visited?''

She chewed disconsolately at her bottom lip. "I'll keep my fingers crossed that he doesn't. I'm not very good at fibbing,'' she said.

"That's a relief. I'd hate to think you'd let them believe I'd fallen off the face of the earth. I have a vested interest in those babies. I don't happen to care who knows it.''

"I'm sorry, Michael. Of course you do. After all, you loved their mother.'' Faith stepped back and gripped the doorknob. "I guess you loved her even after the divorce.'' She avoided looking at Michael as she said it.

He placed a curled finger under her chin, forcing her to meet his brooding gaze. "I've deliberately avoided having this conversation with you, Faith. The truth is, I didn't want you to think less of me. I know Lacy meant the world to you. But our marriage had more downs than ups. While it's true that I wasn't the one who opted out, it's taken me some time to realize I felt a sense of relief when all was said and done. Maybe you'd rather not know it, but I'm telling you anyhow. These last weeks with you have been more enjoyable than all the years I spent with Lacy. Oh, at first, with the move, starting the clinic and arranging her follow-up transplant care, our differences weren't so apparent. I may even discount the second year. After that, though…''

Faith wished he hadn't said a word. And yet she was glad he had. His confession eased some of her guilty conscience over dreaming of things she shouldn't. But she felt a great sadness for her sister, and a disloyalty at her own reaction. Because what he'd said meant he wasn't indifferent to her, and that thrilled her. But poor, misguided, childish Lacy…so unhappy in her marriage.

"Don't look so shocked by my confession." Pulling out his keys, Michael turned toward his door. "I'm camped on your doorstep because of the twins. You don't have to worry that I'll take advantage of you, Faith."

She said nothing. He'd gone inside his apartment and closed the door before she moved. He'd certainly made himself clear. Had burst the bubble on her foolish day-dreams. He might enjoy her companionship, but as far as attraction went…forget it. In bed at night, she'd actually dared to imagine that he might ask her to live with him if it turned out he was the twins' dad. Last night, they'd watched a late movie seated side by side on the couch. The way they'd laughed and talked so comfortably together, she'd let her imagination run wild after he'd gone. Oh, she hadn't kidded herself into believing he felt for her what she did for him. But they got along, and they both loved the babies. A marriage could start with that and build.

Slipping inside the apartment, she quietly closed her door. It was never going to happen, no matter how much she prayed. It was time she stopped being naive.

She finished picking up the place and pulled on a clean T-shirt and a pair of faded denim overalls. Her hair curled over her ears. She needed it cut. Maybe Michael would watch the babies one afternoon next week. She might even treat herself to a facial. Funny how he'd become so entwined in her life in such a short time. How on earth would she manage things like haircuts if he wasn't around?

She carefully dressed Nick in a sailor suit and Abby in a pretty yellow dress. "Wait," she said, slapping her forehead with a palm. Why give the Fieldings greater reason to choose Nick over his sister? She removed the nautical outfit and dressed him in a green-and-white shorts set that had lambs all over it.

No sooner had she finished with the last snap than there was a knock at her door. Scooping up the twins, she strolled through the living room to answer it.

The three who stood there might as well have come for a wake. Kipp nervously pulled at the neck of his polo shirt. His father wore a scowl. Shelby hovered behind them, studying the ceiling, the walls, the floor. Her gaze lit anywhere but on the infants Faith held.

"Welcome." Faith pasted on a phony smile. Actually, it wasn't so phony. There was obviously dissension in the ranks. She shouldn't be happy about that, but it was only human nature, she thought.

"They've grown," Kipp observed after they'd all taken seats around the room.

"Yesterday was their checkup." Faith rattled off a height and weight for each child. "They had their first set of shots. So if they're fussy, that's why." She stopped beside Kipp. "Would anyone like to hold them while I fix us some iced tea?"

No one said a word. Faith whipped a baby blanket off the arm of the couch. She spread it on the floor and laid Nick and Abby down. Both immediately kicked and waved their arms. Abigail blew bubbles and Nicholas began to sputter and drool.

"Why is the boy doing that?" demanded the elder Fielding with a certain degree of revulsion.

Faith tried not to sound defensive—or angry.

"Dr. Sampson said Nick may be cutting teeth. It's early, but the doctor said some babies teethe at six or eight weeks. Drooling is quite common. You've probably forgotten how your son reacted to teething."

"My son never drooled," the pompous man declared.

"Ho-kay!" Faith wasn't about to argue. "I'll get that tea," she said. "Sugar or lemon, anyone?" she asked.

Shelby folded her hands. "Nothing. We can't stay. You said we'd just pop in and out." She aimed her comment at Kipp's father.

Faith thought it was odd that Shelby had appealed to her father-in-law and not her husband.

"Cool it, Shel," Kipp said mildly. He slid to his knees and after some hesitation, picked up Nicholas. Kipp's dad moved to where he could get a clearer look at the boy.

After five silent minutes had passed, Faith hoisted Abby onto her lap. It broke her heart to see that sweet baby being ignored.

All in all, the Fieldings stayed half an hour. Only until the babies began to fuss and Faith said it was time for their bottles. "You can feed Nicholas if you like," she offered magnanimously.

Kipp was indecisive; he might have agreed if his wife hadn't risen and hurried to the door.

"Uh, we really don't wish to disrupt your schedule," Kipp told Faith.

"We only came because Bob Schlegel said we should," Shelby burst out. "Although it makes no sense. All this fuss and you don't even know if that child is your son."

Kipp apologized for his wife's petulance. He placed Nick in Faith's arms and followed his family out. "On Friday I'm off to the Carolinas for another race. I'll touch base when I get back."

"The DNA results might be in by then," Faith said, wanting them just to leave.

They did, without a backward glance, and she went to prepare bottles. Uncommonly depressed, she was reluctant to phone Michael although she'd promised. But within minutes, he was standing in the kichen; he'd obviously been keeping tabs. Faith doubted the Fielding troop had made it down the elevator before Michael used his key and let himself in.

"Short visit. Is old Kipper having second thoughts about daddyhood?"

"Oh, Michael." Faith dropped the bottles and burst into tears.

He caught her in his arms and let her sob against his chest. "Kipp only wants Nick. Shelby doesn't want either baby. How can anyone be so...so coldhearted? Abby's gorgeous. She's going to look like Lacy. Please, Michael, don't let them win."

Michael rocked her, rubbing his cheek across her hair. "I see Abby's resemblance to Lacy, now that you mention it," he murmured. "Maybe that's Shelby's objection. God, I wish I could promise, Faith. I can't." His voice dropped, reflecting his frustration. "Dammit, if I could put a rush on that DNA, I would."

CHAPTER NINE

THEY CLUNG TO EACH OTHER until their heartbeats leveled. One of the babies lying on the blanket in the living room began to wail. Faith separated herself from Michael's warmth, pressing a hand to her lips and running the other through her hair. "I don't know what got into me. Their bottles are ruined. Do you mind seeing to the twins while I mix more formula?" Her voice sounded strained.

He caught her hand. "Look at me."

Her eyes lifted slowly, warily.

"I wish I could promise I was going to win. But you know as well as I do, Faith, the whole custody mess is a crapshoot at this point."

"I know. That's why I'm still carrying my lucky clover. It's called covering all bases," she said as she bent to collect the bottles she'd dropped and then carried them to the kitchen sink.

Michael picked up both babies and snuggled them into his arms. "When I spoke with Lon earlier, he said nothing further can be done on our case until the test results come back."

"David gave me the same story," Faith said, as she handed Michael a bottle and held out her arms for one of the babies.

Michael passed her Nicholas. "Here you go, princess," he said, parting Abigail's rosebud lips with the bottle's milky nipple.

Faith settled into a corner of the couch with Nick. "Kipp's dad had the nerve to imply that something might be wrong with Nick because he drooled."

"I hope you wrote it down. If Kipp does turn out to be the biological dad, you have a better shot than I do at contesting his custody. Lon said I might be able to ask for comparative DNA from a second lab, but the judge could still grant Fielding temporary custody pending any outcome."

Faith used her fingers to brush Nick's dark, flyaway hair. "It's too depressing to dwell on, Michael. I may only have a couple of weeks left as their mom. I'm going to put everything else out of my mind and just savor being with them, watching them develop. They're coming into their own personalities, have you noticed?"

"Yes. Abigail's already an accomplished flirt. Nick is going to rip through life with gusto."

Faith raised her head. "Both of those traits describe Lacy."

"I suppose so," Michael mused. "Fraternal twins only share half their parents' genes, which cuts down on genetic similarities. According to my book, it's too early to say whether Abby or Nick inherited any of their father's features or traits."

"It'd be easier to accept the DNA results if the children resembled the proven biological dad."

"The waiting is getting to us, Faith. I like your idea of forgetting all about custody for now. After the twins finish their bottles, why don't we put them in their carriers and drive down the coast? Fall's going to give way to winter soon and it won't be as easy to take them on outings."

Faith didn't want to say that every time they got in Michael's car and the four of them went somewhere, it made her heart ache. She didn't want to tell him that she'd never felt more poignantly alone than on those occasions. The fact that they weren't now and never would be a real family became more painful with every "family" thing they did. Whenever they went out with the babies, people assumed they were married. There was something about twins that made everyone stop and admire, cooing and smiling. Passersby always took for granted that she and Michael were the parents. Faith thought she'd handled it well at first. Now, because they'd grown closer and they'd fallen into sharing tasks, it got harder and harder to put on an act.

What excuse could she give Michael for preferring to mope around the house? "I'll pack a diaper bag," she said without a lot of enthusiasm. "How long will we be gone?"

"We could drive down to Sandwich. I know a great casual seafood place there. We haven't had dinner out since you brought the babies home. Isn't it time we took the plunge?"

"Why?"

His eyes twinkled. "Well, for one thing, it'll be more enjoyable now than when they're older and can reach everything on the table. For another, you deserve a break from cooking."

"You've cooked as many meals as I have."

Michael fixed her with steady eyes. "Do you argue with every man who asks you out to dinner, Faith, or just with me?"

"Men never ask me to dinner," she said, undergoing a sudden need to flee his inspection. The way he'd put that—*asking her out*—made it sound like they'd be going on a date.

"Then I have serious doubts about Boston's male population. That makes me all the more determined to drag you out today. I've never been through the glass museum, have you? I hear it's filled with items made by the now-defunct Boston Sandwich Glass company. They made the pitcher you have sitting on the kitchen table, you know."

"All right. You win. I'd love to go through the museum and have dinner someplace. But don't say I didn't warn you if Abby and Nick both need to be changed and fed the minute the waiter serves your lobster."

"Success has to do with good planning," he said. "You'll see."

She did, indeed, and couldn't help but rub it in four hours later when both babies set up a howl not two seconds after the waiter served her and Michael steaming bowls of thick clam chowder.

Faith had looked forward to the warm stew. Outside, the day had turned quite blustery. She'd been more than ready to leave the beach and go inside for an early dinner. They'd visited the museum first, which she'd thoroughly enjoyed, and couldn't believe Michael had let her wander to her heart's content.

"What's wrong with them?" Michael whispered, when his attempt to rock the carriers and quiet the infants failed.

"It's called Murphy's Law." Faith loosened the straps holding Abigail in her seat and, after straightening the blanket, picked up the baby and rocked her in her arms. "At the parents-of-multiples meeting last week, the topic was timing. A bunch of parents complained that whenever they sat down to a hot meal or got on the phone or even initiated sex, that was precisely when both babies decided to act up. Or three, in the case of triplets.''

Michael couldn't say why his mind had stalled on her reference to initiating sex. His partner at the clinic, who was always analyzing him, would say it was because he'd been celibate for nearly a year. Michael thought it was more likely because the subject had been on his mind too often lately. Rarely a night went by that he didn't lie in his bed thinking of Faith lying next door in hers. He'd had some pretty vivid dreams after falling asleep, too.

He'd folded enough of Faith's laundry to know what she wore underneath her day wear. She didn't go in for frills. Remembering that made him smile.

Her nightgowns were nothing like the blatantly provocative ones Lacy had preferred. But Faith owned a plain white sleeveless cotton number with a thin bead of lace running around a short hem and a deep V neck that left Michael sweating each time he pulled it out of the dryer.

"Why are you staring at me?" Faith hissed. "Are you going to let Nicholas scream until he wakes the dead?"

Jolted out of his reverie, Michael shot a guilty glance around the busy dining room. "Everyone's looking at us," he said.

"No kidding." Faith delivered a smirk insinuating that he was awfully dense. "Eat your soup," she said, and sighed. "Hand me Nick. I'll go see if the ladies room has a changing table. They might be wet again."

"We changed them before we came in so we wouldn't have to go through this." Michael watched her gather both babies and the heavy diaper bag.

"I could say I told you so," Faith muttered, excusing herself as she banged the diaper bag against another diner's chair.

It was only after she left and Michael plunged a spoon into his soup that he realized every woman in the room glowered at him as if he somehow personified all the articles written about chauvinistic men. It didn't help that everyone in the restaurant could still hear both twins wailing. Michael recorked the bottle of wine he'd foolishly ordered. That, at least, they could take home. As a matter of fact, he thought, motioning their waiter over, they hadn't ordered anything for their main course that couldn't be stuffed into a doggie bag.

"Do you want your wife's entrée delayed?" the waiter asked, nervously glancing toward the alcove from which the chorus continued.

Michael didn't correct the man's assumption that Faith was his wife. He just pulled out a money clip and peeled off a few bills. "Could you box the whole works, including the wine? Here. This should cover everything."

The man backed away from the money. "I could hurry your dinner, sir. No sense both of you eating cold food."

"The idea in coming here was to treat the lady," Michael said, his voice sharper than intended. "We'll pick up our doggie bag on the way out. I'll go give her a hand." Collecting the carriers and Faith's purse, he wove his way through the tables, oblivious to the sympathy directed at him by male counterparts.

Unselfconscious, he tapped once on the door to the ladies' room, then barged in. Faith glanced up, her relief palpable. She balanced both infants on a narrow couch, pinning Nicholas to the back of the seat with one hip while doing her best to keep the screaming Abby from sliding off a slick changing pad. "Michael." Faith blew at a curl that fell stubbornly over her right eye. "This place isn't set up for kids and they were both completely wet again. I'm sorry if we're spoiling your dinner."

Michael lifted Nick and kissed his red little face. "Don't apologize, Faith. It's not your fault. I concede that going out to dinner was a stupid idea."

"It was a lovely idea. Not very practical, as it turned out," she lamented, snapping the last snap on Abigail's pink overalls. "They're so upset, I don't know if we can calm them enough to sit through dinner."

"We're leaving," he said, buckling Nick into his carrier. "They'll be happier at home and so will we."

"I hope so," Faith murmured. "They both seem to have runny noses. More so than I'd expect from this crying jag."

"Do you think it was too windy during our walk on the beach?"

"Too soon for that to have caused problems, I should think. Maybe what Dr. Sampson thought might be teething was really a cold."

"Colds? But the weather's been too mild, hasn't it?"

"Spoken like a surgeon. Colds come from viruses, Doctor. They aren't caused by weather."

"Touché, Nurse. I'm sure I learned that in first-year medical school."

"That's the one drawback to taking the twins to Dr. Sampson. He knows we're nurse and doctor. He expects us to have all the answers." Faith grabbed her purse and the diaper bag. She opened the door, leaving Michael to gather up both infant carriers. "I feel he expects us to know more than we do."

"Well, I'm not above telling him I'm in over my head. The youngest patient I've seen in the last eight years was the girl in Norway, and she's fourteen. Oh, can you grab our sack of food?" Michael asked Faith. The cashier held it out as they passed.

Faith stepped to the front window. A mass of dark clouds had rolled in, and rain pelted the glass. "Why don't you take all the extraneous junk to the car and drive around and pick us up? I'll wait here with the twins."

"I'll do that," Michael agreed. "Boy, this squall came out of nowhere."

"It's a freak storm," said the cashier. "We've been hearing reports all day. They're saying hurricane-force winds. You haven't heard?" Her manner suggested they'd flown in from a different planet.

"Hurricane?" Faith and Michael said together. "We, uh, we've been pretty immersed in the twins, and haven't listened to the news," Michael added. "But we walked on the beach earlier and there were people everywhere."

"Probably still are," the woman said with a grin. "We New Englanders are the hardy sort."

Neither Faith nor Michael responded. They were both too busy staring at the rain that had begun to pound the pavement in earnest. Michael got out his car keys and arranged the items he needed to carry so that he'd have one hand free.

"I put the hoods to the carriers in the trunk, along with some heavier blankets. If it's not too much trouble, Michael, could you bring those after you park out front?"

Nodding, he dashed out into the slanting rain. His

hair and shirt were both wet through when he returned a few minutes later.

"It's downright nasty out there." Turning to the cashier, he said, "You've been listening to the radio. Any word on how far up the coast this extends?"

"The worst of it is supposed to slam into Plymouth within the next hour or so. There are storm warnings posted all along the coast highway. No relief in sight until after midnight." The young woman turned the volume up on her small radio, allowing Michael and Faith to hear the newscaster.

Michael's scowl deepened as reports grew more ominous.

"What are you thinking?" Faith asked. She was unsettled, even though the babies had finally ceased fussing in their carriers, as she swayed them back and forth. Her arms couldn't take much more of the constant strain. Two carriers and babies weren't light.

"I'm not keen on the prospect of getting blown off the interstate," Michael said. "Did you pack extra formula or any change of clothes for the twins?"

"I always pack a variety of outfits. They have one set of bottles left. That should be enough to get us home."

"I'm thinking we should spend the night here."

"But, Michael! We have nothing for the ten, two and six o'clock feedings."

"They're on a fairly common formula. We'll stop at a store."

The cashier couldn't help but overhear their conversation. She interjected a word of advice. "The inns will be filling up. A lot of travelers have been caught off guard. After all, it's barely into October. No one expected this storm. If the wind picks up much, local businesses will start to board up.''

Worried now, Faith pressed her forehead to the window, angling for a better look at the blustery skies. "If it was just you and I," she told Michael, "I'd be tempted to try and outrun the storm. I'm not so willing to take chances with the babies.''

"Exactly my feeling." Michael blew out a relieved breath. "Listen, a cardiologist I know pretty well owns an old saltbox somewhere on the outskirts of Sandwich. He's invited me numerous times to join him for a fishing excursion. The place might be no more than a glorified shack, but it should be reasonably warm and dry. If I can reach him, I'm sure he'll let us stay there for the night. I know it has kitchen facilities.''

"I suppose it would be better than trying to take two babies to a B and B or an inn. But even if you reach your friend, how would we get into his house?''

"He's offered me use of the place on short notice if I'm ever in the area. People who live here are the trusting sort. Porter said he keeps a key hanging on a peg near the front door.''

Faith pursed her lips. "I wouldn't feel right staying there unless you talk to him first.''

"I have his number in an address book I keep in the glove box along with my cell phone. While you're strapping in the carriers, I'll give him a call.''

It so happened that Michael's friend was at home and delighted to be of service. He'd just heard about the storm and been about to phone a neighbor to see if he'd shutter the windows. Now Michael could handle that chore. Otherwise, the two men kept the conversation brief. Michael wrote down detailed directions, including how to find the nearest grocery store.

"I guess we're doing the right thing," Faith exclaimed after Michael eased the car away from the curb and they were rocked by a hefty crosswind.

"I've never seen this place. Like I said, it could be primitive. Porter's a crusty old bachelor. Repairing bad tickers and fishing are all he ever talks about."

They stopped at the store first, rather than having Michael go back out into the storm. Which was a good thing. The proprietor said he and his wife were about to batten down the place and close for the night.

Wind and rain followed Michael into the car. The sack of groceries he plopped into Faith's lap dripped, too.

"Brr." She rubbed at her arms, then reached into the back seat and tucked the blankets tighter around the babies. Both had gone to sleep. "We've lived on the East Coast long enough. We ought to know better than to leave home without taking an umbrella and jacket, Michael. Whatever possessed us?"

"This is our first full day-trip with the twins. We were so concerned with packing everything they needed, we forgot about checking the weather or preparing for ourselves."

"I hope the house has heat," Faith said suddenly.

"It's supposed to." Michael peered through the gusting rain, trying to read the numbers on the houses. "There it is. The gray-and-white clapboard."

"They all look alike, but that one has a porch. At least we can keep the babies dry while you unlock the door."

"I'll go open up and see about heat. You and the babies stay in the car for the time being."

"I'm not helpless, Michael."

"I know you're not," he said irritably. "But I got us into this fix. At least let me see to your comfort."

Faith flinched as he slammed the door and disappeared into a swirl of wind and rain. Should she apologize for stepping on his masculine pride? she wondered. She just wasn't used to having a man look out for her. Furthermore, she shouldn't get out of the habit of looking out for herself. How many more weeks would Michael be around? The call regarding DNA results could come at any time. Four to six weeks they'd said. On Monday it would be four weeks.

Truth be known, she already relied too heavily on Michael for his help with the babies. And for his companionship. She hadn't had any male friend to laugh and share observations and debate ideas with in longer than she cared to remember. She'd miss that once Michael left. Faith had enjoyed their lively conversations. She watched as Michael slogged from window to window, dropping and locking the heavy wooden shutters in place. She'd miss *him,* dammit. Why not admit it?

He arrived back at the car to get her before she had a chance to become too maudlin. "It's not a palace by any means," he panted, hunched over the carriers as he raced with Faith to the porch. "But it's not a total loser, either," he added, his mouth twitching with a grin.

Stepping through the door, Faith wrinkled her nose. "It smells musty."

"Oh? I thought it smelled fishy. But I didn't find one rotting in the fridge or anything."

"Well, it is a fishing cottage," Faith ventured, letting Michael close the door while she did a slow, three hundred and sixty degree turn. Plank floors were covered with bright braided rugs. A leather couch and two overstuffed chairs sat grouped around a cheerfully burning fireplace. Two doors opened off the large square room. One was obviously the kitchen, the other a bedroom.

Faith's gaze skittered around the entire perimeter again. *One bedroom.* Was that why Michael suddenly fell silent and appeared to be awaiting an explosion?

"I plugged in the fridge and put the last two bottles of formula and our leftovers from the restaurant inside," he said, again pausing to give her time to speak. "The stove is ancient," he informed her when she made no comment. "The good news is that we've got a fairly new microwave."

"Now tell me the bad," Faith said, assuming he'd mention that there was only one bed.

"The only heat in the whole house comes from this fireplace. The kitchen, bedroom and bathroom are cold as a polar bear's backside."

Faith noticed then how wet his shirt was across the shoulders and down the sleeves. In fact, he shivered uncontrollably. "This room will be cozy soon. Pull off that wet shirt and drape it over a chair near the fire, Michael. You can sit on the hearth until you warm up. I'll take the twins from their carriers and let them stretch out on blankets on the couch."

"You're a good sport, Faith. But you take the chair. I'd hate for the babies to catch a chill."

"They have terry sleepers in the diaper bag. I will let the room warm up, though, before I change them. They have plenty of extra blankets. It's you I'm worried about, Michael. All those trips to the car and wrestling with those shutters completely soaked your clothes."

"I hate to take off my shirt and, uh, offend you."

"Offend me? Michael, I'm a nurse! I'm afraid there are no surprises left when it comes to the naked body."

"I wouldn't have thought so. But the first night I

showed up at your door, I had the distinct impression you were bothered by my state of dress. Or, rather, undress...."

Faith recalled that night vividly. She *had* reacted badly. Only because she'd liked what she'd seen of his lean, tanned torso. He'd caught her off guard and she hadn't had time to hide a purely sexual response. She certainly couldn't tell him that. "I thought you'd gone back to New York, so I was shocked to see you." There. Faith thought she'd covered quite admirably.

"In that case, I guess you won't mind if I shed my jeans as well as the shirt. Wet denim is colder than wet cotton."

"Be my guest," she said, once she determined he wasn't just trying to get a rise out of her. Being a doctor and all, he probably didn't realize it was easier for her to deal with a half-naked patient than it was to make small talk while staring at the navy blue briefs of someone she had wicked dreams about. She knew the color of his briefs, thanks to their shared laundry chores.

Faith felt her cheeks heat when it suddenly dawned on her that Michael had seen her underthings, too. No big deal to him. He wouldn't fantasize about her white cotton panties. Lacy had always said they were boring. Now Faith almost wished she, too, had developed a taste for silk.

Abigail sneezed and immediately began to fuss, which jolted Faith right out of her flight of fancy. Or it did until Michael stood up and loped across the living room in nothing but those navy shorts.

"Earlier it was Nick doing all the hacking. Should we dilute their next set of bottles? If they're coming down with colds, we don't want to clog them up."

"For pity's sake, Michael. You're the one who'll be

clogged up if you keep prancing around in the altogether. I'm sure there's an extra blanket in the bedroom
you could wrap around yourself." Even as the prim-
sounding suggestion left her lips, Faith admitted that
Michael's bare skin looked toasty warm and touchable.

"Tell me again how you find no surprises when it
comes to the naked body."

Swallowing twice to dampen her dry mouth, Faith
slid her hands around Abigail to keep from flattening
her palms against the crisp dark hair fanning Michael's
chest. A chest hovering all too close to the end of her
nose...

It was the first time Faith could recall being happy
to have both babies crying at once. Thank goodness
Michael scooped up Abby and sauntered back to his
chair, leaving her to soothe Nick.

Good grief, that was worse. Michael Cameron's back
view curled Faith's toes right into the soles of her
sneakers. She went hot, then cold and then hot again.
Her reaction was so intense, she tested her forehead to
see if maybe she'd developed a fever. No, her forehead
felt cool. Clammy, but cool.

"Don't tell me you're getting sick, too?" Michael
said as he studied her, once more from safely across the
room. He'd had to retreat or risk making a fool of himself by hauling her into his arms.

"I'm fine." Faith reached for the diaper bag. "Nick's
wet. I'm going to change him, then I'll switch with you
and get Abby into her sleeper."

"Sounds like a plan. I'll wash my hands and prepare
the bottles."

"Dressed like that?"

Michael frowned. He wasn't at all sure Faith *wasn't*
getting sick. She was acting odd. But maybe it was the
storm. For the past ten minutes he'd seen the lightning

crack through small gaps in the shutters. Thunder vied with the pounding of rain. "If you want to fix the bottles, I'll hold both of the little rascals. Remember to dilute their milk."

"Won't they be up twice as often?"

"Probably. I doubt we'll get much sleeping done tonight, anyhow."

"Because we'd have to share a bed?" Faith blurted.

Michael stared at her flushed cheeks and bright eyes. His mind began flipping back over the recent give-and-take. He started to wonder whether he wasn't the only one having thoughts of a sexual nature. What would happen if he laid his cards on the table? If he admitted to having had dreams about taking her to bed? Still, if he'd misread the signs, Faith could really cry foul to her lawyer.

Maybe he'd just put out feelers and see how she responded. "I don't have any problem with our sharing a bed. Do you?"

"I, ah, no. The twins will be quite comfortable in their carriers. But we'll be exhausted tomorrow if we don't nab a few z's."

Now Michael was afraid she hadn't fully understood that his intention included their making love. Why was this so hard? It wasn't as if they were juveniles.

Nothing more was said. Faith changed both babies and prepared their bottles. Michael fed Abby and she fed Nick. Even though their breathing was raspy, both babies drifted off to sleep.

"Are you hungry?" Faith asked when Michael rose and stoked the fire.

"Not for food," he said boldly, deciding it was time to jack up the stakes.

If Faith had any doubts after their earlier pussyfooting

around the issue of bed, Michael had just made his intentions completely clear. Her heart began to pound as she checked to see that the twins' carriers were set solidly on the couch. Straightening, her back still toward Michael, she clamped a hand across her jittery stomach. She felt rather than heard him walk up behind her. Yet she stiffened when he slid his arms around her waist and nuzzled the side of her neck with his lips.

"Second thoughts already?" he rumbled softly near her ear.

Faith didn't trust herself to do more than shake her head. Then she worried about the sudden way this had come to pass. She'd harbored a crush on him forever. Did he know? Had he figured it out tonight? What was she to him—a dalliance? *A substitute for her sister?* The thought caused Faith to shrug off the clever fingers that had unbuttoned her blouse and unsnapped her bra.

As though reading her mind, Michael eased her back against his rock-solid erection. "For the better part of a year after we first met, Faith, hardly a day went by that I didn't picture touching you like this." A rough chuckle crept past her ear. "I know you'll say all the surgical residents were young and horny back then, but there wasn't another woman on the face of the earth who haunted my waking and sleeping thoughts like you did."

Unexpectedly she turned in his arms, and they both caught their breath as her nipples grazed the hair on his chest. Anything she might have said Michael ended up swallowing as his mouth met hers in a deep kiss.

If he relaxed his shoulders and bent his head, Faith didn't have to quite stand on tiptoe. Which was a good thing, since her knees were shaking. Especially when she suddenly found her jeans pooled around her ankles.

Michael stumbled backward, gripping her around the waist as he carried her to the chair, leaving her jeans on the rug.

"Aren't we going into the bedroom?" she mumbled when he sat and pulled her astride his hips.

"Don't think I can make it," he muttered, trying again to fuse their mouths. His free hand plunged into the pocket of his drying jeans. "I have a condom in my billfold. Something tells me you aren't on the pill. Are you?" Michael hesitated.

The desperate urge to find fulfillment, and the quiver in her stomach, didn't abate even though her mind retreated. "You just happen to carry condoms?"

"Always. Or have you forgotten your sister wasn't supposed to get pregnant?"

The mention of Lacy had the effect of a faceful of cold water. It wasn't easy scrambling off Michael's lap on legs made of sponge rubber, but she managed.

Michael could have bitten off his tongue. He'd realized immediately that he'd been a damned fool to bring up Lacy's memory. And he should've known better; he'd long since figured out that Faith felt overshadowed in the presence of her younger sister. "Ah, hell, Faith." He dropped the gold foil packet he'd finally extracted, and swiped a shaking hand across his face. "My marriage was over a long time before the divorce. But as I said earlier, you played havoc with my mind a lot longer, from the first day I met you. Dammit, you're not Lacy's stand-in!"

Faith's hands shook equally hard, making it almost impossible for her to climb back into her jeans. "Then maybe you won't mind telling me why, if you spent so much time thinking about *me,* you chose to marry

Lacy.'' Anger made the fingers hooking her bra and buttoning her blouse swift and sure in their movements.

Michael decided his jeans had dried enough, and as this attempt at lovemaking was obviously going nowhere, he might as well put them on. He spoke through gritted teeth while struggling to fasten his zipper. ''Unlike you, Lacy needed me. You were always so damned self-possessed, Faith. You didn't need anyone.'' He'd lashed out in frustration—and he knew that his words sounded more vitriolic than he'd meant.

Hurt, and feeling her dreams dissolve around her, Faith snapped back. ''Then nothing's changed, Michael. I can still get along fine on my own.''

He might have refuted such a declaration, but just then both babies woke up screaming and coughing. Michael's earlier prediction had come true. Neither he nor Faith did more than doze off for the rest of a very long night.

By morning, the storm had passed and moved up the coast. A neighbor told Michael the winds were now battering the coast of Maine.

He and Faith set out for Boston. Conversation was kept to a minimum. The babies both sounded congested, so she asked Michael to swing by Dr. Sampson's office. By the time his staff was able to fit them in, Michael's nose had begun to drip and his head ached like fury. He noticed that Faith had bought a decongestant and cough drops for herself at the pharmacy.

''I've got a slight sore throat,'' she said in answer to his raspy question about how she felt. ''Go back to your apartment and get some sleep,'' she told him in cool tones. ''I've worked many a night feeling worse. The babies and I will get along fine. Just fine!''

CHAPTER TEN

IF MEN WERE LOUSY PATIENTS, doctors must be the worst, Michael decided. He stumbled into his apartment and fell across the bed. Then he climbed out again and sat in the kitchen with a cup of coffee. He didn't drink it, just hung his head over the cup, hoping the steam would clear his sinuses. He felt like crap in more ways than one. Things had been going well between him and Faith. He'd screwed up royally.

He'd moved too fast. Had let his interest in her overpower his good sense. But Michael had no idea how to straighten this out. If he'd been equipped with the ability to deal with hurt feelings, Lacy might still be alive and none of this would have happened. No Kipp Fielding. No messy triangle. No legal battle.

No babies.

He listened for any sign from next door that Faith needed his assistance with the twins. All was quiet. The medicine must have done its job. Good. Considering how they'd ended the outing, Michael wasn't anxious to knock on her door and get his head bitten off. For two cents, he'd stay away until she begged for his help. As if Faith would break down and ask *any* man for help. Dammit, she couldn't bend, wasn't capable of it, and he had a history of failure at compromise. Any relationship between them was doomed. It was high time he admitted it. He might—if he could get her out of his head.

Groaning, Michael wished he'd followed Faith's lead and bought himself a decongestant. He hadn't had a head cold like this in twenty years. How long did the damned things last? he wondered as he dumped the now-cold coffee down the sink and flung himself across the bed again.

After tossing and turning for more than two hours, he piled up a stack of pillows and fell asleep virtually sitting up.

AS THE NIGHT DRAGGED ON, Faith did her best to minister to both fussy babies. Her own head felt like a helium-filled balloon. When the light of dawn streaked the sky, she'd reached her wits' end. Nick and Abby had slept in fits and starts. They were hungry but had little interest in their bottles. Abby refused to drink at all. Faith worried that she'd become dehydrated. ''Come on, sweetheart,'' she pleaded with the hot, fussy child. ''I know you feel rotten, but if you don't take in some fluids, you'll feel worse.''

Between rocking and pacing the floor, Faith listened for any sign of life in the apartment next door. As the morning wore on, she began to wonder if Michael had packed up and gone back to New York. She wouldn't blame him. She'd acted like a twit. She'd acted jealous of a sister who was no longer a threat. Guilt slammed through her. Guilt because for so long, she'd denied being jealous of Lacy. Guilt because now that Lacy was dead, Faith had been about to take what had belonged to her sister. Maybe the guilt was irrational, but Faith still felt it, compounded by the tragedy of Lacy's death. And Faith had dumped all *her* guilt on Michael.

Boy, she was something. If he never spoke to her
again, it would serve her right. Tears began to run down
her cheeks. Hugging Abigail close, Faith rubbed her
face over Abby's soft hair. Ultimately she would be the
loser if Michael won custody and never let her see the
twins again.

By late afternoon, Faith was certain Michael had
gone. There wasn't the slightest sound from his apartment. Her cold had worsened, as had those of the twins.
Though both babies had taken in some of the electrolyte
drink Dr Sampson's nurse had told Faith to buy at the
pharmacy, they were still extremely fussy.

Following a second night without sleep, Faith decided she couldn't do this alone. She hauled out the
telephone book and started down the list of advertise-
ments for agencies providing mother's helpers. Her own
throat was so sore she could barely croak out her questions. It turned out she'd wasted her breath. Not one of
the agencies had a mother's helper available for short-
term assignments.

Faith was tempted to promise them she'd pay a
month's wages even though she hoped she'd only need
someone for a few days.

Just when she thought her arms would fall off from
holding the babies and walking the floor with them, she
heard the shower running next door. If Michael had
been gone, he was now back. The joy she felt in her
heart was overwhelming—and pathetic, she told herself.

He'd probably laugh in her face if she phoned to ask
for his help. Practically the last thing he'd said to her
had been a bitter comment about her self-sufficiency.
And she'd more or less told him it would be a cold day
in hell before she needed *anything* from a man.

Words. False pride. They could really get you in trouble.

She waited fifteen minutes after hearing the shower shut off to pick up the card on which he'd written his cell phone number. Twice she punched in the first three digits, then went into a fit of coughing and hung up without completing the call.

As she flexed her fingers and tried again, Nicholas woke up screaming and pulling at his ears. He probably needed to go to the doctor again for something stronger than a decongestant. Faith didn't think she could manage bundling both babies up and calling a cab to go downtown. She'd have to call Michael—but she found it easier to beg for his help on behalf of the twins rather than herself.

Jiggling the distressed baby on one shoulder, Faith quickly punched in Michael's cell number. The phone rang and rang and rang. She hadn't hung up yet when a knock sounded at her door. Trailing the long cord to the entry, she balanced the receiver and Nick, while trying to peer out the peephole. To Faith's surprise, Michael stood there, a frown on his face, one hand splayed against the wall.

She dropped the receiver and flipped open all three locks. Faith found herself offering a teary apology to Michael's back. He'd turned and headed back into his apartment.

He glanced over his shoulder, shock on his face. "Wait a minute, Faith. Don't close the door. I left my cell phone in the apartment and I hear it ringing."

"It's me," she said breathlessly, pointing to the receiver at her feet.

"You? You're calling me?"

She nodded and closed her eyes. Michael looked so

wonderfully healthy. He was clean and shaved, while she hadn't had time to shower since they'd arrived home from their outing. She'd changed her blouse because both babies had spit up on it, but she wore the same jeans. "Oh, Michael! You have every right to tell me to get lost, b-ut...but I need you. Nick has to see Dr. Sampson. I think he's developed an ear infection. I'm so light-headed from lack of sleep, I feel faint. Please..." She extended a hand, then quickly drew it back. The man must think she was a stark, raving maniac.

"God, Faith. Why didn't you phone me earlier? I slept for twenty hours straight."

"So that's why I didn't hear any noise coming from your apartment. I thought you'd gone to New York."

"You really were calling me?" he asked, stooping to pick up the buzzing receiver.

Faith clung to Nick and stared at Michael. "I'd hoped even if you were still mad at me, you'd take pity on the twins."

"I'm not mad at you, Faith." Reaching out a finger, Michael ran it tentatively over the trail left by her tears. "I never was angry at you. I'm sorry I pushed too fast. I had no right to do that when our lives are so up in the air over the custody agreement. I'm hoping we can forget it ever happened and go on as we were before."

Bad as she felt, his declaration ripped through her heart. Or maybe it was her stomach. Faith felt very much as if she was about to throw up.

She was.

Thrusting the crying baby into Michael's arms, Faith covered her mouth and ran for the bathroom.

Michael paced outside the bathroom door listening to her retch, and feeling helpless. He'd poked his head inside once, only to have her plead to be left alone. He might have drawn her a glass of water or gotten her a cool washcloth if Abigail hadn't awakened and joined her brother's chorus. Both babies were stuffy. Michael checked the medicine schedule Faith had clipped to one of the cribs. They weren't due more for another hour.

He listened to them cough and cry for five additional minutes, then made up his mind. He was taking all three of them to the doctor.

"Get a jacket," he told Faith when she finally emerged from the bathroom, pale and shaky. "The babies are already in their carriers. I'll load them up and meet you at the front entrance. Can you make it that far alone?" he asked sharply.

"I just need sleep," Faith said. "Can you manage both babies?"

"I am man," he joked, beating a fist on his chest. Faith swayed then, and he cursed and scooped her off her feet. "I'll put you to bed myself. And I'll ask Dr. Sampson to prescribe something for flu and cold. Are you allergic to any medications?"

"No," she mumbled. She was sound asleep by the time he stripped back the spread and put her carefully down. He brushed the dark curls off her forehead, thinking she looked terribly fragile. Remembering that he'd slept better on a pile of pillows, Michael lifted her tenderly and arranged several pillows at her back. "I'll return as soon as possible," he whispered, pulling off her shoes before covering her with the spread.

AGAIN, DR. SAMPSON'S OFFICE had to work the babies into an already overfull schedule. "Sorry I didn't call ahead," Michael said when Hal finally got around to seeing them. He explained how they'd all been sick and that Faith still was.

"Flu and colds are both going around," the doctor acknowledged "Faith was right. Nick has developed oitis media," he said referring to an infection of the inner ear. "We caught it early. I'll want him on an antibiotic for ten days. Continue to push fluids with this young miss," he said, after noting that Abby's ears were fine. "Abigail's lost a little weight. She doesn't have much to play around with."

Michael, who'd been holding Nick, now cuddled the choking girl under his chin. She settled in, curling close to her brother.

"You're a natural at this, Michael," Dr. Sampson said. "If your esteemed colleagues could only see you now."

Michael gave a short laugh. "My partner should see me. He's badgering me to come back to the clinic."

"I didn't mean to make light of your situation. I take it there's no word yet on the DNA?"

"No." Michael shook his head. "Next week, or so I'm guessing. You know," he mused, "I want the results, but I'm afraid to get the call saying they're finally in."

"I can understand that. You've gotten really attached to the twins. So has Faith. And the two of you function well together. It'll be tough if you have to fight each other."

Michael said nothing, but Hal's statement echoed in his ears as he stood in line at the pharmacy. The prophesy nagged at him even after he'd returned to Faith's apartment.

He looked in on her shortly after settling the twins in a crib. Faith was dead to the world. She didn't twitch a muscle. Didn't know he'd come in. Since she was sleeping so soundly, Michael decided not to wake her to give her a dose of the medicine Dr. Sampson had prescribed. Michael had long subscribed to the belief that sleep was a profound healer.

As the afternoon waned, Michael figured he'd be spending the night here. Slipping out while everyone slept, he collected enough clean clothing to last for several days, and a book he'd been reading, along with the latest cardiopulmonary journal. It was a magazine that frequently published his articles, although he hadn't written any since before the divorce. The Norwegian girl's case had some anomalies worth publishing. Funny, but the intense desire that used to drive him seemed to have deserted him. He hadn't thought about performing surgery in over three weeks. What did it mean? Was he burned-out?

He was doing too much introspection. Grimacing, Michael dumped everything in the guest bedroom.

He checked in on the babies and happened to discover that their laundry hamper was full. This was as good a chance as any to go next door and throw a load into the washer.

Before he could toss the clean clothes into the dryer, however, things changed. The twins woke up wet and hungry. While Michael was in the middle of feeding them, Faith stumbled out of her room and made it only as far as the bathroom door, where she upchucked again. All over the floor.

Michael felt so sorry for her. "Don't worry about cleaning up," he murmured. "Take care of yourself. I'll scrub the floor in a minute. Hal prescribed some medicine to help you ward off the nausea. I left it in the bathroom. Can you manage to get into a nightgown by yourself? I'm sure the babies have already been exposed to whatever you have, but just in case they haven't, I'd as soon they not get too close to you."

"I think this is rather more than you bargained for, Michael. You didn't sign on to take care of me."

"Like I haven't dealt with worse as a doctor?"

"What would I have done without you?" she asked in all seriousness, gazing at him as she slumped against the door casing.

A wry smile tugged at the corners of his lips. "I promise not to tell a soul that you aren't a superwoman, Faith."

"Joke all you want. I honestly don't know how I would have gotten through this siege. Handling the twins by myself is tough. Add to that everyone being sick…" If she had anything to add to the statement, she didn't. "Oh, no, I'm dizzy again." Teetering, she wove her way back to her room.

Michael held his breath until he heard the squeak of her mattress. "Thank God she made it," he murmured to the wide-eyed babies.

It was nearly dark by the time he had a chance to clean the tile floor in the bathroom. He quietly entered Faith's room to check on her again and discovered that she'd taken a second dose of her medicine. She lay sprawled atop her covers, still in yesterday's sweaty, wrinkled clothes. Michael debated with himself a respectable few minutes. Then, gritting his teeth, he opened her dresser drawers and searched until he found a nightgown. He was a doctor, he reasoned. Faith didn't have anything he hadn't seen before. It was just too bad that the gown he pulled out happened to be the one he'd had fantasies about.

Michael snapped on the bedside lamp. If she woke

up, she could take care of this herself. She tossed a bit. Even mumbled and licked her lips. Her eyes remained closed.

Her skin now felt warm and dry. She probably still had a fever. Once he'd slipped off her blouse and jeans, he bathed her face and arms in cool water.

As fast as possible, he drew her gown over her head, tucked her arms through the armholes, and rearranged her in the bed. Since the room was warm, he covered her with only a sheet.

Leaving a light on low, he wandered into the kitchen, where he heated himself a can of soup. There was something hugely satisfying about knowing he'd met the needs of three people he cared about a great deal. Oddly enough, despite his medical successes, he'd doubted his ability to nurture for quite some time following the divorce. He'd stayed in Europe for a couple of months, throwing himself into the lecture circuit. His lengthy absence then contributed to his partner's concern about the current situation; Dominic felt he'd been left to manage the clinic on his own for too long. But Michael had needed to stay away after Lacy's rejection. The divorce had shaken something elemental in Michael—his confidence in his own ability to comfort and support. If he hadn't discovered the twins, Michael thought he might have lost a vital portion of himself. The part that allowed him to be a true healer, not just a technician, performing medical procedures. The words *physician, heal thyself* were never more prophetic. In a way, Lacy had given him a wake-up call. Michael didn't think he'd ever compartmentalize the areas of his life again.

The feeling that he'd accomplished something—that he'd made a few life-altering decisions in these past hours—remained with him for the rest of the night.

Toward morning, after cajoling Faith into taking another dose of medicine, he thought she seemed cooler and slept more deeply. She had tried to get up once when the babies cried for their two-o'clock bottles. When Michael assured her he didn't need assistance, she'd burrowed beneath the covers again.

Now it was nine in the morning, and Faith snoozed on. Michael got the twins up. He dressed them and fed them diluted formula. They smiled and kicked their legs happily—obviously on the mend. Nick had slept between feedings, which meant his ear wasn't bothering him as much.

Michael noticed that now the babies were a bit older, they stayed awake for longer periods of time. Both held their heads up without assistance, and they laughed aloud with very little prompting.

Michael opened out the playpen Gwen had lent Faith. He put the babies inside and hunted up a few rattles and squeaky toys. He'd just sat down with a second cup of coffee and begun leafing through a medical journal when he remembered the laundry he'd thrown in the washer yesterday. The darned stuff probably needed to be rinsed again.

Rather than haul two babies over to his apartment, Michael propped open both doors so he could more easily run from one place to the other. That way, he could still hear the babies if they cried, and from Faith's living room he'd hear the washer shut off.

An hour later, on the fourth trip, he dashed out of his place carrying a basketful of newly dried baby clothing and ran smack into a man and a woman headed for Faith's apartment. "May I help you?" he asked coolly, not recognizing them. At least, he didn't until the couple took a second look at him and seemed to do a double take.

"Oh," he exclaimed. "Daniel Burgess and Barbara Lang." Shifting the basket to his other hip, Michael stretched out a hand. "Faith didn't tell me to expect a visit from Social Services."

"We were, ah, in the area and decided to stop by," Burgess said. He opened a notebook and glanced pointedly at the numbers on both apartments. "Are you visiting the Cameron twins today, Doctor?" the man asked.

"Yes," Michael said. Lon Maxwell knew he'd rented the apartment next to Faith. Other than Lon and Faith, no one knew. It was no one's business.

He'd never had to contend with visits from Social Services. He decided to be polite but not go out of his way to be too hospitable. What he hoped was that they'd quickly see the babies were doing well and then leave. Because Michael didn't buy their "in the area" story. Burgess had hesitated too long.

"Judge Brown ordered all parties to phone ahead before visiting," he pointed out as he seated the couple. Michael dumped the basket of clean clothing on the couch, sat and began to fold things.

"Oh, but this isn't an official visit," Ms. Lang assured him. Even as she stiffly balanced her briefcase across her knees, her eyes roamed the cluttered room.

Michael knew how it must look. Burgess had been forced to clear two sets of bottles, various burp cloths and a soiled set of Nick's terry sleepers out of one chair before he could sit down. There was a hodgepodge of blankets lying about. The two carriers were stacked by the door; Michael had left them there following his visit to the pediatrician. Glancing around, he saw books and magazines, assorted toys, a coffee cup. Outside of that, the room didn't look too bad...if one discounted the layer of dust on the coffee and end tables.

Daniel Burgess peered into the playpen. "According to my notes, the babies have seen a doctor twice this week. Colds and ear infections." He shook his head. "And yet it's been a warmer than usual fall."

Michael pushed his medical journal aside to make room for a clean stack of receiving blankets. "Bottle-fed babies are more prone to ear infections." Michael had read that in a parents' magazine in Hal Sampson's office.

Burgess cleared his throat and jotted a notation in his notebook.

Barbara Lang put her case down and bent to pick up Nick. She held him aloft at arm's length and talked baby talk.

"Nick's been known to spit up as long as an hour after feeding." Michael warned, sneaking a peek at his watch. He was getting antsy. They hadn't asked about Faith, but he had no doubt they would if they stayed much longer. Or maybe they'd assume that, because he was here, she'd taken the opportunity to get out of the house and do some shopping.

Ms. Lang returned Nick to the playpen. She wagged a rattle in front of Abby and seemed pleased when the baby grasped the toy. "Well, Daniel, Dr. Cameron appears to have things under control. Maybe we should go."

Yes! Michael said to himself. Rising, he took two steps toward the door, hoping they'd follow. They might have if Faith hadn't chosen that moment to stagger into the living room. Her hair looked thoroughly mussed. Her feet were bare, and she couldn't seem to hit the armholes of a pale yellow, summery bathrobe.

"I can't believe the time, Michael." Her husky, sleepy voice sounded garbled around a huge yawn. "You should've dragged me out of bed." As she covered her open mouth with a hand, Michael was sure she had no idea they even had visitors.

Gurgling helplessly in his throat, Michael sprinted to her side before she could start scolding him for taking off her clothes and putting her in a nightgown. A gown that left all too much of her glorious self exposed. Michael thought she looked delightful. He wasn't, however, overjoyed to see Daniel Burgess's eyes popping out of his head.

"Faith, Mr. Burgess and Ms. Lang from the State Department of Social Services have dropped by."

She gasped, choked, started coughing.

"Faith's been sick," Michael added, aiming an apology over his shoulder at the gawking couple. "Combination of cold and flu. Dr. Sampson ordered her some medicine and said she should stay in bed. Sampson said there's been a lot of different viruses going around the area."

Blotches of red crept up Faith's neck. Hopping backward toward the hall, she pulled at Michael's shirtfront, trying to keep him solidly between her and the pair seated in her living room. "Why didn't you warn me?" she sputtered.

"Didn't have time," he whispered back.

Rising on tiptoes, Faith connected with Barbara Lang's still-shocked gaze. "Give me a minute to dress," she said brightly, doing her best not to hyperventilate. She let go of Michael's shirt and escaped down the hall, leaving him to deal with their visitors.

"Brother." Faith gripped her still muzzy head with both hands. "Throwing up in front of Michael was bad enough," she moaned. "Now I've paraded past state workers in my nightie. Can my day get any worse?" What was Michael telling them? she wondered as she pawed through her dresser drawers in search of fresh underwear. She really needed to shower. She'd worn the same clothes for— Her head shot up and the last thought scrambled and stopped as if it had hit a brick wall. In a sense it had. Her last conscious memory was of throwing up outside the bathroom door. She'd been wearing a blouse and jeans at the time.

"Oh." Her fingers plucked at the lace trim on her nightdress. *Michael. He'd undressed her and put her to bed.*

Faith needed a clearer head to face that fact, if not to face their visitors. She elected to take the time to shower and wash her hair. What could those two want? In her experience as a girl, a surprise visit from Social Services meant trouble. It meant well-meaning neighbors had reported that her mother's condition had worsened, and they thought someone other than a child should look after Lacy.

Standing under the hot, stinging spray, Faith could only worry. Maybe the Fieldings had issued a new complaint. It would be just like Kipp's father to want the babies fostered elsewhere. All kinds of frantic and suspicious thoughts ran through Faith's mind as she showered, then toweled dry.

The whole process of showering, dressing and blowing her hair dry had taken no more than twenty minutes. Still, it was on shaking legs that Faith approached the living room.

Michael sat, a baby balanced on each knee. Otherwise, the room appeared empty.

"Where are our guests?"

Glancing up, Michael took in her wide eyes and colorless face. Even then, Faith looked beautiful to him and he couldn't take his eyes off her. "I think we provided more excitement than either of their hearts could handle," he drawled. "I can't tell you how glad I am to see you looking better."

"What did they want? Who filed a complaint? Have the babies been crying too much?"

"Burgess knew we'd made two trips to the doctor."

"Darn and blast." She flopped suddenly into one of the chairs. "They were gathering dirt. And boy, we gave it to them, didn't we?" Closing her eyes, Faith sighed.

"Dirt? I'll grant you the tables are dusty and the place looked a little untidy." He grinned. "But if they were looking for dirt, they didn't find any. I bathed the babies this morning. They could see the laundry was done."

"Not *that* kind of dirt, Michael. Don't joke about it. I mean scandal. They'll think we're living together."

"We are, sort of. I moved some stuff into the guest room after you got so sick."

"You told them you were sleeping in the guest room?"

"No. They didn't ask. They didn't ask much of anything. In fact, I can't figure out why they bothered to come."

Faith threw up her hands. "I told you. They were snooping."

"For whom? And what conclusion could they draw that would be so bad? Look around you, Faith. Baby things, car carriers, playpen. From where Ms. Lang sat, she could see the rack of bottles in the kitchen. Plus, I had enough clothes spread out here to outfit quintuplets. These babies are obviously well looked after. Anyway, who would report us? And why?''

"Lacy probably didn't tell you—I doubt she was old enough to be aware. Social Services wanted to take us kids away from Mother and Daddy more than once. It was awful."

"What I'm telling you is they'd have to really twist things to make you seem unfit."

"They don't lie, but they can word the truth so that a judge might wonder if we're doing a good job. For instance, the report could read, Dr. Cameron *appeared* to have fed the twins. He *left* the babies in a playpen and folded clean clothes throughout our visit. At ten to eleven, Miss Hyatt *wandered* out of the bedroom in her nightgown. Look at the inferences that can be drawn."

"I see. Someone looking for dirt, as you phrased it, might conclude a number of things." He ticked them off on his fingers. "We aren't married. Possibly cohabiting. We're neglecting the babies. I'm doing all the work and you're a lazy bum."

Faith's lips thinned. "Right. Why did they show up this morning of all mornings, Michael? Did you call them?"

"What?" He yelped so loudly Abigail started to cry. "Shh...shh, honey." Rocking her to calm her, Michael glared at Faith over the top of Abby's fuzzy head. "You don't really think such a thing, I hope."

She linked her hands and stared at them. "While I was in the shower, I started adding up a few things."

"Like what? Why do I have the feeling I don't want to hear this?"

"Whose idea was it to drive down the coast? Yours. Maybe you knew about the storm in advance. Maybe you set me up. It wasn't *my* friend who so conveniently had a cabin nearby. Ha! I ruined your plan to seduce and discredit me. How lucky for you I got sick when I did, Michael. Because you still managed to damage my reputation with Burgess and Lang—especially when they saw me waltz out wearing a see-through nightgown."

"For crying out loud! With that imagination, why are you a nurse? You ought to write novels."

"Really? If my idea's so far-fetched, how come I never saw any sign that you were interested in me? Not before you met Lacy, or in the past five weeks."

"The signs were there, Faith. I can't help it if you only see what you want to see. And I don't know how to prove what goes on in my head while I sleep. But I can tell you that if you had a window into my mind, you wouldn't like what you'd see."

She blushed at that. Her fingers flexed several times. She did not lift her head to meet his eyes. If she had, Michael figured she'd see the hunger in them. He considered getting up off the couch, putting down the babies and taking her in his arms. But the phone rang, shattering his intentions.

Faith crossed the room and snatched it up. "David," she said in obvious surprise. "How good of you to call and check on us. I'm recovering from the flu. The babies both have colds. One of Nick's ears is infected. Yes, I'm much better, thanks, and so are they."

Michael saw her grip the phone more tightly. She put out a hand to steady herself against the wall. He knew something was wrong and felt his own stomach tighten in response. If Lang and Burgess had caused trouble, they hadn't wasted any time. He stood and paced the floor behind Faith until she hung up. "Well?" he exclaimed the minute she'd replaced the receiver. "What's going on?"

"The DNA results are back, Michael," Faith said in a flat tone.

"So what did it prove? Am I the twins' father?" he asked.

"David didn't know the results. The judge has them. Apparently they'll remain sealed until we all meet in her chambers again."

"When?" He barely mouthed the word.

"Tomorrow at two o'clock. I'm to arrange for a sitter, David said."

A pent-up breath escaped Michael's lips. "At least, the wait will soon be over. This waiting's making everyone nuts."

"Before I went in to take my shower, I remember thinking my day couldn't get any worse. I was wrong." Tears pooled along her lower eyelids as Faith cuddled Abigail close and kissed her fiercely.

CHAPTER ELEVEN

THE PHONE CALL FROM DAVID REED cast a pall over both of them for the rest of that day. She and Michael fell silent for long periods of time. Then one or the other would burst out with a question.

"Why can't someone just open the envelope from the lab and telephone everyone with the results?" Faith sneezed several times into a tissue after asking.

Michael pulled a handful of tissues from a box that sat on the table beside him, and handed them to her. He uttered what passed as a noncommittal grunt.

Faith blocked a final sneeze. "What does that mean? Do you agree or disagree that we shouldn't all be left hanging?"

"I want to know the results. But at this stage, we can't afford to have anyone cry foul. If Judge Brown opened the envelope, our lawyers could claim grounds to suggest tampering."

"But a judge?"

"Judges aren't all squeaky-clean, Faith. I'd rather wait and watch the envelope being opened." Michael sat forward and rested his elbows on his thighs. He laced his fingers and idly twirled his thumbs. "But part of me wants to put off knowing."

"Why? Earlier you said the wait was hard on everyone."

"I know," he said in a shaky voice, reaching over to

rub the back of Faith's neck. "Guess I'm not as confident about the outcome now as I was during our initial
hearing."

Faith moved away to escape the hypnotic touch of
Michael's fingers. She placed Abby in the playpen next
to her sleeping twin. Nick had drifted off while batting
at a soft toy. "Whichever lawyer said it would be harder
to give up the twins once I brought them home was a
hundred percent correct. I thought I was attached before,
but now all I want to do is pack them up and run far,
far away."

Michael dropped a soft yellow blanket over the infants. "Funny, those same thoughts have been running
through my head. I don't even like the idea of leaving
them with a sitter tomorrow while we attend the hearing."

"A sitter! Oh, Michael. I still need to do that. I wish
there was someone in the building," she said half to
herself. "Most of the people I'd trust will be at work
during the time we need someone."

Michael pulled Faith against his chest. They stood in
contemplative silence for a moment. Until Faith slipped
away and rummaged in the cupboard for a new tissue
box.

"This is doubly hard on you, I guess," Michael said,
his gaze sympathetic.

"Because I'm sick, you mean? The medicine helps.
I'll get in three more doses before the hearing. You
know how it is with nurses. Unless we're dead, the hospital expects us to work. It becomes habit to keep on
going while we're sick."

"Same with doctors. You'd think the medical profession would be more tolerant of staff illness."

"I remember one time Gwen had pneumonia and our

supervisor scheduled her for back-to-back shifts. Hey.'' Faith snapped her fingers. "Gwen might know of a reliable sitter. She's particular about who looks after her kids.'' She immediately grabbed the phone and dialed her friend.

Michael listened to one half of the conversation. He heard enough to realize their sitter dilemma was solved. "Gwen came up with someone, I take it,'' he said when Faith got off the phone.

"It's her day off and her kids are in school all day. Gwen offered to come over here and stay with the twins. Said she's been meaning to call and give me an afternoon out, anyway. Wow, I feel so much better having that settled.''

"Do you feel good enough to eat something? I think you've lost weight. More than I'd expect from the bout of flu you had.''

"It's these sweats. They're really baggy.''

"I don't think so.'' He eyed her critically and it flustered her. He'd seen almost every inch of her, and his look now reminded her that he, too, was aware of it.

"How can you think about food?'' she asked as an obvious diversion. "I'll be a wreck until after tomorrow's meeting. As a matter of fact, shouldn't you go back to your apartment and call Lon Maxwell to work out your strategy?''

"What good will it do? Any appeal we might file hinges on the DNA results. I don't know about you, but my philosophy is that misery needs company. I was about to suggest I run down to the video store at the corner and rent a couple of movies to get us through the long night. How does that sound?''

She glanced at the babies. "I probably won't sleep,'' she said. "And after tomorrow we may not be on speaking terms. Depending on those DNA results, this may be the last night you spend with the twins.''

"Why are you trying to cut our ties, Faith? Regardless of the outcome, we'll continue to see each other, I promise you.''

Faith's eyelashes swept down, hiding her thoughts. Michael was treading in deep water. He knew Faith's physical response to him in that cabin hadn't been accidental. He also realized their situation gave them a lot to overcome. In fact, he had reservations himself. Not about the passion he felt toward Faith. The more time he spent with her, the more sure he was that he'd married the wrong sister. However, he wanted to be a father to Lacy's babies more than he'd ever expected. Michael certainly didn't want Faith confusing his two pursuits. Wanting her had nothing to do with wanting the babies. It was important she understand that.

Considering how strong his feelings were, Michael wasn't sure he could keep his hands to himself if he and Faith sat side by side watching old movies.

"I won't stay," he said abruptly. He began to collect his belongings. "You still look pretty peaked, Faith. You could crash at my place tonight if you want. I can sleep here and do the night feedings again.''

Faith couldn't keep up with Michael's fluctuating offers. First he wanted them to spend the long, lonely evening together. Now he couldn't seem to be rid of her quick enough. Did it have to do with her fantasy of stealing off with the babies? Or had something triggered a memory of their indiscretions at the cabin? Were his regrets finally surfacing? Faith decided to make it easy for him. "We'll rest better in our own beds," she said. "Don't worry, I'll hear the babies. Last night the medicine knocked me out. Today I've adjusted to it.''

"You're sure?" He hesitated at the door until she nodded. "Until tomorrow, then, Faith." Michael undid all the locks. "You will let me give you a lift to the courthouse?"

Faith caught the door before it closed. "I'll take a cab. I'm not sure what time Gwen will get here. Not only that, there's no need to give Burgess and Lang any extra fuel for speculation."

"Those two will be history once Judge Brown opens the envelope from the lab."

Faith set her jaw stubbornly. "So you say, Michael. Have you forgotten I plan to contest either way? Lacy named me guardian. Me." She tapped a fist over her heart.

"I'm sorry Lacy felt so bitter. But the judge will see that and take it into account before rendering a verdict." Michael's dark eyes burned with compassion for Faith.

She read the look as pity. "Good night, Michael. You won't win. My position is too strong. But for what it's worth, I think you'll make a great father someday."

"Someday I'll be a good husband, as well," he informed her. Then, because he faced a closed door, Michael wondered if she'd heard. If she had, would she put two and two together? She was wrong if she thought that slamming a door in his face meant she'd seen the last of Michael Cameron.

ANOTHER OCTOBER STORM SWEPT IN from sea the next day, matching Faith's mood. The nearer it came to the hearing, the more Faith's stomach pitched. The sensation was reminscent of the flu she'd just suffered, but she knew it was nerves. Pure and simple nerves.

It was too bad Michael hadn't popped over for coffee. As he'd said, misery did indeed love company. In spite

of how they'd parted last night, Faith was surprised not
to hear from him.

Fortunately, Gwen arrived an hour early. "I thought,
given how important it is to make a good showing today, you might need extra time to get spiffed up." Hugging Faith, she added, "Knock 'em dead, okay? Show
them what you're made of."

"Gwen, you're wonderful. I've been so rattled all
morning, I think the twins sense there's something
wrong. They've been fussier than normal."

Gwen tossed her purse and car keys on the table and
gathered a crying Nick into her arms. "It's baby radar,"
Gwen advised sagely. "Kids act out every time mom
has a chance to go out. The little charmers can turn on
the waterworks at will. Their aim is to make mom feel
so guilty she'll stay home." Laughing, the mother of
four buried her lips in the baby's neck and blew him a
raspberry. He snorted several times in response. "See?"
Gwen said. "What did I tell you?"

Faith didn't look convinced. "Nick and Abby are too
little for that sort of manipulative behavior."

"Don't kid yourself, honey. Babies come out of the
womb knowing how to manipulate mom and dad.
Speaking of dad, where is that gorgeous hunk of man?"
Gwen peered into rooms as she followed Faith to her
bedroom.

"Which man?" Faith pretended not to understand her
friend. "Until Judge Brown opens the all-important envelope today, Nicholas and Abigail are fatherless."

"You know perfectly well I mean Dr. Cameron. Did
you know Cicely's sister works in Hal Sampson's office? Carrie overheard Michael telling Hal the two of
you and the babies had spent the night in some fishing
cabin down the coast."

Faith's sharp exhalation brought a smile to Gwen's face.

Suddenly smug, she dropped a kiss on Nick's nose. "Hey, Faith, remember how we all used to fantasize what that man would be like in bed?" she said. "Is he as good as he looks?"

"I wouldn't know. We never got that far." Faith's muffled reply came from beneath the folds of a jade-green velour dress she'd dived into. "Hey, you were happily married when we both held retractors for Michael. Back off, Gwen, or I'll tell Jerry what you said."

"Ouch, the girl plays hardball." Abigail let out a wail from the nursery then, ending the women's chat.

But Gwen wasn't one to give up easily. "You look great," she told Faith as Faith swiped on pale lipstick and raced for the door to go meet her cab. "I'll bet Dr. Cameron won't be able to concentrate on anything but you today."

Faith balanced half in, half out of the door. "Gwen! Pu...lee...se! Nothing happened in that cabin."

"Of course not. *One* baby can throw a wrench into any lovemaking plans. But two..." Gwen rolled innocent gray eyes. "The thing you need to remember is that Michael *tried* to get something going. Right?" She smiled widely. "You're not denying it, I see. He's interested, and you know it. Think long and hard about that, Faith. Especially if he ends up winning the daddy pool."

Faith raised both hands in exasperation. "My cab is waiting," she said. "I showed you where the bottles and diapers are. If the hearing runs late, I'll call." Tempted to slam the door, Faith sighed and shut it softly instead. Gwen would have her say, no matter what.

THE STORM CAUSED a traffic snarl-up. Faith arrived late, nearly fifteen minutes after the meeting time. An unsmiling clerk hustled her down the dreary hall and into an already full chamber.

She felt Michael's gaze. Staring straight ahead, Faith slipped into the vacant seat left between him and David Reed. If she'd arrived early, she could have engineered the seating better and found a place well away from Michael. Now she'd have to act stoic while waiting for one or both of their lives to be ripped to shreds.

"I guess Gwen got there okay," Michael murmured. "I'd begun to worry. Is she all right with the twins?"

"Fine. Shh." Faith brought a finger to her lips. "Barbara Lang and Daniel Burgess are watching us." Faith wondered if they thought she looked entirely too well to have been as sick as she and Michael had claimed. Or, on the other hand, did they think she resembled something no self-respecting feline would drag in? As if to emphasize the lingering effects of her cold, Faith's nose twitched and she sneezed several times in succession.

Even Judge Brown glanced up. "Are you all right, Ms. Hyatt? Shall I ask the clerk to bring you a box of tissues or perhaps a glass of water?"

Faith shook her head. Michael had already unzipped her purse, and handed her a plastic-wrapped packet of tissues. "Thanks," she whispered.

"In that case," the judge said, pausing to run a last glance around the room. "I believe we are ready to begin. It pleases me that you were all able to make it on short notice. It shows that your interest in the welfare of the twins has remained strong."

"We're all here," one of Kipp Fieldling's lawyers growled. "Please enter in the record that our client flew home from the Bahamas in order to comply with the request that we all assemble on short notice, as you aptly put it.''

The judge seemed to take a long time to acknowledge Keith Schlegel. ''So entered,'' she said at last, directing a nod toward the stenographer. ''I've also received a report from Daniel Burgess and Barbara Lang as to their preliminary custody recommendations. I'll make copies available to all parties, along with today's transcript, if that's agreeable?'' Judge Brown appeared to be focused on getting a response from each team. If she heard Faith and Michael's audible groans, she didn't let on.

David conferred with Faith in low tones. Lon Maxwell did the same with Michael.

''We can always file a rebuttal later,'' he said. ''I know you were sick. Dr. Sampson will probably attest to that in a signed affidavit if Burgess and Lang get nasty. I suggest we agree to the copies in order to move on to the primary issue—what's in the envelope.''

''If that's what you think,'' Faith said, shredding a tissue. ''As I explained yesterday, they showed up without calling first. I—I suppose the damage from their report is done. I mean, the judge has already read it.''

''Brown is known for her fairness. Look, Faith. I'd hate to make a big fuss about something that might not even be an issue.''

''Does your client have a problem with including the Burgess-Lang report in today's transcript, Mr. Reed?'' Judge Brown asked.

''No, Your Honor,'' David said firmly. ''I assume we'll be able to counter the report if I deem it necessary?''

''You mean, if we don't conclude this case today?''

''I sincerely doubt that's possible, Your Honor,'' David said. "You hold the answer to the question of the Cameron twins' biological father—information which in no way changes my client's claim to custody of the babies, based on her sister's last will and testament."

"So you're saying regardless of DNA, your client will press for custody."

"Yes, Your Honor. That is what I'm saying."

The Schlegel brothers hunched around their partner, Nancy Matz. All shielded Kipp, Shelby and Kipp's father. The six jabbered, gestured and shook fingers. In contrast, Lon Maxwell and Michael relaxed in their chairs as if they'd already anticipated Faith's next move.

The judge spent a few minutes flipping pages in a day planner. "It would please the court to have the domestic fate of these children settled before the holidays begin. Mr. Reed, can you prepare an adequate case for your client by mid-November?"

David studied his own calendar. "That depends, Your Honor."

"On what?"

"On which gentleman fathered Lacy Hyatt Cameron's babies. I hope you aren't asking me to disclose my strategy?"

"Of course not," the judge conceded, her frown easing. "I understand it will take you longer to research case histories that have gone against a married couple than the more conventional cases that have ruled against single dads."

"Could we get on with the reason we're all here today?" Kipp's father complained loudly. "Well, what's the sense in dragging this out?" he said, tossing down his pen. "There are peoples' lives on hold here."

Judge Brown picked up the envelope. Turning to a

clerk who hovered at the back of the room, she said, "Ms. Carlson, could you please walk this envelope around? I want every counselor and client to verify that the seal on the envelope remains unbroken."

The elder Fielding threw an arm over the back of his chair. "Ye gods. We trust you, Judge. Open the damned thing, already."

The judge's well-shaped eyebrows drew down sharply. "Mr. Fielding, another outburst like that and I'll have to ask you to leave. The principals in this case have waited nearly six weeks for these DNA results. Ten additional minutes shouldn't cause anyone hardship."

The young clerk started with the state Social Service representatives. Burgess and Lang each checked the seal and also the postmark and return label.

David and Faith did the same.

Michael gave it a cursory glance, while his lawyer jotted the pertinent details on his legal pad. Finally, every member of the Fielding group examined the envelope. As the young clerk returned it to Judge Brown, Faith slid to the edge of her chair and noticed that everyone else did, too. "The anticipation is nerveracking," she murmured to David.

Michael heard. "Why are you concerned?"

Faith clamped her teeth over her bottom lip. Under the table she had her fingers crossed that Michael's name would be inside that envelope. Not because she relished a fight with him, but if she ultimately lost, she'd far rather Michael raise the babies than Kipp and Shelby. By now, she would have thought he'd know how she felt.

The silence in the room was taut with suspense as Judge Brown slid a letter opener under the envelope flap. Her agonizingly slow rip of the paper had the same effect on the room's occupants as running a fingernail down a blackboard.

All drew in deep breaths when the judge extracted two sheets of paper from the envelope. "For the benefit of the record," the judge stated, "let it show that I've removed individual reports on blood drawn September fourth by a hematologist at Good Shepherd Hospital laboratory. One report is for Kipp J. Fielding III, the other for Michael L. Cameron, M.D."

Judge Brown perused first one sheet of paper, then the other as the keys to the stenowriter clicked softly. "My stars!" she burst out. Both papers slipped from her fingers and fluttered to the floor. The judge's eyes, indeed her whole face, reflected her shock. Composing herself with an effort, she bent and retrieved the pages. She seemed at a loss for words for several seconds, though she had to be aware that her entire audience leaned forward in their chairs.

"In my twenty years of serving in various capacities with Family Court, I've never run across anything like this. Lacy Hyatt Cameron's twins were fathered separately."

The clients all swiveled and looked to their lawyers for clarification. The legal counselors, in turn, peered confoundedly at Judge Brown.

The elder Fielding tumbled first to what Judge Brown meant. He clapped his son on the back. "I knew it. I knew it all along. The boy is yours. I have a grandson at last. Praise be!"

Pandemonium erupted with his declaration. The noise level in the room rose to deafening heights. In the absence of a gavel, Judge Brown pounded her fist on the desk and shouted for silence. "Stop this!" she ordered in her most imperious voice. "This is not a free-for-all, ladies and gentlemen. This is a child-custody hearing. Now then," she said sternly, tugging down her suit jacket. "Mr. Fielding has the right idea, only he's incorrect in his deduction. According to the DNA test results, the cord blood of the female child who, for the record, bears the name Abigail Dawn Cameron, matches the blood drawn from Kipp Fielding III. Whereas, cord blood of the male, known for the record as Nicholas John Cameron, bears the exact imprint of Michael Cameron's DNA."

Following a stunned silence, voices again escalated throughout the room. Again the judge pounded for order, this time with less success.

Bob Schlegel jumped to his feet. He stood, scowling around the room until talk tapered off, then stopped altogether. "Those tests are obviously erroneous," he bellowed, his face florid. "I've handled custody cases for over twenty years, and I've never heard of anything so preposterous as separate fathers of twins."

Nancy Matz placed a hand on her partner's arm. "I believe it's possible, Bob. Not long ago I saw a television documentary that dealt with this very thing."

He gaped at her. "Twins—with *different* fathers?"

Lon Maxwell, Michael's attorney, straightened his tie. "I can't quote names or dates, but my wife read a true account in one of her women's magazines recently. It dealt with twins having two fathers. She found it so fascinating, she read me most of the article at breakfast one morning. Ahem…we'd need to each document this for ourselves, of course, but here's the gist of how such a phenomena is possible, if I remember correctly." He paused, drawing a hand through his hair. "In a typical ovulation cycle, one or more eggs are released into a woman's fallopian tubes. After that, there's a window of two or three days during which conception can occur. So, as you can see, this phenomenon—two babies, two fathers, one birth—is certainly possible, although it's very rare."

Judge Brown reread both reports and then thumbed back through her notes. "In our initial hearing, both Mr. Fielding and Dr. Cameron claimed to have been intimate with Lacy Hyatt Cameron within a two-day period. Naturally I'd want to see some expert corroboration before we proceed. But a good place to begin, Counselors, might be with the American Society for Reproductive Medicine."

"Proceed?" shouted Keith Schlegel, who'd remained mute during the previous uproar. "The place to start is with new DNA blood work. This must be some lab technician's idea of a joke."

"It's no joke, Mr. Schlegel," Judge Brown informed him. "I'll have my clerk run copies of these data sheets right now for everyone involved. The testing lab is reputable. They do the work on some of our most sensitive criminal cases. What we have is unusual, possibly even a test case involving dual paternity."

Michael groped until he found Faith's hand. They clung together mutely. Kipp and Shelby both slumped back in their chairs, while the separate attorneys rallied and began to argue loudly.

Nancy Matz, after hastily conferring with her partners, paced before the judge. "This case is really open-and-shut. If we all buy into the premise that the DNA testing is valid, then dispensation is simple. Kipp and Shelby should be awarded custody of Abigail, and Dr. Cameron gets Nicholas. Let's end this today."

David slammed his hand flat to the table. "Such a

decision doesn't *begin* to address my client's claim. I don't give a damn if the babies have separate biological fathers. They had a common biological mother. A mother who clearly stated, while she was of sound mind and body, that she wanted her sister, my client, to receive custody of her offspring."

Lon Maxwell punched an index finger in the air. "I believe that even your client said Lacy Cameron wasn't aware she carried twins. That fact, if nothing else, should nullify her wishes."

Bob Schlegel's voice rumbled from the far side of the room. "My client's father has offered to pay for new DNA tests. He and his son both feel a strong kinship to baby Nicholas. They aren't prepared to accept this lab's report."

The judge glanced over sharply. "I'm not sure I'll agree. Further testing would necessitate leaving the twins in foster care another four to six weeks. That's assuming any lab you all agree on could draw blood today. And since the cord blood has already been used, you'd have to petition the court to draw blood from the infants."

"Couldn't they have mouth swabs?" This suggestion came from Nancy Matz.

"As complicated as this promises to be," said the judge, "my bottom-line concern is to impact the children as minimally as possible."

"We agree," chorused the two state social workers. Barbara Lang pulled out her notebook. "The twins have settled in nicely with Ms. Hyatt. Daniel and I recommended in our report that she be allowed to continue caring for the twins until custody can be finalized. In fact, she and Dr. Cameron did a fine job of co-parenting, as we noted."

Faith and Michael both gasped. They hugged spontaneously, expressions of amazement etched on their faces.

A flurry of activity erupted in the Fielding camp. Bob Schlegel hitched up his pants and cleared his throat. "On behalf of our client, Your Honor, we object to Dr. Cameron being allowed a larger role in the twins' lives than are Mr. and Mrs. Fielding. They have a substantial estate to run in New York, as well as other pressing obligations. It places a hardship on them to commute to Boston."

"What would you suggest, Counselor?" Judge Brown shot back. "If you recall, Dr. Cameron's home and surgical practice is also in New York. He obviously thought the babies were worth an investment of his time."

"Surely you aren't taking sides, Judge?" Keith Schlegel interjected in a calm, reasonable voice. "Haven't the DNA results moved us into completely new territory? I suggest we all need time to adequately prepare appeals."

Nancy Matz, who'd been in a huddle with Kipp's father, again got slowly to her feet. "In fairness to all concerned, we respectfully request the babies be placed in state-approved foster care for the duration of this custody settlement."

"No!" Faith's cry pierced the air, echoed by David Reed.

"This is obviously not in the children's best interests," he went on. "And it is unacceptable to my client." Faith gripped the sleeve of Michael's suit coat and implored him with tear-filled eyes.

White-faced, Michael covered her hands. His thumbs rubbed warmth into the backs of hers. "Lon," he directed, never taking his eyes from Faith, "I'll agree to return to New York if I must. But why disrupt the babies' lives? They aren't to blame for how this turned out."

Bedlam broke out again, with the Fieldings' lawyers shouting to be heard. Judge Brown again demanded order.

"You all seem to forget that I'm the one who makes the decisions with regard to placement of the Cameron twins. I say we leave things as they are for now and reconvene in these quarters three weeks from today at the same hour for the purpose of presenting expert testimony." She held up a hand when Bob Schlegel started to register an objection.

"My decision is final. Mr. and Mrs. Fielding are welcome, urged, in fact, to spend time with Abigail and Nicholas. Furthermore, I'm ordering Ms. Hyatt to allow them free access to the babies. By that, I mean whenever they can get to Boston." Her tone held a finality that brooked no requests for change or any dissension.

However, Bob Schlegel was like a dog with a bone. "If the same applies to Dr. Cameron, he'll be in Boston every day. It's evident from the report filed by Social Services that he's been shacking up with Ms. Hyatt."

Michael bounded to his feet, fists clenched. Lon Maxwell yanked him back into his chair. "Don't play into his hands," he hissed.

David said virtually the same to Faith, who'd also bristled at the accusation.

The judge sent Schlegel a withering glance. "I'll ask you to refrain from using crudities in these hearings, please. Mr. Burgess and Ms. Lang verified that Dr. Cameron rented an apartment in the building where Ms. Hyatt lives. Your clients are equally free to take up residence in Boston until this matter is settled, if they so choose. As a matter of fact, I realize I've forgotten to set child support payments.'' She named a monthly fee. ''Both Mr. Fielding III and Dr. Cameron will pay that amount to the court, retroactive to the children's birth.'' This time she slammed down a gavel, which a young clerk had hastened to bring her.

Reed gathered his legal pads and stuffed them inside his briefcase. He all but kicked up his heels in glee. ''Man, oh, man. What a case. Whoever wins this will be assured a niche in legal history.''

Lon Maxwell did rub his hands together. ''Don't get too far from the phone,'' he advised Michael. ''Oh, and refuse to speak with reporters. They'll turn this into a sideshow if we let them.''

''Reporters?'' Michael, who'd stood and caught Faith's arm, turned back. ''Why would reporters show any interest in a simple custody case?'' he asked Lon.

''Old son, there's nothing simple about this case now. It's a lallapalooza.''

He'd no sooner spoken than the door flew inward and reporters and cameramen streamed into the room. Ignoring the judge's admonition to leave immediately, the men and women stuck microphones in the faces of lawyers and clients alike.

Shelby Fielding shrank into her husband's side. Pushing at the microphone, she began to sob against Kipp's shoulder.

''Who leaked this information?'' Bob Schlegel roared.

''Good question,'' Michael echoed. Reaching for Faith, he sheltered her under his arm and began shoving his way through the mass of bodies toward the back door.

At a frantic call from the judge, policemen armed with nightsticks muscled their way into the room. "All right," one sergeant shouted. "This is private chambers. Let's clear the room."

A particularly determined fellow and his cameraman stuck close behind Michael and Faith. Out of breath, Michael handed Faith into the front seat of his car. "No comment," he growled after each question. "Get out from in front of my car, buddy, or I'll run you over."

"What's wrong with these people?" Faith gasped as the flashes blinded her. "Michael, we have to go back to the apartment. Gwen won't know anything about this. We can't have her opening the door and letting these jerks get pictures of the babies."

"Those chamber walls must have ears," Michael said. "There are always reporters hanging around a courthouse waiting for a big story."

Faith looked stricken. "Now they'll exploit the whole sordid mess leading up to Lacy's death." She covered her face with her hands to avoid being photographed by a woman who stepped off the curb as Michael wheeled the BMW around the corner of the courthouse.

His expression grim, Michael took the last corner on two wheels. Once they'd left the prying eyes behind, he slid an arm around Faith and pulled her against his shoulder. "The stories can't hurt Lacy now, sweetheart. My main concern is keeping you and the babies from being hurt."

Faith hauled in a deep breath. Michael's jacket smelled of wool and a light, earthy scent she'd come to connect with him…and with a feeling of safety. It was odd, given the volatility of their relationship till now, but she did trust Michael to make the right decisions when it came to protecting the babies. But could *anyone* protect them from the battle that was sure to heat up over the next three weeks?

CHAPTER TWELVE

GWEN LEAPED OFF THE COUCH as Faith and Michael let themselves in the front door and stripped off their coats. She bounced a twin on each hip. "My word, guys, I turned on the TV in time to hear your story break. There was a mob of reporters at the courthouse. The channel I watched tried to interview Kipp Fielding and his wife. His dad took a swing at a cameraman. How did you two escape the party?"

Faith dropped into a chair. "My knees are still shaking, Gwen. Those photographers are nuts. Michael almost ran over one who stepped in front of the car."

"The media types did seem obsessed. So, the lab found that the twins don't have the same father. A real bummer, huh? What'll happen to the kids?" she asked, handing one of the twins to Michael.

He kissed the baby's downy hair. "It's anyone's guess at this point," he said, heaving a sigh. "Everything's up in the air again."

"Sorry," Gwen interjected, "but aren't congratulations in order for you?"

Faith listened closely. She wanted to hear what Michael had to say, as he hadn't mentioned the DNA results on the way home.

He shrugged. "If you want the truth, I haven't had time to absorb it all."

"If you understand the findings, Gwen, maybe you

can explain," Faith said. "I'm skeptical. Only on rare occasions do some women release more than one egg. Why this time? Why Lacy?"

"I worked in endocrinology for a couple of years," Gwen said. "Extra eggs aren't all that uncommon. What's unusual is for the eggs to be fertilized by sperm from different men," she added dryly. "During the broadcast, one lawyer told a reporter the judge ordered your legal teams to consult with a reproductive expert. I say, good luck. In our clinic, the doctors couldn't even agree on how long eggs stay in the fallopian tubes. Some said three days. Others four. I should think a day could make a huge difference if these lawyers decide to get down and dirty."

"In what way?" Michael asked.

"To put it delicately, if they decide to make each man prove when the deed was done."

Faith took the other baby from Gwen and realized it was Nick. She wondered if Michael even realized he held Kipp's daughter and not his son. "That may have been an arguable point without the DNA, Gwen. But those results were conclusive. Besides, both men submitted depositions before the first hearing, listing the dates they and Lacy were intimate."

"Then what's the problem?" Gwen sounded puzzled. Collecting her purse and her sweater, she kissed each baby, hugged Faith and moved toward the door.

"I'm the problem," Faith said forthrightly. "Lacy signed over her custodial rights to me. And I take that responsibility seriously."

"You aren't totally to blame for the brouhaha, Faith," Michael reminded her. "Kipp's dad is demanding additional DNA testing. He thinks Nick, not Abigail, is his grandchild," he added for Gwen's benefit.

She stopped at the door. "Now who would care which child was theirs? They're both perfect little angels."

The phone rang before either Faith or Michael could respond to her statement.

"I know my way out," Gwen said. "Go catch your phone."

Michael deferred to Faith, since it was her phone. He walked Gwen to the door. "There may be reporters hanging around the main entrance. If you take the elevator all the way to the basement, there's a back door that opens into the parking lot. Try not to let anyone slip inside. That's assuming the media bird-dogs have found us."

"They have," Faith said. "That was a reporter on the phone." Even as she broke off speaking, the telephone rang again.

"Unplug it," Michael suggested. "Lon has my cell number. You can give it to Reed and also Fielding."

"Bye, guys. Sounds like you two have all you can handle." Gwen wiggled her fingers and stepped into the hall.

"Hey, thanks for baby-sitting," Faith called. "I owe you one."

"Honey, I'll collect if you ever get your life in order. Right now, I'd say you have more than enough to keep you busy." With that, she slipped out and closed the door.

Frowning at the insistent telephone, Faith disconnected it as Michael had urged. "How long do you suppose this will go on?"

"I don't want to sound negative, but probably until Judge Brown hands down a final decision."

"Three more weeks?" Faith blanched. "How will we

shop or get out to take the babies for walks in the park? Will I be followed again when I go to visit my dad?''

In a spontaneous move, Michael bent and kissed away the frown that creased Faith's forehead. ''Three weeks only gets us to the next hearing, sweetheart, which I'm afraid will turn out to be another round of arguments resulting in further delays.''

Slipping an arm around his waist, Faith leaned into him. The babies' chubby fingers entwined. Both seemed content to be held by adults they trusted. ''Judge Brown won't really separate them, will she, Michael?'' Faith asked worriedly.

''Separate them?'' Michael seemed to have lost his train of thought. In actuality, he felt more relaxed than at any time since he'd walked out on Faith and the twins last night. When they were together like this, their problems seemed to dwindle in scope.

Faith tipped back her head and searched Michael's face. ''You didn't hear Nancy Matz demand an open-and-shut case? You were sitting there when she proposed awarding Abigail to Kipp, and Nicholas to you. What did you *think* she meant?''

''I didn't hear her say that. I'll admit that after the judge read the DNA results, I was in a fog for a while. What was Kipp's reaction?''

''None that I recall. He and Shelby both seemed shell-shocked by the DNA reports. From what I observed, their attorneys couldn't agree among themselves. I'm hoping that'll be a strike against them with the judge.''

''What planet did that Matz woman fall from? What kind of person proposes separating twin infants for any reason?''

Faith's gaze cut back to the babies. ''If that seems to

be a serious possibility, I'd drop my case before I'd see them split up. I'd recommend they both go to Kipp and Shelby.''

''No.'' Reacting to the pain in her eyes and the tremor in her voice, Michael angled his head and settled his lips softly over hers. He meant it as a kiss to show support. Things changed when Faith's mouth opened under his. Desire, banked for too long, flamed out of control, triggering a restless longing in Michael. One impossible to quench while they each held a baby.

When Michael finally lifted his head, he discovered his free hand buried in Faith's feathery curls. Her eyes were closed, her breathing quickened—and it was all he could do not to kiss her again.

Faith, who hadn't realized she'd risen on her toes, dropped slowly back onto her heels. She opened her eyes and uncurled the fingers crushing Michael's lapel. Unable to stop a blush, she directed her attention to smoothing the fabric. ''It's almost time to feed the babies, and here we are still in our dressy clothes.''

Michael exerted a little pressure on the back of Faith's head and forced her to meet his eyes. ''It happened, Faith. We kissed and both felt the floor sway. You have to stop denying honest attraction.''

''Don't you mean lust?''

''Are you so sure it's not more than that?'' Michael continued to knead the tense muscles at the back of her neck.

She drew in a shaky breath. ''We're trapped together in the middle of a combustible situation. Emotions run high.''

When Michael refused to make light of what had happened, Faith directed his gaze from her to the infants. ''Ask yourself why you kissed me now, Michael. Can you honestly say it wasn't a result of our discussion involving the twins?''

"It was, but not in the way you mean. I share your pain and disappointment, Faith. When you hurt, I hurt. I can't speak plainer than that "

Faith's smile was brittle and she knew it. A foolish part of her had hoped Michael might say he loved her. What was it about that silly little word that made it so important? In the next heartbeat she answered herself. If a man and a woman truly loved each other, all of life's problems could be conquered. Her parents had shared such a love, and they'd built a happy marriage, in spite of overwhelming odds. Darn it all, Faith wanted no less.

"I'm going to change into sweats," she said, handing Nick to Michael.

"Running away is another form of denial, Faith." Michael's cell phone rang before he launched a second barrage at her retreating back. Placing the twins in the playpen, he flipped open the phone. "Cameron here," he snapped, feeling on the verge of combustible, as Faith had kindly termed it. "Lon, hi," Michael expelled a breath. "Sorry I left you to fend off the piranhas. We had a sitter here at Faith's. I wanted to get home before reporters started bugging her."

He listened a moment.

"Just Kipp and Shelby?" Michael asked in response to Lon's information. Apparently the couple planned to swing by for an informal visit before they returned to New York.

"We can't very well stop them, can we, Lon? I mean, the judge gave everyone unlimited access."

Faith reentered the room while he was still talking.

"Your lawyer?" she asked when he'd clicked off. Her stomach tightened as she waited for his reply.

"Kipp and Shelby are stopping here on their way out of town. They've been trying to phone, but of course we have the phone unplugged."

"What do they want?"

"To see Abigail, I guess. Shall we put her in a dress?" he asked, shoving his cell phone into a side pocket of the diaper bag.

Faith watched the babies batting at plush black-and-white cows tied to the slats of the playpen. Gwen must have brought them. "Abby's clean. She looks cute in that pink terry sleeper. And comfortable. Let's leave her."

"Okay." Michael walked over to the window. "There's a van from a local TV station parked out front. I'm going down to wait for the Fieldings in the lobby. We don't want reporters following them inside."

Faith had a bad feeling about this impromptu visit. "Why are you suddenly being so accommodating of our enemies?"

"Enemy? Kipp is Abigail's father."

As Faith watched the door close on Michael's heels, she leaned down and kissed both babies. Then she straightened the magazines on the coffee table and plumped the sofa pillows, wondering how she'd get through the visit.

The couple must have been in the area when Lon phoned. Michael was back all too quickly with Kipp and Shelby in tow.

They'd barely voiced stilted greetings when Kipp made a beeline for the playpen and picked Abby up. He sat on the couch. Instead of joining him, his wife perched on the chair farthest from the babies, and inspected her flawless fingernails.

Kipp stared at the baby for a long time, as if memorizing every feature. "I was hoping by now to recognize something of myself in her."

"She's the spitting image of Lacy," Faith blurted. On hearing a sharp hiss of air to her left, where Shelby Fielding sat, Faith guiltily twisted her mother's ring around her finger. She could have bitten her tongue.

A slow dawning of the truth flashed in Kipp's eyes seconds before he doused it and looked at his wife. "I read that children, even adopted ones, come to resemble the people who raise them," he stammered, seeking support from Michael and Faith.

They remained tense and silent, continuing to hover on either side of the playpen.

"Uh." Kipp cleared his throat. "I have a proposition for you, Cameron," he said, eyes locking with Michael's, closing Faith out.

"What kind of proposition?" Michael crossed his arms and widened his stance. He tried but failed to catch Faith's eye. Michael was pretty sure neither of them was going to like what the man had to say.

Kipp lowered his voice. "Take some time to consider what I'm proposing. I'm sure when you examine all the facets, you'll agree it's the best possible solution."

"Spit it out," growled Michael.

"All right. As you, Shelby and I all live in New York, I'm recommending my wife and I take both babies to live with us. You'd need a live-in au pair, anyway. Whenever you can escape work, it'd be a simple matter of coming by to pick up the boy."

Michael practically tripped over his tongue in his

haste to answer. "What gives you the idea I'd ever agree to such an arrangement?"

Kipp smiled. "My dad is your partner's stockbroker. Dominic is floundering without you. If you don't go back soon, your clinic will collapse. Understand, we aren't asking to adopt Nick. If, after the twins are older, you find more time in your schedule, it'll be easy enough to move him in with you. Under my plan, the siblings can eventually attend the same private school. Last, but not least, family courts generally place children with a couple when faced with an either-or choice. Since the babies technically belong to you and me, if we can reach some kind of terms, it'd save everyone time and expense. Judge Brown pitched a fit over the media blitz. I'd bet big bucks she'll rubber-stamp any reasonable system you and I work out."

Faith couldn't believe how neatly he'd cut her out of the triangle. Frozen inside, she finally dared to look at Michael. She expected, no, prayed he'd be gearing up to explode. The icy knot in her stomach froze even tighter. Michael calmly stroked his chin with a thumb and forefinger. He appeared to be considering Kipp's deal. But why shouldn't he? Faith thought numbly. After all, she'd said she'd bow out rather than separate the twins. Until this very minute, she hadn't a clue how impossibly hard that would be. The room swelled and receded as her world slowly crumbled.

"Tell you what. Give me some time to weigh the pros and cons." Michael aimed a polite smile at Shelby Fielding. "Does Kipp's proposal meet with your approval?"

The woman hesitated too long, in Faith's opinion. But when Shelby did at last issue a scratchy "ye-es,"

Michael apparently found it satisfactory. Otherwise he wouldn't have extended his hand to Kipp.

Whatever else passed between the two Fieldings and Michael escaped Faith. She felt sucked into a muddy vortex. She was vaguely aware of Michael walking the couple to the door. She might have managed a cordial goodbye, or maybe not. The first real emotion that registered after her stomach hit bottom was when Michael struck the living-room wall with a fist, exclaiming, "That pompous son of a bitch!"

Faith's head reeled. She flinched, listening to the inventive curses rolling off Michael's tongue as he paced the room.

"But you treated them so civilly," she gasped. "Why...why didn't you tell him no?"

"Because while he was spouting off, I devised a plan of my own."

"What kind of plan?"

"I...well, never mind. It has a few snags I'll need to work out. We'll talk about it later. Maybe over dinner, after I have time to fill in some of the holes."

"Holes or not, it can't be any worse than Kipp's preposterous plan," Faith insisted, pausing to try and read in his eyes whether his unnamed idea was as one-sided as Kipp's. "I'm not going to like this, either, am I?" she asked, tensing at the nervous way Michael scraped his fingers through his hair.

Both babies, who'd been quietly contented up to now, kicked unhappily and began to squall, allowing Michael a reprieve.

"I'll fix their bottles," Faith said over the din.

Michael scooped the two infants into his arms. "When do they get real food?" he asked, the query coming out of left field.

"Dr. Sampson prefers to start cereal at three months. Maybe later for these guys, since they were premature."

In the flurry of activity centered on changing diapers and preparing to feed two hungry babies, Faith forgot about Michael's plan. What stuck in her mind was something Kipp had said. It surfaced again when she and Michael were settled on the couch, each feeding a baby. "Michael, your clinic isn't really in danger of folding, is it? I mean, you are keeping in contact with your partner."

"Yeah. Dominic's called a number of times."

"So, then Kipp was lying? Or else his dad?"

"Dom may well have complained. My partner goes through a lot of money. He's a confirmed bachelor and switches girlfriends every few months. A guy like that can't fathom why I'd leave a booming practice to spend time with crying babies." Michael grinned. "They were crying every time Dominic phoned."

"Kipp got the story right in another sense, too, I guess," she said. "I never stopped to think, but technically you are just on holiday."

"Where's this conversation leading, Faith? Have I ever implied otherwise?" Michael's dark eyes pinned hers.

"No. No, you haven't," she agreed readily.

"So what's troubling you? I can almost hear the wheels turning."

Faith changed gears without blinking. "Did you ever want to do anything other than be a surgeon?"

Michael laughed. "Sure. When I was six I wanted to be a priest."

That was probably the last career Faith would have expected. But at six... He was probably pulling her leg. "Huh. I'll bet that notion didn't last long."

"Until I was fourteen."

"Really? Fourteen? What happened then to change your mind?"

"Well, my dad caught me necking on the porch swing with a sixteen-year-old neighbor girl. He said with the interest I showed in anatomy, I ought to spend my free time in his office learning to be a doctor. Then he proceeded to lecture me on sex and celibacy. I knew, of course, that priests were celibate. I suspect I gleaned enough about the female anatomy during my swing encounter with Tammy Hurley to decide on a new career path then and there."

"Yeah, right," Faith snorted. Lifting a sleepy Abby to her shoulder, she drummed her fingers lightly on the baby's back, trying to get her to burp. "How long before you and Tammy found a more private place to finish that anatomy course?"

"We didn't." Michael let his son slurp down the last of an eight-ounce bottle. Burping had never been a problem for Nicholas. He let out a big one, then closed his eyes. "This kid's ready to crash. I'm going to stick him in the crib. I'll turn on the monitor, so all you have to do when Abby finally burps is put her down."

As though she didn't want to take a back seat to her brother, Abby emitted three in a row. "I'll go with you," Faith said. "That way I won't risk waking Nicholas later."

The babies still slept together in one crib because they preferred it. Michael placed Nick down first and covered him with a blanket. While Faith settled Abigail, Michael flipped on the monitor, which allowed them to hear the babies from the other room.

Faith led the way to the door. She realized Michael hadn't followed and turned back to see why not. Hands thrust into the pockets of his suit pants, he stood gazing at the sleeping babies. A raw look of love softened his masculine features. "Is everything all right?" Faith whispered. Michael's expression had triggered a coiled ache in her abdomen.

Michael pulled one hand from his pocket and motioned Faith toward him. He slipped the same hand around her shoulder once she stood beside him. "Look at the way Abigail burrows against Nicholas," he murmured. "Have you noticed that their heads and arms always touch when they sleep? I defy anyone to look at this picture and say they should be separated."

"I have film in the camera. Maybe I ought to take some snapshots for the court record," Faith said, resting her own head on Michael's broad shoulder.

"Yes, do," he urged. "There's no way anyone with a heart could see how attached they are and then turn around and split them up."

Good sense told Faith that in the case of three people vying for two small babies, someone had to lose. Not wanting to burst Michael's optimistic bubble, she padded off to get her camera.

Michael was obviously stressed by some worry of his own. He barely said two words during their meal of tangy, taco-baked potatoes and small garden salads that Faith prepared after she'd used an entire roll of film on the babies.

Watching Michael toy with the cheesy topping on his baked potato, Faith decided he must be more worried about the situation at the clinic than he'd let on. It had become easy to forget that either of them might ever have to return to demanding jobs. The fact remained that the long, erratic hours Michael spent attending to patients had been the catalyst for Lacy's leaving him.

It hadn't taken Kipp Fielding long to figure that out and capitalize on Michael's hectic life.

It hurt too much to think about strangers raising her sister's babies. Realistically, Faith knew that was what would happen if the court gave Abby and Nick to their fathers. Neither man was ever home. Although, maybe Shelby would eventually come to love the twins—one or both of them. After all, as Gwen had said, who wouldn't lose their hearts once they got to know these precious little ones?

A dish Faith had always loved and looked forward to fixing suddenly seemed tasteless. Excusing herself, Faith rose and scraped her food into the trash.

Michael wasn't any more able to eat than she was. "Something has to give, Faith," he said, joining her in clearing the table. "Do you agree we can't go on the way we are?"

Faith gripped the edge of the sink, and her throat jammed so she couldn't speak, could only nod.

Michael gathered her hands and turned her around. "At the risk of sounding like Fielding did earlier, I'd like you to listen to me, Faith. Don't interrupt until I finish, then you can have your say."

A ripple of hope coursed through her body, followed by a shiver of fear. Faith did her best, nevertheless, to muster a smile. "I'm trying hard not to be scared, Michael. But I've rarely seen you this intense."

He rubbed his thumbs over the white knuckles of her hands. One at a time, he lifted her narrow hands and pressed a reassuring kiss into each palm. He was grateful that she came easily into his arms. That way he could bury his face in her sweet-smelling neck and not have to face a refusal he was awfully afraid would show first in her eyes.

Faith settled comfortably with an ear to Michael's chest. She had no idea what he was about to spring on her. Nestled in his arms like this, she thought even the most horrible news would be palatable. Her lips quirked in a smile as the first strains of his deep voice rumbled beneath her ear.

"There was one thing Kipp said that grabbed me and refused to let go. Do you remember how he sounded so positive about the court placing the twins with a couple rather than a single parent?" Michael laid a row of kisses along her ear.

Faith stilled, taking comfort for a moment in the steady beat of Michael's heart. She fingered the points of his crisp shirt collar. "Kipp was making a case to suit himself. According to David, the judge will study a range of factors before rendering a decision. Lon must have told you we all have strong points."

Michael's arms tightened around her. "I asked you to listen, Faith."

"Then stop asking me questions," she scolded softly, reveling in the comfort of being held. Hugs had been infrequent in Faith's life.

"But suppose a married couple does look like the better option?"

Faith knew to keep quiet this time. Michael had made it clear he wanted to work through to his conclusion without interruption.

"If I was the one deciding, I might think two people were more capable of caring for two children," he said. "I read the report Burgess and Lang submitted. More than once they praised us for working together."

Loosening his hold, Michael ran his palms in lazy eights over Faith's back. She practically purred and hoped he'd continue.

"What I'm getting at, Faith is straightforward. If we were married, we'd actually look better than Kipp and Shelby. You *are* their aunt, and both of us have experience taking care of the twins, while they have none. What do you think?"

In a stupefied corner of her brain, Faith realized that this time Michael expected some response. She lifted her head. Still, he held her so tightly she couldn't see past his chin. "I'm sure you think you've hit on the perfect solution. But, Michael, I haven't even dated anyone in over a year. Maybe it's easy for you to snap your fingers and come up with a wife. In fact, it probably is." Faith's stomach dived again as she wriggled out of his arms and said in a shaky voice, "Whoever she is, she'd better be sincere about wanting children. Judge Brown doesn't strike me as someone easily fooled."

Michael's face went through various stages of shock before sinking into dismay. He doubled back over what he'd said and how it had come out so wrong. He saw now where he'd made his mistake. Slipping an arm around Faith's stubbornly rigid shoulders, he navigated her into the living room. There, he turned her and pressed her onto the couch. Sinking down on one knee, he again gathered both of her hands. "Faith, honey," he said, with only the most minimal tremor, "I meant that we should marry each other."

"Each other?" Faith practically swallowed the question. Disengaging one hand, she pointed first to herself, then to Michael and back to herself again. Words failed her completely this time.

A smile finally kicked up one corner of Michael's mouth. He managed to nod before he placed a hand on either side of her and leaned forward to capture her lips in a reassuring heartfelt kiss.

The kiss went on and on. Michael followed her lips when Faith toppled backward into the soft cushions.

She tried and failed to get a grip on her senses. At some point, without even being aware of it, she kicked off her shoes. It seemed as if his kisses burned everywhere, from the top of her head to the soles of her feet. Cradled in his arms, she felt her entire body tingle in anticipation of *more* than kissing and being kissed.

Married. Such a beautiful word. It tumbled around and around inside Faith's head, gathering hope. It had been several years since she'd allowed herself to think, to plan, to dream about a husband. About walking down the aisle at the church in Marblehead, where her parents had begun their married life. Oh…Michael probably wouldn't want a church wedding. He'd been content to marry Lacy in her dreary hospital room.

Now that the niggling worry had wormed its way into her mind, Faith thought it quite likely that she and Michael had widely differing views concerning this possible marriage. The word *love* had not crossed his lips. Of course, she'd been rather dense about his proposal at first and after that, his lips had kept her mind on his kisses.

Ooh, and now he was doing remarkable things with his mouth against her bare breast. *Did love matter, after all?* she wondered as she tunneled her fingers deep within the satiny strands of his thick hair.

The thoughts spinning in Faith's head soon gave way to feelings. Feelings she'd flirted with a few times, but mostly had only imagined. The few times the accountant had slept over at her apartment, their fleeting encounters had been nothing like this.

Michael's skin felt slick and soft—on his arms and shoulders and where it stretched over his muscled back and narrow hips. His palms were warm and heavenly on the inside of her thighs. One of his thumbs edged higher until it caressed her moist panties. Faith wanted to weep. She did cry out and felt as though she'd been caught in a downward spiral.

At that moment, she didn't think anything in the world could possibly compare. Especially when his searing kisses moved down her body, and his hands slipped behind her, lifting until he gently removed the cotton barrier and covered her with his mouth.

"Is this your first time?" he murmured.

Unable to speak at first, Faith shook her head. Then she found her voice. "No. But it's been a long while." She was a mature woman, and a nurse. Faith knew the facts of life. Yet she couldn't believe what Michael was doing with his tongue.

He blew softly on her stomach and groaned. "Ah, Faith…"

Faith writhed beneath his mouth. Could a man who wasn't in love do this to a woman? Michael's lips wreaked pure torture. Pure rapture. In a tiny still-functioning corner of her brain, Faith envisioned herself and Michael spending a lifetime of nights like this.

Gwen said babies invariably decided to cry and interrupt their parents during lovemaking. Faith listened carefully but heard nothing except the babies' soft breathing on the monitor. Nothing except the pounding of Michael's heart and then her own moan of pleasure as, moments later, she flew apart.

Michael, her lover. *Could life get more perfect?*

CHAPTER THIRTEEN

THE DISTANT SOUND OF a crying baby prodded Faith awake. The room was black. Normally at night she could see the night-light in the nursery, so either she hadn't turned it on or it'd burned out. She started to get up but was stopped by a heavy restraint across her middle. A moment's panic abated as the memory of how she'd spent the preceding hours filtered into Faith's sleepy brain. Fondly she recalled being initiated into numerous new ways of love and then falling asleep in Michael's arms.

That was why she couldn't see a night-light. This was the living-room couch and not her bed. Michael lay on his side facing her, an arm pinning her to the back cushions. She ached from lying in the same position all night. Well, that was only part of the reason she ached, Faith thought with a blush and a smile as she eased out from beneath Michael's arm.

AN INSISTENT NOISE—crying—penetrated Michael's sleep-fogged brain. He lifted his head and squinted at his watch. Four-thirty according to the night dial. He didn't stop to wonder why he was naked except for his watch. His mind only grasped the fact that the twins had slept for a good long stretch. Michael eased oddly tight muscles. That was when it began to dawn—his limbs were tangled with another pair. Smooth, cool legs and a soft warm body. "Lacy?" he murmured, far from being fully awake.

The body beside him had been stirring, too, slipping away from him. Suddenly it stilled, and a light snapped on, blinding Michael. Behind the harsh glare, a voice filled with pain, answered him. "Faith. Not Lacy. How could you, Michael? How could you?"

His bed partner scrambled over top of him. Michael watched her grab clothes from the coffee table and the floor, stirring a cool breeze across his naked backside. Emitting the cry of an injured animal, Faith exited the room in a flash of bare legs.

Recollection of the night flooded back. An incredible, incredible night. It had come on the heels of their latest custody hearing, followed by an infuriating visit from Fielding, the arrogant bastard.

Michael struggled to sit up. It had been weeks— months maybe—since he'd slept so soundly. More awake now, his question from minutes before kicked him in the heart like a Missouri mule. God, yes, he was awake. Michael groaned and scrambled to find his pants. Faith's unhappiness as she fled the room flowed over him and hammered in his blood. *How could he,* was right. How could he call her by another woman's name after the wonderful way, the welcoming and giving way, she'd received him last night?

"Cameron, you ought to be shot," he muttered as he stumbled out to find Faith. He hadn't dreamed of Lacy in months. Not even in the unsettled days after she'd divorced him. Not even after her death. So what in hell possessed him to say her name and ruin the fragile trust he'd finally won from Faith?

"Faith?" She didn't answer, but Michael saw her rocking the babies in the nursery rocking chair. The light of a waning moon silvered noiseless tears that coursed down her cheeks. Both babies sucked on their fingers. Michael knew they needed bottles. He'd get them, but not until he made an effort to explain to Faith something he didn't understand himself.

"You're not a substitute for Lacy, if that's what's running through your mind," he said urgently. "You're the only woman I've been with since my divorce, Faith." His voice pulsed with emotion as he spoke.

The rocking never slowed, nor did Faith look at him or acknowledge his presence in any other way.

"I was half-asleep, Faith! Tell me—what more do you want from me?"

She buried her head in one of the babies' necks. Abby's, Michael thought. "I already explained that my relationship with Lacy was going down the tubes before we split up." Michael knew she had to be taking this in. Stepping closer, he emphasized his appeal with outstretched hands. "My getting Lacy pregnant was a fluke. She initiated sex that day only because she thought I'd come home early to take her to a party. She went ballistic when she found out I'd come to pack for another medical expedition. We hadn't slept in the same bed for three months, I swear. Dammit, Faith, look at me. It's important that you believe me."

He gave up when both twins started to wail. Time. She needed time to work this through. Once she did, she'd be fair. That was just one of the many things he loved about Faith. She didn't harbor grudges.

Faith heard Michael rattling around the kitchen and assumed he was preparing bottles for the twins. She didn't know why she was acting so...so childish. Michael had never said he loved her. His marriage proposal had been more of a business deal, along the lines of the plan presented by Kipp Fielding. Now that she thought about it, she recalled Michael's saying, after Kipp had left, that he had his own plan to win the custody suit.

Kissing the babies, Faith rocked harder. Michael had never promised her love. At the most, he candidly pointed out a shared attraction. A new trickle of tears squeezed from beneath her closed eyelids. It was her own silly dream that made her want more. She loved these babies and she loved Michael. She wanted them to be a real family.

Michael walked back into the nursery carrying two bottles. Faith wished he'd taken time to put on a shirt. If they were going to make a success of his business proposal, she had to keep a level head.

"Do you want to feed Abby or Nick?" she asked. These were her first words after shedding copious tears and her voice was hoarse.

"It doesn't matter which. You do know that, don't you, Faith? I don't love Nick more than Abigail because he shares my blood."

So, the word love *was* in Michael's vocabulary. He wasn't like some men who could never utter the word. She handed him Nick, anyway, and busied herself settling Abby in the crook of her arm. "I saw something in your face the first day you held them at the hospital, Michael," she said quietly. "I knew then that they'd both found a home in your heart."

"They did." He sat on the carpeted floor and leaned against one of the dressers. After testing the bottle on the inside of his wrist, he offered it to Nick.

Dawn began to spill first light into the colorful room. The primary colors were soothing to Michael, as was listening to the rhythmic sucking of the babies. His babies. He thought about the night he'd spent making love to the woman he envisioned spending the next fifty years with. That filled his heart with a sense of peace. It came to him, then, that he'd been walking a precarious tightrope between his marriage to Lacy and his work for a lot longer than he'd realized. His life had lacked balance. Whatever had been the cause—his fast climb to the top of the prominent community of specialists or Lacy's growing dissatisfaction with his involvement in his work—Michael didn't intend to repeat his mistakes. He'd find more hours to spend with Faith. It was time to make changes in his life. He didn't want to miss these all-too-fleeting moments with his family.

His family. A term that held no meaning without Faith. Alarm edged out the feeling of peace. Did Faith seem mellower? Maybe he ought to give her more time, but something inside warned Michael to act now. "My timing probably stinks, Faith. But you didn't answer my question last night."

Her eyes met Michael's and skittered away quickly. "We should have done more talking."

"I'm not complaining." There was a smile in his voice.

Faith sighed. "Nor am I, Michael. Let's start over."

Her statement started the blood pumping through his veins again. "Will you marry me?"

Faith rocked forward and back and forward again. The only other movement she made was to stroke Abigail's ear and cheek and silky hair. "On paper, Michael. I'll marry you on paper."

"On paper?" Michael scowled. "What the hell does that mean?"

"It means I'll fill out the forms at a justice of the

peace. In the eyes of the court, we'll legally be husband and wife. That's all.''

Maybe he hadn't slept as well as he thought. Michael had trouble understanding Faith's terse little speech. Or...maybe not. He was afraid he knew exactly what she was saying. "I want more," he said softly. Gruffly. "I want our marriage to be real."

Oh, so do I. Faith's lips trembled. So did her hands. And her heart cracked and bled into a chest already filled with pain. "Those are my terms, Michael. If we don't win custody we'll have an annulment. In the interim, there'll be no repeat of last night."

"Last night was good," he said lamely. He had to fight the pressure of tears at the backs of his eyes.

"Nick's finished his bottle," Faith chided. "You're letting him suck air."

Michael tipped the bottle up fast. As he hoisted his son to his shoulder, he noticed the sheen reflecting off Faith's eyes. He'd won his point for now. Any fool could see she hadn't recovered from the blow he'd dealt her in accidentally calling her by her sister's name. He'd make it up to her if he had to work at it a lifetime. Which he had every intention of doing.

He would have started his quest then and there had his cell phone not bleated unceasingly until he extracted the instrument from the diaper bag and flipped it open. "Dominic?" Michael fumbled the phone and the baby, whose back arched as Nicholas burped and pooped simultaneously. "Hold on a minute, Dom." Michael climbed to his feet, trying to shuffle the phone to the hollow of one shoulder.

Taking pity on him, Faith rose gracefully and took the baby from his arms. "I'll change him. Talk to your partner."

Michael did, but he watched how deftly Faith dispatched diapers. "All right, Dominic, calm down. Admit Cynthia to I.C.U. Put her on the usual monitors. If you think she's rejecting the heart, she probably is. I can be there in two hours. You know the routine—bump her to the top of the emergency list. I left my medical bag at the apartment. If you'll go by and pick it up, I'll tell my housekeeper to have it ready. See you at Mercy General. Tell Cyn I'm on my way." He clicked off and turned to Faith.

"I heard. You have an emergency, Michael. Go. I'll be fine."

"Who'll help with the babies?"

"I'm quite recovered, Michael. I really can do this without help. It's what I intended before you moved in next door."

"But…" The ravages of indecision accentuated the deep creases bracketing his mouth.

Faith waved him away. Bending, she blew a kiss on Nick's exposed belly. The baby laughed out loud, galvanizing Faith and Michael with the thrilling sound.

"Oh-oh," Faith exclaimed delightedly. "I'll have to log that in his baby book. He's giggled some, but I think this is his first real laugh."

Michael held out a hand to the babies. They not only followed his movement with their eyes, each latched on to one of his fingers. "I'll call you tonight," he promised Faith. He didn't want to leave them. Not any of them, but most especially Faith. "Cynthia Fitzhugh was my first dual-organ transplant after I set up practice in New York. It was a near-perfect match. She shouldn't be rejecting."

"So go find out why she is," Faith said gently.

''That's your work and you're good at it, Michael Cameron.''

He pulled his fingers away from the babies and leaned down to kiss Faith goodbye. She saw his intention and turned, so his lips barely skimmed her jaw. He knew then that he had a long way to go to dig himself out of the hole he'd fallen into this morning. From experience, he knew how difficult that was to do long-distance.

Still, he had no choice. He'd taken a healer's oath. ''I *will* telephone,'' he said again as he strode out of the nursery. Within minutes he was gone, leaving nothing behind but the faint scent of Lagerfeld that Faith always associated with Michael.

By nightfall, even that small trace was gone. He didn't call, even though Faith had plugged in the phone again and suffered through too many calls from obnoxious reporters. What had she expected? That Michael would somehow be different from other doctors who buried themselves in their work to the exclusion of all else? That he would change his life for her when he hadn't done so for Lacy?

As midnight came and went, Faith sat alone and lonely, staring out the window at a dark, rain-soaked landscape. She'd had her first taste of how Lacy must have felt the many nights she called just to talk. To connect with another voice, she'd said.

Unlike her sister, Faith wasn't one to wallow in self-pity.

Next day, the storm had passed. She bundled the babies, put them in their stroller and headed for the library. She'd no sooner set foot out the door than reporters climbed from two different vehicles and boxed her neatly between them.

"We knew you'd surface one of these days," the younger of the two men announced.

"I'm not making any comment with regard to the case," Faith told them both.

"Did you read the story in the morning paper?" The older man flipped open his notebook and read to Faith from notes he'd obviously jotted down. "According to a news flash out of New York, Kipp Fielding's lawyer declared his client and Dr. Cameron have joined forces against you."

"That's not true," Faith exclaimed. As soon as she'd spoken, she wished she could take back her words. Especially when both men turned to clean pages on their pads, overt interest in their eyes. "I'm not saying anything else. If you want to know my position, talk to my attorney, David Reed."

"We've talked to the lawyers. Schlegel, Schlegel and Matz went over Judge Brown's head yesterday and got her visitation edict changed. Superior Court Judge Reuben Kline overturned Brown's decision. Kline has ordered you to travel to New York with the babies once a week. Cameron's attorney said they couldn't be happier, since the doctor has now returned to his practice. I suppose Reed plans to counter?"

Faith's head spun. Was Michael aware of this? Was that why he hadn't called? If all along he'd planned to side with Kipp, she had certainly played the fool. It was plain what Maxwell could do, if Michael revealed how easily she'd fallen into bed with him.

Her breakfast of toast and coffee threatened to come up. David had once said that Bob Schlegel could neutralize her position by discrediting Lacy. What stopped them from applying the same "loose woman" label to her?

Even if she countered and insisted that Michael had proposed marriage, it'd be her word against his. The sick feeling returned.

"Hey!" the young reporter called as Faith whirled around and walked quickly back to her apartment building. "So far all of you are letting the lawyers run this case. John Q. Public cares about what happens to those kids. They're calling our office in droves. If you play your cards right, Ms. Hyatt, you could probably come up with a book or movie deal. This is the hottest news on the Eastern Seaboard."

"No comment," she muttered, grateful the door opened without a hitch today. Some days, especially following a rain, the door tended to stick.

Upstairs again, she peeled the twins out of their jackets and placed them in the playpen. She picked up the receiver, but the phone rang before she could dial out. It was David calling her.

"What's going on over there, Faith? I couldn't get through to you all morning."

"I unplugged the phone. I've been plagued by reporters. But you're the person I was about to call. Why do I need to travel to New York with the twins every week?"

"So you read today's newspaper? Dammit, Faith, I might have seen it coming and thrown up a roadblock if you'd told me Cameron went back to New York."

"He only left yesterday. His partner at the clinic called with an emergency. One of Michael's patients."

"Huh, probably a lie he and Maxwell concocted to get the ball back in their court."

"What do you mean?" Faith had to sit. Her knees buckled.

"I mean they're making you haul the babies into their

territory because it gives them an advantage, a chance to work a deal. Next they'll say that two of the three principals reside in New York, so the hearings should be moved there. If that happens, it cuts our chances of winning.''

Faith's pulse thundered in her ears. ''What do you foresee happening?''

''The truth? My guess is Dr. Cameron will get the boy and Fielding the girl.''

''Nicholas and Abigail,'' Faith snapped. ''They have names, David,'' she said, sniffling and blinking furiously.

''Yeah, well, that could change, too. Everything could go topsy-turvy. Kipp's father wants the DNA repeated. That man's ruthless. Cameron's a fool to climb into bed with them. Those old Wall Street types have no scruples. Money greases any wheel, if you get my drift. Next thing you know, the first DNA tests will be declared invalid, and Fielding has himself a grandchild.''

The more Faith listened to David, the more certain she was some mistake had occurred. ''You aren't giving Michael credit. He'd never allow that. He agrees with me that it'd be horrible to separate the twins. Hasn't Mr. Fielding seen the studies? Even as adults, most of the twins who were separated as babies said they felt a piece of themselves was missing.''

''The man wants his own flesh and blood, regardless. You have to stop being so gullible, Faith. Cameron has his own agenda. I'll admit those twin studies may be our best defense. If we can keep the case in Boston Family Court, odds are we'll get a fair hearing. But I've got to tell you, the way things have gone in the past two days doesn't bode well.''

Faith hardened her heart. "I'm not paying for gloom and doom, David. We have right on our side. Now, when do I have to transport the babies to New York? And where do we go after I get there?"

"The first visitation is tomorrow." He gave her the address of the Fielding estate. "I believe you know where Cameron lives. Their attorneys have requested the babies spend a full hour at each residence. I'm sorry, Faith, but you'll need to fulfill your obligation this one time, anyway. I've filed a counter that, in essence, says with fall weather turning to winter soon, the new order places an undue hardship on the infants."

"What about the hardship it places on me? I have to take the train because I don't have a car."

"I tried to play down that aspect. We don't want Schlegel or Maxwell challenging your position as temporary custodian. Frankly, the longer the babies remain in your care, the more pressure a judge will feel to leave them be. I'm drafting something now that says the kids are getting used to their surroundings, et cetera."

"I hope it works." Faith couldn't help feeling anxious, given present circumstances.

"I'll phone tomorrow night and let you know how my appeal's been received. Kline is a tough judge. But I happen to know he has five grandchildren he dotes on. I'm not above making a few comparisons to tug at his heartstrings."

"All right, David. I'll be waiting to hear. I'm not exactly sure of the train schedules, but I'll go early and try to be home before dark. I'll call you, okay? Remember I have my phone unplugged. Because of the reporters."

"Nothing like a good court bloodbath involving kids to stir a media frenzy. Plus, half the world knows this

could be a trend-setting case. That's why all the lawyers
have been interviewed on CNN. We're all in negotia-
tions to appear on *Larry King Live*. It's a good thing
you aren't answering your phone. They'll be after you,
Kipp and Michael, too. But you should refuse.''

''Why would *you* appear? The media only wants to
exploit innocent babies.''

''Remember at the beginning I told you we had a hot
case? Those DNA results upped the temperature.
Whichever lawyer or legal team wins—hey, he'll be
writing his own ticket. Ours isn't the first case of its
kind, but it has unique features.''

''I had no idea there were any similar situations.''

''Yes, well, this quite possibly is the first twins-
with-different-dads battle where the biological mother
doesn't factor in.''

''If Lacy had lived, the court wouldn't be so eager
to split up the twins, I'll bet,'' Faith murmured, unable
to hide the sad tremor in her voice.

''At least she had the foresight to appoint you her
surrogate stand-in. Which has given me an idea for another angle. I'll do my best to see Judge Kline tomorrow.'' He paused. ''We should conduct our next strategy session in person. Leave my name with your
building manager. I'll drop by around seven or eight.
Good luck in New York, Faith. Don't let the men in-
timidate you.''

''No, I won't,'' she murmured. But David had already hung up. Leaving the receiver off the hook, she
sat for some time watching the babies kick and coo.
Nick tried several times to turn over. Faith didn't expect
him to succeed, and when he did, she grinned and
clapped spontaneously. She sobered as she realized

she'd been wishing Michael was here to see Nick's big accomplishment.

"Oh, Michael," she sobbed, covering her face with her hands. "Oh, Michael." *I know you don't care for me the way I care for you. But I believed you when you said you loved Nick and Abigail equally. I really thought they were hearts and souls to you, not biological oddities or...or some stupid test case.*

IN SPITE OF A SLEEPLESS NIGHT, Faith was determined to look her best and brightest when presenting herself in New York. Unfortunately, the logistics of transporting two babies for two hours by train had her rethinking her plan to wear a dress. In the end, she changed into comfortable drawstring pants and sneakers. She wore a cardigan sweater over a cotton T-shirt. Instead of taking the stroller, she placed Abby in a front pack and Nick in a backpack she'd been given at her shower. That left her hands free to carry the monster diaper bag. Faith also dispensed with a purse. She tucked her ID and money into one of the bag's pockets and had to smile. No mugger would steal a lumpy diaper bag.

The train ride was actually quite pleasant. A baby always managed to coax good humor from the grumpiest of the grumpy. Two babies who'd just discovered their own ability to smile and flirt garnered much more than twice the interest. She was careful to conceal the children's identity, though. It had taken a bit of ingenuity to sneak out of the apartment house and bypass the reporters who hung around the front entrance. There were even more of them today than yesterday. It still shocked her that so many people found their case riveting. But then, when it came to this case, Faith was thrown off balance a lot.

She allowed herself the luxury of taking a cab to the Fielding address. It was awkward traveling by car without the infant carriers. She buckled in securely, sitting well forward on the seat, and left the babies in their respective packs. Both were fussy. They needed changing and it was time to eat. Faith hated the fact that Kipp and Shelby wouldn't be seeing the twins at their best. On the other hand, maybe if they discovered the babies weren't always perfect, they might have second thoughts about their vigorous pursuit.

Faith's cab pulled into the massive circular driveway at the same time Shelby Fielding slipped behind the wheel of a sleek Jaguar parked in front of the three-story brick home. The woman saw Faith, frowned, climbed out of the Jag again and drummed her fingers on the roof of the automobile.

"What are you doing here?" Shelby demanded, when it appeared obvious that Faith had paid her driver and was set to dismiss the cab.

Jiggling the now loudly crying babies, Faith wasn't inclined to be generous. "As if you didn't know your lawyers and Michael's overturned Judge Brown's visitation ruling! I'm complying with the latest court order—making the requisite weekly visit to your home."

Shelby paled underneath her layer of carefully applied makeup. "You must be mistaken. Kipp left yesterday for a race in Antigua. He'll be gone a week and a half." She inspected a diamond-encrusted watch and exclaimed, "If I don't leave this minute, I'll be late for my final evaluation at the fertility clinic."

"Fertility…" Faith hurried around the front of the Jag and backed Shelby against the car. "I've ridden two-plus hours with two restless babies. One of whom was fathered by your husband. If this is some kind of passive-aggressive game you and he are playing, I'd appreciate being dealt out of it.''

Color flared across Shelby's narrow cheekbones. "Kipp wouldn't have set something up like this and expected me to handle it. He wouldn't." In jerky motions, she extracted a cell phone from her Donald Pliner handbag and punched in a series of numbers.

Meanwhile, Faith did her best to quiet the babies, who'd joined in a crying chorus.

Shelby tapped the toe of the strappy heels that matched her purse. "This is Shelby Fielding," she said haughtily in a tone suggesting she was someone special. "Put me through to Bob Schlegel immediately."

Faith patted Abigail's back and made soothing sounds over her shoulder at Nick.

"Bob, thank heavens, I caught you," Shelby exclaimed, sounding for all the world as if she meant it. "The Hyatt woman has arrived at my home with the twins. Kipp's out of town." She paused in the middle of her hysterical outburst and listened to the masculine drone on the other end of the line.

"You mean to tell me Kipp isn't aware you overturned the original visitation order? No. That's impossible, Bob. I have an appointment. In fact, I'm late. I can't cancel and entertain her for an hour. All right. All right. I'll give her a lift to Dr. Cameron's apartment. Yes," she said in meeker tones. "I understand Kipp is paying you a lot of money to do a job for him. But you can't expect us to comply with a decree we didn't know about." The scowl she wore when she clicked off soon blossomed into a placating smile.

"There's been a mix-up on our side, Ms Hyatt. Bob thought Keith had informed Kipp and me of the change. The news fell through the cracks, I'm afraid. Today the

twins will only be visiting Dr. Cameron. Hop in. I'll
run you by his place."

Faith knew that if she said what she felt like saying,
she'd be the one who ended up looking bad. She held
her tongue for the short ride to Michael's building, even
though buckling her and the bulky baby-packs into the
sports car proved to be harder than in the cab. Plus, not
even the car's movement appeased the wet and hungry
infants.

Shelby swung close to the curb outside Michael's
luxury complex. She didn't cut the engine, but tapped
shell-pink fingernails restlessly on the steering wheel.

"Did Mr. Schlegel know for certain that Dr. Cameron's home?" Faith craned her neck and eyed the upper windows, all of which looked dark. Michael could
be in his den. Faith knew from past visits that it faced
the opposite street. "Could you wait while I ask the
doorman if he's home?" she murmured, leaning back
inside the car to haul out the diaper bag she'd wedged
by her feet.

"I went out of my way to bring you here. I'm going
to learn the results of my latest procedure, and I'm already late. Look, I'm sorry. I really must go."

Faith slammed the door and jumped back from the
curb to avoid the backdraft from the car's muffler.
"Thanks for nothing," she muttered, hunching to hoist
Nicholas higher on her back as the Jag roared out of
sight.

The doorman wasn't one Faith had ever met. Of
course, it'd been more than a year since she'd been to
the Cameron suite.

"Dr. Cameron did not leave word to expect a person
with two babies," the man said. The nasal way he said
person made Faith feel as if she was in the same cate-

gory as the garbage collector. Or perhaps the garbage itself.

"Will you ring his apartment, please? The babies need attention. Even if Michael isn't home, I'm sure Mrs. Parker will authorize a visit. Tell her it's Faith Hyatt, Lacy Cameron's sister."

"The doctor is at the hospital," the man said after a brief conversation he'd taken pains to not let Faith hear. "Mrs. Parker received no instructions to allow you in. She reminded me that Dr. Cameron and his wife divorced earlier this year. You'll have to have Dr. Cameron get in touch with one of us, I'm afraid."

"Would you explain to Mrs. Parker that I have Dr. Cameron's son with me?"

"Are you going to leave peacefully, miss, or shall I phone the cops? The doc doesn't have a kid." The attendant reached for the phone inside his work station.

"Good grief." Faith started to say something smart-alecky in return, but decided there was no use. Media frenzy or not, it figured she'd run into the one person in New York who apparently didn't read the paper, gossip or watch headline news on TV. "Look, I'm sort of stranded. I promise I won't trouble you if you'll get me a cab."

"Sure thing." The man still didn't seem to trust her. He didn't invite her to stand inside the foyer, and he kept her in sight until the cab pulled up.

The cabbie showed greater sympathy. "Twins. You've got your hands full, missus. Me and my wife had our flock one at a time." He shook his head. "Where to?"

Faith named the hospital where Michael practiced. At least, she hoped that was where she'd find him. Prominent as he was, he'd have privileges at many hospitals in the city. For just a minute, her resolve faltered. She reminded herself that even if he didn't want to see *her*, he'd never turn his back on Abby and Nick.

Faith's head ached from the twins' constant crying. They were hungry and she was tired. She was angry, too. Who wouldn't be? She'd complied with a court mandate, only to be turned away at the two homes she'd been ordered to visit.

"Hope the little guys get better," the cabbie told Faith as she paid her bill. "I don't have another fare, so I don't mind lending a hand to help you get them into the emergency room."

Faith almost cried. Kind words right now had that effect on her. What did it say for her situation that a New York cabdriver—one of a clan reputed to be consistently rude—had been nicer to her than the people who might one day have a hand in raising Abigail and Nicholas? "Thank you, but we'll be fine," she sniffled.

Inside, Faith made a beeline for the main desk. Instead of asking for a ladies' lounge where she could change the babies, she asked to have Michael paged. She did so with authority. Let him see what these games he was playing through their attorneys had done to the babies he professed to love.

She rained kisses down on Abby's red face and paced the lobby, bouncing the heavy carrier on her back to try and quiet Nick. Suddenly Michael loomed in front of her, looking wonderful to Faith even though he appeared to be a bit bleary-eyed himself.

"Faith, what's wrong? Are the babies sick again? Are you?" Michael's questions ran together as he pried Nicholas out of the backpack and helped her remove Abigail from the sweaty front carrier. When, surprisingly, Michael leaned over and kissed Faith soundly on the lips, tears threatened to spill from her eyes for the second time in only minutes. Yet she was determined to stay mad at Michael. After all, he'd had a hand in sending her on this wild-goose chase.

"What did you all think," she asked, clenching her fists. "That I'd ignore Judge Kline's orders to bring Nick and Abby to New York so they could spend time with you and Kipp? You ought to know me better than that, Michael."

"Who's Judge Kline?" Michael seemed genuinely baffled. "These babies are soaking wet. No wonder they're crying."

Michael strode to a bank of elevators. There was nothing for Faith to do but follow him. "Judge Kline is the Superior Court Judge who overruled Judge Brown's visitation decree. Oh, why am I explaining this? I'm sure you already know it. David said the Schlegels and Lon Maxwell filed a joint appeal."

Herding Faith into an empty elevator, Michael rode up two floors, then motioned her off and into a quiet room where there were two soft leather couches. The scent of fresh-perked coffee permeated the air.

"Those packs look incredibly uncomfortable," he said, relieving her of the heavy diaper bag. "I'll change the babies while you shed those things, unless you need help getting out of them."

Faith shook her head. The straps had cut off circulation to her arms, and her fingers had trouble undoing the buckles. *Why was Michael being so nice?*

As if he'd read her mind, he glanced up from pulling diapers and changes of clothing from the bag. "I really don't know what you're talking about, Faith. I haven't left the hospital since I got here. We couldn't get a heart for Mrs. Fitzhugh. Last night I decided to try repairing hers. We've never tried a five bypass on a transplanted heart before. It's been touch and go all day. An hour ago we saw the first sign of improvement."

"I'm glad," Faith said sincerely. "Wait a minute." She turned from the sink where she was running hot water over the two bottles of formula. "Kipp's out of town and Shelby Fielding claimed she had no clue Bob Schlegel had filed the appeal. Now you're denying you asked Maxwell to act on your behalf? Have the lawyers gone berserk?"

"I don't know, but when we're done here I'll find out," Michael muttered. He accepted a bottle from Faith and stuck it in Abby's mouth. "There, there, honeybunch. God, I've missed you guys," he said with feeling, staring at Faith as she sat down to feed Nicholas.

Still smarting from being rebuffed twice—by Shelby Fielding and also at Michael's home—Faith wasn't ready to forgive him. "Apparently you didn't miss us enough to have one of your staff phone."

He looked abashed at that. "You know how it is when a doctor has a patient at death's door. I'd figured on doing a lot of things. Truth is, I haven't had a minute to myself. I'd planned to go to Tiffany's and choose your ring, too. Since you're here, and as Cynthia is somewhat improved, maybe we can go together."

"Ring?" Faith felt the room recede. "I—I assumed you'd decided not to proceed down the marriage avenue. I mean, according to David, Kipp's legal team and yours are working to get the hearings moved to New York."

"What's that got to do with our getting married?"

More confused than ever, Faith automatically burped Nicholas. "So, we're still working from plan A, Michael?"

He smiled and the tired lines that had dulled his eyes fell away. "You, I and the twins are going to be a family, Faith. There isn't going to be any plan B. I promise."

Faith's heart battled her head. Her heart wanted to believe, but her head remembered all the things that had gone wrong already. Michael was back to his hospital routine. How long before he forgot her and the babies again? For the moment, however, his smile set her world right.

Faith wanted so much to believe that things would work out, exactly the way Michael had promised.

CHAPTER FOURTEEN

THE BABIES FELL ASLEEP almost immediately after eating. Faith fussed over them, smoothing the tufts of hair sticking up on each tiny head. Nick sucked so hard at the bottle whenever he ate that he perspired. He also twisted the fingers of his left hand in the longer strands of hair that fell over his ear. Abigail did the same, only she had less hair to grasp. She pinched her ear, leaving it red and sometimes scratched.

"One of us needs to clip their fingernails," Michael noted as he inspected Abby's scratches and the little fingers he splayed out over his larger forefinger.

"I'll let you do the honors." Faith laughed. "You're the surgeon with nerves of steel."

"Oh, ho. Surgeons never work on their own families."

"I bought special baby clippers. Supposedly there's less chance of slipping and cutting fingers and toes. I guess I could do it. I am a nurse, after all."

"I'll do it. I was only teasing. Remind me when we get home. Are you ready to leave? I need a minute to check on Cynthia and give the nursing supervisor my cell number, then we can take off. The car seats are still in the back of my car."

"You're needed here, Michael. I didn't stop by to ask for a lift home. It was more that I needed a place to feed and change them—and that I was mad about no one being aware of the court order except me.''

''Don't remind me. When I calm down, I intend to phone Lon Maxwell and find out what possessed him. He takes his orders from me and no one else. I'll set my housekeeper and the security staff straight, too. I don't want you ever to have to go through that again. There's no excuse for what happened today, Faith.''

''Gr-r-reat! Then I'll be on everyone's bad-guy list. It wasn't my intention to cause trouble.''

''Well, I don't mind at all. Mrs. Parker knows you're family, and she's well aware that I'm involved in a custody suit. I don't understand her actions and I'll be discussing this with her.''

''That's between the two of you. I could have pressed harder, I suppose, but I remember how much she intimidated Lacy.''

''That's news to me. Lacy never said a word. I hired Mrs. Parker so Lacy wouldn't have to worry about cleaning and cooking so soon after her surgery. It worked out well, and I assumed Lacy wanted to keep Mrs. Parker on.''

''That woman would only ever take orders from you, Michael. And you were so rarely home. More often than not, *she* set the house rules, not Lacy.''

He shook his head in amazement. ''As I said, Faith, things are going to change.'' Digging in his pocket, Michael pulled out a set of keys. ''I'm parked on level one in the fifth slot from the west exit. If you load the babies, I'll be there in less than ten minutes and we can get underway.''

Faith had protested all she was going to. If Michael was determined to drive her back to Boston, she was grateful. The afternoon commuter trains were always full and they stopped at every station. The trip home would be much more pleasant in the luxury of Michael's car.

After he returned, they set off, only to be stuck in heavy traffic for some fifteen minutes. She again apologized for intruding on his day. "I feel guilty, Michael. You look exhausted. Are you quite sure you want to make the round trip to Boston?"

"I have to. Tonight will be critical for Cynthia. I wish I didn't have to turn right around and come back. You do know, I hope, that I'd much rather stay with you and the kids."

Faith didn't know that. She wasn't even thoroughly convinced after he'd said it. After all, who knew more about the pressures on a doctor than a nurse? If it'd been any doctor but Michael, she'd never have agreed to marry him. The man bewitched her. He always had and probably always would. Faith found it impossible to think rationally when he was around. She held no illusions about marriage to Michael Cameron; she knew it meant she'd carry the burden of raising the twins practically alone. She'd heard doctors' wives complain about not receiving any emotional support. Now she would join their ranks.

On closer examination of her feelings, Faith admitted she'd settle for small snatches of shared time with Michael. After all, she understood the importance of his work. And she'd expected to be a single parent to Lacy's babies, in any event. But could anyone blame her for wanting more from marriage?

"I almost forgot," she said, a genuine smile chasing away her troubled thoughts. "Nicholas rolled over this morning! He did it more than once, so I know it wasn't a fluke."

"I haven't been gone *that* long. I can't believe I missed such an important milestone. Did you think to record it on video?"

"No. I don't have a video camera. It would be a good idea to get one, though. The twins will be going through a lot of firsts in the months to come."

"They've gone through a lot of stages just since you brought them home. What's after rolling? Crawling?"

"Dr. Sampson's nurse gave me a brochure with an approximate timetable. She said not to worry if they develop faster or slower than it says."

"That means we shouldn't worry because Nick smiled before Abby and now he's rolled over first?"

"Right. She may walk or speak before he does. Then again, because she was smaller at birth, she may always be developmentally slower than Nicholas."

"Another reason I'd really hate for the Fieldings to end up with the twins. Maybe I'm wrong about them, but I can see them pressuring Abigail to do better than her brother. I mean, she does have that superior Fielding blood running through her veins," Michael drawled sarcastically.

His words brought Faith a whole new set of worries. David had said if the Fieldings managed to get the hearings transferred to New York, they'd be able to influence the outcome. Because Michael's clinic and his legal residence were in New York, he fit into their schemes. If Michael loved her, if he hadn't offered to marry her just to try and win custody, she'd suggest he relocate his practice to Boston. But why would he? He had name recognition where he was, and a partner who was probably more important to his life than a wife of convenience would ever be.

"I shouldn't have said anything," Michael muttered,

darting sidelong glances at Faith. "Now you're worried about the Fieldings placing unrealistic demands on Abigail. It won't happen, I swear. They'd have to get her first. And the babies hardly know Kipp or Shelby. Just because old man Fielding tops the list of rich and famous, that doesn't automatically give them an edge."

"Is there any chance he didn't earn his millions legally?"

"Admirable thought, but Kipp-the-first made a killing in real estate. He married into an old banking family. Our Kipp's father increased their wealth on Wall Street. He chose a wealthy socialite wife, too. Kipp has trust funds from both sides of the family. Shelby's folks had a pedigree, too, but I understand they left her cash-poor when they died. She was at Bryn Mawr when their yacht went down in a storm. Kipp was at Yale. He may have married Shelby for her contacts in the boating world, but that's not a crime."

"Schlegel, Schlegel and Matz can make her sound tragic then, can't they? At least if it were me, I'd play up that angle. Young woman lost her parents, wants desperately to have a family of her own. According to David she's had every fertility treatment known to man. That's where she was going today in such a rush. To a fertility clinic. She was quite obsessed with making the appointment. That's why she threw me out on the curb by your apartment and tore off like a madwoman."

"The story fits Lacy's explanation. I recall hearing you say that Kipp broke off their affair because he felt he owed it to his wife to let her try a new fertility method she'd discovered."

"Yes. It was the final blow, so to speak. The reason Lacy left without telling Kipp she was pregnant."

"And yet," Michael said thoughtfully, "it showed

character that the man would be concerned enough for his wife to stick by her through another process. Fertility tests and treatments aren't any fun for either the man *or* the woman. Some are quite painful.''

"I wasn't under the impression that Lacy thought Kipp stayed out of a sense of love or concern for Shelby. More likely it was because his father demanded an heir to carry on that exclusive Fielding bloodline.''

"I know you want to believe Kipp and Shelby will make horrible parents, Faith. He might be weak and she's snooty, but basically they're above average when it comes to looking at where to place kids. I really don't think we have a prayer of discrediting them in the eyes of a judge. If we tried, our efforts might backfire. We'd be better served to concentrate on making ourselves look *more* desirable.''

"You're right. I have nothing against the Fieldings except a gut feeling that Shelby would rather not be stuck with a reminder of Kipp's infidelity. In a way I feel sorry for her. All her friends and acquaintances must be talking behind her back. They must know every sordid detail, considering how the case has been dissected by the media.''

"Friends, strangers, everyone has an opinion. I still think that, in the end, the judge will weigh all facts and do what's right.''

Almost two hours later, Michael pulled into the parking lot behind Faith's apartment. "I'll carry the kids upstairs. Then I need to leave again.''

Faith had toyed for over an hour with telling Michael there was no way the two of them would look better than Kipp and Shelby. Kipp might be off sailing in Antigua, but Shelby was home attending to duty. She didn't say anything, however. She had no right to chastise Michael for dashing back to New York. His life and work were there.

"Hey, we weren't harassed by reporters. Do you suppose that means you can keep your phone plugged in?" Michael asked as they slipped jackets off the still-sleeping twins.

"I did last night. You'd promised to call me, remember? When you didn't, I disconnected it again."

Michael looked contrite. "I meant to call. If Cynthia's recovery continues, there's no reason I couldn't phone tonight." He tried to pull Faith into his arms, but she ducked out and missed the kiss he aimed at her lips.

"You'll be back when?" she asked, busying herself with hanging the jackets in the closet.

"In time for the hearing. A few days before that, if I can manage. I have a list of things to do and a short period of time in which to do them." Walking up behind Faith, Michael curved his hands over her upper arms and tilted her back flat to his chest. He laid a cheek in need of a shave against her smoother, softer one. "I wish I didn't have to go at all," he murmured. "I'm ready to get on with the wedding."

Faith allowed herself the pleasure of snuggling into his arms. His solid strength and the steady beat of his heart offered a sense of safety. Turning slowly, she slid her arms around his neck and raised her lips to accept the kiss she'd shied away from earlier. Michael's shirt still carried the faint aroma of the hospital. But Faith wasn't put off. Some might find the antiseptic odor oppressive; Faith found it comforting. She briefly touched her tongue to his lips and then when he groaned, she kissed him as if there was no tomorrow.

Michael was the one to call a halt this time. Heart beating fast, he exhaled a stream of air and permitted only their foreheads to touch. "It wouldn't take much of this to tempt me to stay. But I can't."

Michael took a giant backward step. His gaze lingered on her hungrily, before sliding to the cribs where the babies curled together. "I don't ever remember wanting to ignore responsibility so badly," he sighed. "But I can't. We both know that wouldn't play well with the judge, either. Goodbye, sweetheart. I'm counting on you to keep the home fires burning." Hurrying into the outer hall, he walked quickly to the elevators.

Faith stood with one hand pressed to her knotted stomach and the other to her quivering lips long after Michael left. By initiating that kiss, she'd bared her soul. Hadn't he seen that, or didn't he care? He hadn't said he loved her. Foolishly, she had clung to the hope that he'd at least acknowledge the *possibility* of love in their proposed union. She could only conclude that he wouldn't be offering marriage if he thought he could win custody of the twins without it.

So, what did it say about her that she'd marry him on any terms? Faith weighed the matter in her mind for the remainder of the evening. She finally admitted that she'd loved him for so long, she would accept a one-sided match in order to spend even tidbits of time with him.

If that made her pathetic, so be it. If that made her a traitor to Lacy, so be it.

She was prepared to hear nothing from Michael until whatever day he managed to return to Boston. True to his word this time, Michael phoned that night to let her know he'd arrived safely, and Cynthia had continued to improve. "I can't tell you how many times I almost turned back," he confided in a husky, sexy voice that practically unstrung Faith.

"I'll bet the hospital staff is happy you didn't. It probably makes them nervous to have their star surgeon out of reach." Faith had begun to distance herself from him. It was possibly the only way she'd survive a marriage without love.

If Michael noticed a change in her attitude, he didn't remark on it. "You know how hospital administrators are when someone on staff breaks new ground, Faith. After the surgery, the P.R. department sent out a press release. I could do without the added publicity. I prefer not being in the limelight."

"Boy, can I relate." Faith fell back on the couch and wound an overlong curl around one finger. "I've hung up on five reporters who called since you left. Apparently they found out you'd driven me home. Two of them knew about the mix-up in today's visitation. What do they have, a pipeline to our lawyers?"

"That reminds me. I phoned Lon. Our lawyers are out of control. He tried giving *me* orders, until I reminded him I was the guy paying his bill."

"They all want to win this case, Michael. David told me it'll be a huge legal coup for the law firm whose client ends up with a favorable ruling."

"Yeah. Well, the one working for me had better not go behind my back and cut deals with the other team. Lon blew up when I told him to get me out of the new visitation agreement. I have my doubts that he's attuned to the best interest of the babies. If I didn't think firing him would create total confusion at the next hearing, I'd have done it. I hung up without telling him we'd decided to get married, Faith. I hope you haven't mentioned it to David."

"No." Faith's stomach rolled. A woman on the brink of marriage should be shouting it from the rooftops.

And Michael wanted her to keep it quiet.… No doubt as part of his strategy.

His next words proved her right, "Good. It'll have greater impact if you show up at the hearing wearing an engagement ring. Do you have a preference in cut? Emerald? Marquise? Standard?"

"Not emerald," Faith said quickly. That would remind her too much of the ring he'd given Lacy. "Nothing showy. A ring isn't important, Michael."

"It is to me. I'm also in favor of our wedding being as soon as possible. Most people involved in the case ~~probably~~ think we're sleeping together as it is, so the sooner we make it legal, the better."

Better for whom? Faith wondered. Oh, he meant it would look better to a judge, of course. "Will you arrange a marriage service with a justice of the peace in New York, or shall I arrange one here?"

"Do you mind if we have a church wedding? I never felt right marrying Lacy in the hospital."

"Is that really necessary?" Faith's throat was tight.

"Humor me. I want to see my bride walk down the aisle. Besides, someday the kids will expect to see pictures of our wedding."

"Weddings are costly, Michael." Faith bit her lip as a sharp reminder not to let the excitement that had begun to build get out of hand. His wanting a church wedding meant nothing. Another show for his custody quest.

"Faith, I have money. I've been too busy to spend much of what I made. I told you things were going to change. I'll send you my charge card. Use it for whatever you need. I'm sure Thanksgiving is too soon for a wedding. Shall we shoot for Christmas Eve? Morning, with a brunch afterward for guests? That way we can spend Christmas as a family.''

"All right, Michael.'' The old dream called for a honeymoon in some exotic locale. She guessed honeymoons weren't part of Michael's plan. Not with less than two months to get everything ready. This wasn't a love match, she reminded herself, but a marriage to establish a home for the twins. Fine. She loved the babies. She'd make their first Christmas a special event.

"I have to go, Faith. I'm being paged. I'll overnight my card. We'll finalize any other details after the hearing.''

Faith's heart tripped faster as they said their goodbyes. Somehow, knowing that she'd be planning their wedding made marriage to Michael seem more real. She longed to tell someone, even though he'd said they shouldn't until after the hearing. She sat down and wrote a letter to her aunt Lorraine, who worked in a mission hospital in Tanzania. Tomorrow, she'd visit her dad and tell him. He liked Michael. At one time, Dwight Hyatt had been aware that she carried a torch for Lacy's husband. Sporadically aware, anyway. Her dad had offered his sympathy and his shoulder for her to cry on after Lacy's wedding. If he was having a good day tomorrow, he might share the joy that filled her heart. No one else would, as she'd kept her feelings for Michael well hidden. Maybe her father would even be able to walk her down the aisle.

But the next day, when Faith and the twins visited Dwight, he referred to her by her mother's name. And he thought the twins were Faith and Lacy as babies. The fact that one was a girl and the other a boy meant nothing to the old man, who lived more and more in his own world.

Faith didn't linger at the rest home. Seeing her father's condition deteriorating cast a pall over her already fragile joy. From there, she did go to book a small chapel at the church, but she spent more time lighting candles for her father and Michael than arranging her special day.

During what remained of the week, Faith tried to recapture her earlier delight in planning for her future with Michael. She just couldn't seem to shake the sense of anxiety that surrounded her every move. She lived with the cloying fear that Michael wouldn't show up in time for the hearing and that she'd never see him again.

The fear stuck with her in spite of the fact that he called every night.

"If we didn't have these conversations, I'd go crazy in New York with you guys in Boston," he said one evening when she mentioned how long they'd been talking on the phone. "I can't be there to help you start feeding Abby and Nick cereal. Listening to you scrape the spoon on the bowl puts me closer to the experience."

At that very moment, Nicholas spewed rice cereal and formula all over Faith. "Oh, yuck! I hope you felt that shower, Michael." Laughing, she juggled the phone to her other ear as she wiped Nick's face and her own shirt and chin.

"If you need to clean up, I'll call back later."

"That's not necessary, Michael." The few times he'd phoned after she'd gone to bed, he'd said things that made it impossible for her to sleep afterward. He'd asked what kind of nightgown she had on and had commented on how he'd like to remove it. Slowly...

"It is necessary, Faith. I won't risk losing you from inattention."

Faith closed her eyes. Although Michael hadn't spoken Lacy's name, he might as well have. But she guessed her sister would always be between them.

"Faith, dammit, I can feel you pulling away from me. You do it every time I touch on anything personal. Talk to me. If you're having seconds thoughts, we need to figure out why."

Second thoughts. And third. But not for any reason that must be running through his mind. She tossed the empty plastic cereal bowl into the sink. Bustling around the kitchen, she ran water over washcloths and wiped the babies' faces and hands. "I don't know what you expect, Michael. You call when I'm in the middle of caring for the babies so you can feel involved. But I only have two hands, and between the kids, they have four—all of them trying to push the spoon away. And yesterday Dr. Sampson agreed that Nick's cutting three teeth at one time. I spent the night walking the floor."

"Look, I'm doing my best to wind things up here so I can get back to Boston. Barring unforeseen complications, Cynthia ought to go home next week."

Faith rubbed two fingers across the furrows forming between her eyebrows. "Are we fighting, Michael? I don't want to make your life miserable." She burst into tears.

"Stop. I ought to be shot for leaving you to deal with so much. You need a mother's helper, Faith. Why don't you call an agency tomorrow?"

"It's not that, Michael. I can take care of the twins. But…but David phoned today. He's positive you and Kipp are in cahoots. Nancy Matz told him I don't have a prayer of winning. She suggested I'd be smart to let Shelby have the babies before the hearing. According to Nancy, if I show that much good sense, the rest of you will be more inclined to allow me future visits with the kids.''

"Rubbish. Where in tarnation does that woman come up with her half-baked ideas? More likely she's trying to rattle my cage. Kipp's team doesn't like it that I stopped Lon from negotiating with them. You hang in there, honey. Everything's going to work out fine, you'll see.''

"I hope.'' Faith scrubbed at the unwanted tears. "Sorry, Michael. I think we're all walking a fine line, and it's difficult.'' She sighed. "I feel I'm being unfair to David in excluding him from our plans. Frankly, I just want a final decision. If Kipp's team does anything to prevent the judge from deciding on a permanent placement at the November hearing, I'm not sure I can continue on as we are. I'm getting too attached to the babies...even though I promised I'd consider myself a temporary foster parent. How do real foster moms let go? Losing the twins will break my heart.''

"You have to keep a positive attitude, Faith.''

"I can't. There was a sidebar in this morning's paper that listed twenty reasons why family court will favor Kipp and Shelby over either you or me.''

"Stop reading that stuff. The reporters have nothing concrete, so they sit around and speculate. They like to sprinkle sand in an oyster. It provides a constant irritation, if you know what I mean.''

"Right. And who gets the pearl in the end? Michael, these babies are more precious than pearls. I keep thinking maybe none of us should be playing god with their lives.''

"You're tired, sweetheart. Hang in a while longer. I believe our getting married will impress the judge. Social Services already reported that we work well as a team.''

''I'll try to be more optimistic. Maybe we should talk about something other than the case for a change.''

They did just that. They talked for two hours, covering subjects of interest to both of them, everything from books to movies, politics to art. ''Wow, it's midnight,'' Michael exclaimed around a yawn. ''I haven't talked on the phone this long since high school.''

''I never have. Not even to Lacy, and we sometimes used to spend an hour on the phone. I don't remember her ever saying you liked paintings of seascapes and old lighthouses. But then she did her best to talk me out of buying the ones I have.''

''Wait until you see what I have stored. During one of Lacy's interior renovations, she took down three favorite watercolors I'd hung in my den.''

''Why didn't you tell her hands off?''

''Because decorating was something she loved to do. I gave her so little else,'' he said quietly. ''I'm glad now that I let her have free rein with the apartment.''

Silence fell between them. Then Michael cleared his throat and Faith thought he was going to say goodbye. She hated parting on a sad note. ''It's okay if you still love her, Michael.''

''Looking back, I'm not sure I ever loved her as I should have. I know that now. Apparently she recognized it much sooner.''

''It's a closed chapter in your life.''

''It is that. And thanks to you and the twins, I've been given a chance to correct my faults in part two of the saga of Michael Cameron.''

Faith didn't know what to say. It was only after

they'd each yawned in the other's ear that they agreed it was time to hang up.

Tuesday, a week before the hearing, an ice storm hit, greatly curtailing Faith's ability to complete the final tasks in arranging the wedding. On her list had been choosing flowers for the chapel and a bridal bouquet. Michael had suggested they serve brunch rather than cake and coffee. She had planned to check out the menus of three restaurants near the chapel. Instead of going out in the wind-driven sleet, she phoned and asked to have copies of the menus mailed to her.

The storm raged for three days. Fortunately, it let up on the fourth, and a south wind blew in and melted the ice on the streets, or Faith's cupboards would have been bare. At least, preoccupation with the weather had taken her mind off the hearing, which was now only a week-end away. As she pushed the babies through the corner grocery store and people stopped to exclaim over them, Faith underwent a sudden, strange longing to have Michael at her side.

And where was he? She'd grown used to their nightly phone visits. The three days she'd needed most to connect with him, he'd seemed to drop off the face of the earth. No calls, and no answer at home or on his cell phone.

It wasn't until Faith stood at the cash register to pay for her groceries, that the morning's headlines caught her eye—and sent her stomach plummeting. Taking Michael's advice, she'd avoided reading articles having to do with the case. What she read now made her physically ill. Bold typeface stretching across six newspaper columns read Attorneys For Kipp Fielding III Expect A Private Settlement Between Their Client And Dr. Michael Cameron In Custody Case Involving Twins With Separate Fathers.

Rooted to the floor, Faith barely managed to produce the cash to pay her bill. Her fingers shook so badly that the clerk asked if she was ill.

She didn't trust herself to respond. She bought the paper and hurriedly loaded the sacks into the stroller, then raced blindly from the store. On the trek home, her knees felt as limp as one of Abby's rag dolls. Her mind refused to comprehend what those headlines might mean.

When Faith reached the safe haven of her apartment, she methodically stored her groceries and changed and fed the babies before she felt calm enough to more closely inspect the article beneath those shocking head-lines.

She'd no more than spread the paper out on the kitchen table when her telephone rang. It was a reporter for an opposing paper, asking if she intended to press on with her lawsuit. Faith hung up without giving her standard "no comment." She quickly dialed David before another call could come in.

He claimed ignorance. "I have calls in to Bob Schlegel and Lon Maxwell. So far, no one's contacted me. Last I spoke to Maxwell, he was adamant that Cameron wasn't interested in working with the Fieldings. The article is devoid of pertinent facts, Faith. This could be some reporter's stab at turning up the heat before Monday's hearing."

"Doesn't that open his paper up for a possible slander suit?"

"Not really. Since those guys don't have to disclose the name of their source, they could later print a retraction and say their source was mistaken."

"All the same," Faith said, having difficulty swallowing, "I'd feel better if you'd heard from the other camps. I'm leaving my phone off the hook. If you find out anything, will you send your clerk by to bring me up-to-date?"

"Sure. But Lacy's custody papers have stood up under scrutiny by the Superior Court commissioner. I received his ruling yesterday. Since then, my assistant and I have been working around the clock to build your case. Relax, Faith. I can't believe that any split agreement Fielding and Cameron could dream up would look good to a judge. Public sentiment is all for keeping the kids together."

Faith hung up and then took the receiver off the hook, wishing she shared David's confidence. Of course, David didn't know she and Michael had been plotting together in order to increase their odds. That was precisely what made her so uneasy. If Michael dickered behind the scenes with her, what stopped him from doing the same with Kipp? Over the last couple of weeks, she'd let her late-night chats with Michael, and all the wedding talk, lull her into complacency.

Her stomach and legs still felt as if they belonged to someone who'd just climbed off an amusement park ride. Faith grabbed a couple of the babies' favorite squeaky toys and went to sit beside the playpen. Playing with Abby and Nick lifted her spirits. She was actually laughing at Abigail's attempts to roll over when she heard voices in the hall. Someone rapped soundly on her door.

"I'm coming," Faith called. She climbed to her feet and straightened her blouse before releasing the locks. David must have heard back from one of the other lawyers. That was fast. Faith yanked open the door, and it took her a second to realize it was Michael, and not David's clerk, standing there. Kipp Fielding and his father hovered in the space behind Michael.

"Look who I found wandering through our parking lot, Faith," Michael said with a grin.

He carried his medical bag and a black suitcase, Faith realized as he stepped past her. Kipp's hands were shoved into his pants pockets. His father gripped a brown leather briefcase. Neither man cracked a smile.

Michael piled his things in a corner and turned to look at Faith, who'd gone white and still gripped the doorknob. He returned to tug it gently from her hands. After closing the door, he slipped an arm around her waist. "Are you ill?"

She dragged a shaking hand through hair that badly needed cutting. "Please," she said tightly, "Sit, gentlemen. And so will I." She pushed Michael's hand roughly aside and stumbled into the chair nearest the playpen. Idly massaging her arms, Faith murmured, "I have a feeling that what you're about to say is going to knock me off my feet, anyhow, so I may as well sit."

Michael sank into the matching chair, leaving the couch to the Fieldings. "Maybe someone would be kind enough to clue me in. None of you seem surprised by this gathering. Am I the only one in the dark here?"

"Come off it, Michael," she snapped. "I know you said I shouldn't read the newspapers but I did. Sorry, but they let your little cat out of the bag."

Folding his hands between his knees, Michael threw a puzzled glance at Faith and then at the men on the couch. Kipp's eyes shifted to the babies and stayed there. The elder Mr. Fielding opened his briefcase and removed five or six pages of paper. He flicked a thumb across his lips a few times. "We're sorry about the leak

to the media,'' he said at last. ''Bob Schlegel has tried
for two days to contact you, Cameron. My son and I
finally drove over to your apartment today. Security said
you'd sublet the place and were headed for Boston.''

''My business in New York took longer than I
thought to tie up, or I'd have been here earlier. I assumed Lon told you.''

It was Faith's turn to look startled. ''So you three
haven't already met, the way the newspaper implied?''

They all shook their heads.

''Why would we meet?'' Michael asked. ''The hearing is Monday.''

The senior Fielding divided the papers and handed
Michael a set. ''My son is prepared to sign over full
and complete custody of the female twin to you, Doctor.
It's all here in black and white.''

A collective gasp exploded from Faith and Michael.
Unthinking, she grabbed Abigail and cuddled her pro-
tectively, as if such a move would shield her from a
father who was announcing he didn't want anything to
do with her.

''I don't understand.'' Michael flipped through the
pages, then settled down to reading the top one.

''Shelby's pregnant,'' Kipp blurted. ''She found out
while I was in Antigua. If she's to carry the baby to
term, she has to be off her feet.''

''You always planned to hire a nanny, I believe,''
Michael pointed out.

Kipp turned to his father, as if for help explaining.
The older man had no trouble being blunt. ''This agreement comes as a condition of Shelby staying with my
son. You'll notice on page two that Bob Schlegel has
arranged a sizable trust for the girl. And a generous
monthly maintenance fee.''

"Dad!" Kipp glared at his father. "For goodness' sake, she has a name. Call her Abigail."

"All right. Abigail will be monetarily provided for until age eighteen."

Michael interrupted. "This reads very much like you're handing Abby over to me with no strings attached."

Faith began to feel faint. The Fieldings were offering Michael everything he wanted. He'd have clear rights to both babies. He no longer needed her to act as his wife. A trembling gripped her and wouldn't let go as she saw all her dreams drift away, like so much smoke up a chimney. It was all Faith could do to listen to Kipp's explanation.

"At the risk of sounding like a jerk," Kipp mumbled, "I experienced the true excitement of being a real father when Shelby made her announcement. That forced me to take a good look at where I was in this custody fight. It struck me that I have no paternal feelings for the baby I made with Lacy." He sucked in a breath. "Believe it or not, I want my marriage to survive. It's what I've always wanted, even though I did stray the one time. But I'd like a solid assurance that Abigail will be raised by someone who loves her. I think that's you, Cameron."

Kipp's dad butted in again. "From the beginning, Kipp had grave concerns about splitting up the twins. What do you say, Doctor? Do we have a deal?" Extracting a gold pen from his suit jacket, Mr. Fielding thumbed out the last page on both packets. His son had already signed.

Michael spared Faith a glance before he accepted the pen. As her face remained unreadable, he put the pen to the page. Hesitating, he asked, "God forbid it should happen, but what if Shelby loses the child she's carrying? Can I expect to be dragged through court again?''

Kipp III stood and paced to the window. He jingled the change in his pockets. ''Shelby will never love Abby as she deserves to be loved. If you've got no objection, Cameron, I might call you from time to time to ask after her welfare. But you have my word as a gentleman that I'll never make waves in her life. It's up to you whether or not you choose to tell her about me before she comes into her trust.''

''Done,'' said Michael.

As he pulled the papers toward him and scribbled his name, Faith fought back a sob. All the love she felt for the twins squeezed the breath from her lungs. But the love she bore Michael withered as he uttered that one damning word.

CHAPTER FIFTEEN

UNABLE TO BEAR LISTENING to the men seal the fate of the babies she would now lose, Faith swept them both into her arms and carried them to the nursery. They were beginning to fuss for bottles, anyhow. She wanted, needed, to feed them one last time.

After they ate, it would be nap time. There was sanity in routine.

Suddenly panic tore at her soul. Oh, God, she'd still have to face Michael. She'd have to hide this terrible, wrenching pain.

Blocking out the low murmur of male voices from her living room, Faith mixed formula by rote. She warmed it for Abigail and barely took the chill off for Nick. Since he'd started cutting those three teeth, he preferred his formula on the cool side.

Tears sprang to her eyes, obscuring her view of their sweet faces as she sat in her mother's rocker and offered a bottle to each baby. How long would it take whatever nanny Michael hired to discover each baby's idiosyncracies? A few raced through Faith's mind. Abigail wanted to be tightly cocooned in a blanket before being placed in bed. Nick sprawled across his portion of the crib. If covered, he soon kicked his blankets off. Certain kinds of disposable diapers gave Abby a horrid rash. Nick, on the other hand, had tougher skin and wore any brand. But he woke up and fussed if the night-light burned out. His sister, unless she was sick, could probably sleep through a rocket launch.

Faith hummed one of the babies' favorite lullabies. Her voice cracked, so she stopped humming and rained kisses down on the perfect little heads. Kisses mixed with salty tears.

Both bottles were empty, and the babies had fallen fast asleep by the time Michael appeared in the doorway leading into the nursery. "There you are, Faith." He bent his head forward and rubbed a hand over the back of his neck. "With all the excitement of the last hour, we haven't even said a proper hello." He started walking toward her, but she stopped him by placing a finger to her lips.

"Sorry," he whispered. "Do you need help getting them into the crib?"

She shook her head wildly. Already she felt sick. She'd never be able to hang on to any portion of her pride if Michael touched her.

While she sat in the babies' room, which she'd fashioned with such love, Faith was forced to examine what would ultimately be best for the twins. Their future as it appeared now was the exact opposite of the life she'd dreamed about for the past several weeks. Definitely opposite of what she wanted. A kind word now, or the barest brush of Michael's hand, would risk shattering her resolve to let him have Abby and Nick without a fight.

Michael whispered that he was going into the kitchen to prepare a pot of coffee and that once Faith put the babies down, he'd meet her there.

She rocked for another five minutes. Abby and Nick were already sound asleep, but she needed the extra time to compose herself. Even then, she hoped Michael didn't stay in her apartment long. Things should move fairly fast for him once she stepped aside and called off David Reed. Of course, the court would approve his taking both babies. As she'd told Michael, she had no heart for trying to split up the infants.

The babies could be gone by as early as next week. Faith got up and moved around in a daze. She laid the twins down and crept out of the room.

Michael had perked a pot of the new coffee she'd bought that day. Faith followed the fragrance into the kitchen. It seemed longer than three hours since she'd ground the beans and filled the half-pound bag.

Hesitating in the hallway outside the kitchen, she closed her eyes and smoothed her fingers across them, taking care to rid herself of any last tears clinging to her eyelashes. With a false smile on her face, Faith breezed into the kitchen and plucked a cup off the mug tree.

Michael bolted up from the table, where he'd been reading the article that took up most of the front page. "Here, let me pour you a cup. That's some article," he acknowledged with a jerk of his thumb. "Now I can see why you were upset when I showed up at the door with Kipp and his father in tow."

Folding the paper, Faith tossed it in the trash. She drew in a tired-sounding breath, accepted the full cup and then sat as far from Michael as possible, given the small diameter of her kitchen table. "I really don't see any need to cover old ground, Michael. It's a lucky break for you that Kipp followed you to Boston and didn't wait to drop this bomb until we'd wasted time gathering at Monday's hearing."

"Lucky break for me?" He stopped with his cup

halfway to his lips and stared at her through a curl of steam.

"Yes." She waved a hand over her own cup, keeping her eyes averted. Then she fingered the watch on her arm and cleared her throat. "I, ah, still have time to phone David and tell him he's dismissed from the case. You'll want to call Lon. It's important to get the permanent fate of the twins settled. The sooner the better."

"I think so, too." Michael gazed at her oddly. The moment Faith reached for the telephone that still lay off the hook, not meeting his eyes, he clamped a hand over her wrist.

She flinched but was unable to control a shudder. When he remained silent, Faith was forced to turn and look at Michael, against her will.

"We can sit here and you can tell me what's going on inside your mind," he said carefully, "or we can take our coffee into the living room and duke this out in more comfortable surroundings. Either way, we will get to the heart of the problem, Faith."

"There's nothing to duke out, Michael. You've won. There's no reason for me to appear in court."

"Whoa!" He held up a hand. "That's the wrong pronoun. Don't you mean *we've* won?"

Tears welled again and slid down her cheeks. "Why are you dragging this out? Why are you torturing me? I won't hold you to any of the promises you made before you learned that Kipp was going to relinquish custody of Abigail."

"Big of you, I'm sure." Flinging off his suit jacket, Michael loosened his tie before crossing his arms defiantly. "Could you be more specific? Exactly what promises are we referring to?"

Faith had sucked in her upper lip. She released it with

a sigh. "The wedding farce. There's only the chapel to cancel. It's lucky for you the weather turned bad. I never arranged for flowers or the brunch."

"Wedding farce, you say?" His dark eyes, normally so sympathetic, burned like two smoldering fires. Digging into his jacket pocket, Michael hauled out a blue velvet box. He snapped it open with one finger and thrust it under Faith's nose. A two-carat warm-pink diamond glowed softly against a backdrop of white satin. The ring's setting was unique. Threads of gold wrapped the prongs holding the diamond, and intertwined, forming two hearts around smaller stones in a wide gold wedding band.

A less ornate man's ring with three similar diamonds embedded in its curve, completed the trio of wedding bands. "I would have been here a day earlier, Faith, but the jeweler at Tiffany's, who agreed to make this to my specifications, had a few finishing touches. He knew I wanted them to be perfect before I slipped it on the finger of the woman I love."

Faith's chin rose, then her mouth gaped open. "Love," she breathed in the shallowest of whispers. "But you've never said you loved me."

"Asking you to marry me, to be the mother of my children, isn't telling you I love you? I thought we both felt how much I loved you that incredible night we spent together in bed."

"I, ah, you never said you did. Love me, that is. I…I…thought you just needed a wife to parade past the judge."

Michael leaned over the table and bracketed her face with his hands. He settled his lips on hers briefly, but with feeling, then straightened away. "I love you so much. These last two weeks without you have been pure hell." He pursed his lips slightly. "I loved your sister with the impetuousness of youth. What I feel for you is what a man feels for a woman he can't bear to live a day without. What a man feels for a woman he intends to spend the rest of his life with." He kissed her again, as if to punctuate his words. "I wanted to do everything right for you, Faith."

"It's all right, Michael. I agreed, with my eyes open, to marry you for the sake of the twins. If you haven't changed your mind, and...and especially if you love me, I'll be happy to keep your house, and cook your meals—and I promise never to say a word about the hours you spend with patients."

"Faith, hush." Dropping his thumbs, Michael ran them lightly over her lips. "I sold my half of the practice. I'm moving to Boston for good. I've negotiated a teaching post at the medical school. I did it because I want more time with you and the twins. I want us to be a regular family. Is that what *you* want, Faith?"

"Oh, Michael." Faith's eyes shimmered with unshed tears. She said with an emotional catch to her voice, "All I've ever wanted is you. You, and the twins. I want to cheer Nick at football games and Abby at soccer. I want to help them grow into fine adults. I don't need backyard barbecues and weekend camping trips, or...or even a silly little word."

"I do. I want it all." Michael slipped the engagement ring on the third finger of her left hand and pulled her out of the chair and into his arms. Then...then he put all the love that filled his heart into a kiss. His hands skimmed the cool skin hiding beneath her white blouse. Buttons gave way, and Michael's palms soon brushed the fullness of her breasts.

Strident cries erupted from the nursery, driving them

apart. Clearly fighting passion, Michael stepped back and took a moment to repair Faith's clothing.

Smiling wryly, she trailed her fingers lovingly along his smooth jaw. "If we can get through the twins' teething, Michael, I predict we'll be together fifty years from now."

"I'm in for the long haul, lady. The twins will eventually sleep through the night. So make a note of where we left off, please."

"After teething comes potty training," she reminded him gently.

"Yeah, yeah. And sixteen years from now, someone's got to teach two kids to drive cars."

Faith glanced over her shoulder at him as she approached the crying twins. "I don't drive, remember?"

Michael stopped her with a loud, wet kiss. "Make that three learning to drive. I know you're trying to shock me into reality, but honey, I'm looking forward to every minute I get to be a father and a husband. By the way, I love you. I love, love, love you. Let me know if you ever get sick of hearing me say it."

"I never will. Oh, Michael, I love you, too."

Coming in March 2000
Two precious stories...
Two cherished authors...
One specially priced volume!

LOVE CHILD by ANNETTE BROADRICK & JUSTINE DAVIS

They knew about
making love...
But what about
making babies?

WHERE THERE IS LOVE by Annette Broadrick
A frantic phone call had secret agent Max Moran on
the first plane to a faraway country. The caller: his
never-forgotten former lover. The mission: the
rescue of a kidnapped child. His son!

UPON THE STORM by Justine Davis
Amid a raging hurricane Trace Dalton found passion in the
arms of a beautiful stranger...then she vanished without a
trace. His search: three long years, no stone unturned.
His discovery: the mystery woman who'd haunted his
dreams...and their child conceived upon the storm....

Available March 2000 at your favorite retail outlet.

Silhouette®
Where love comes alive™

Visit us at www.romance.net

PSBR2400

Looking For More Romance?

Visit Romance.net

Look us up on-line at: http://www.romance.net

Check in daily for these and other exciting features:

Hot off the press

View all current titles, and purchase them on-line.

What do the stars have in store for you?

Horoscope

Hot deals

Exclusive offers available only at Romance.net

Plus, don't miss our interactive quizzes, contests and bonus gifts.

PWEB

Return to the charm of the Regency era with

GEORGETTE HEYER,

creator of the modern Regency genre.

Enjoy six romantic collector's editions with forewords
by some of today's bestselling romance authors,

**Nora Roberts, Mary Jo Putney,
Jo Beverley, Mary Balogh,
Theresa Medeiros and Kasey Michaels.**

Frederica
On sale February 2000
The Nonesuch
On sale March 2000
The Convenient Marriage
On sale April 2000
Cousin Kate
On sale May 2000
The Talisman Ring
On sale June 2000
The Corinthian
On sale July 2000

Available at your favorite retail outlet.

HARLEQUIN®
Makes any time special™

Visit us at www.romance.net   PHGHGEN

HEART OF THE WEST

Every Man Has His Price!

Lost Springs Ranch was famous for turning young mavericks into good men. So word that the ranch was in financial trouble sent a herd of loyal bachelors stampeding back to Wyoming to put themselves on the auction block!

July 1999	*Husband for Hire* Susan Wiggs	January 2000	*The Rancher and the Rich Girl* Heather MacAllister
August	*Courting Callie* Lynn Erickson	February	*Shane's Last Stand* Ruth Jean Dale
September	*Bachelor Father* Vicki Lewis Thompson	March	*A Baby by Chance* Cathy Gillen Thacker
October	*His Bodyguard* Muriel Jensen	April	*The Perfect Solution* Day Leclaire
November	*It Takes a Cowboy* Gina Wilkins	May	*Rent-a-Dad* Judy Christenberry
December	*Hitched by Christmas* Jule McBride	June	*Best Man in Wyoming* Margot Dalton

HARLEQUIN®
Makes any time special ™

Visit us at www.romance.net

PHHOWGEN

Back by popular demand are

DEBBIE MACOMBER's

Hard Luck, Alaska, is a
town that needs women!
And the O'Halloran brothers
are just the fellows
to fly them in.

Starting in March 2000 this beloved series returns
in special 2-in-1 collector's editions:

MAIL-ORDER MARRIAGES, featuring
Brides for Brothers and *The Marriage Risk*
On sale March 2000

FAMILY MEN, featuring
Daddy's Little Helper and *Because of the Baby*
On sale July 2000

THE LAST TWO BACHELORS, featuring
Falling for Him and *Ending in Marriage*
On sale August 2000

Collect and enjoy each MIDNIGHT SONS story!

Available at your favorite retail outlet.

HARLEQUIN®
Makes any time special™

Visit us at www.romance.net   PHMS

Mother's Day is Around the Corner...
Give the gift that celebrates Life and Love!

Show Mom you care by presenting her with a one-year subscription to:

 For only $4.96—
That's **75% off the cover price.**

This easy-to-carry, compact magazine delivers 4 exciting romance stories by some of the very best romance authors in the world.

Plus each issue features personal moments with the authors, author biographies, a crossword puzzle and more...

A one-year subscription includes 6 issues full of love, romance and excitement to warm the heart.

To send a gift subscription, write the recipient's name and address on the coupon below, enclose a check for $4.96 and mail it today. In a few weeks, we will send you an acknowledgment letter and a special postcard so you can notify this lucky person that a fabulous gift is on the way!

Yes! I would like to purchase a one-year gift subscription (that's 6 issues) of WORLD'S BEST ROMANCES, for only $4.96. I save over 75% off the cover price of $21.00.   MDGIFT00

This is a special gift for:

Name _____

Address _____ Apt# _____

City _____ State _____ Zip _____

From _____

Address _____ Apt# _____

City _____ State _____ Zip _____

Mail to: HARLEQUIN WORLD'S BEST ROMANCES
P.O. Box 37254, Boone, Iowa, 50037-0254 Offer valid in the U.S. only.